DUPLICITY

SIBEL HODGE

Published by Thomas & Mercer, Seattle

www.apub.com

Amazon, the Amazon logo, and Thomas & Mercer are trademarks of Amazon.com, Inc., or its affiliates.

ISBN-13: 9781503941106
ISBN-10: 1503941108

Cover design by @blacksheep-uk.com

Printed in the United States of America

DUPLICITY

PART ONE
OBSESSION

THE OTHER ONE
Chapter 1

People always complain about their childhoods. *My mum wouldn't let me have any freedom. My dad wouldn't buy me the latest trendy gear. My sister was the favourite.*

Honestly, they have no fucking idea how shit it can really be.

I grew up on a rural dairy farm in the middle of nowhere. My dad was this big, beefy man. Always angry. Always wanting something different out of life but never willing to change anything. Always taking it out on my tiny little mouse of a mum. He was bitter and twisted. But it was never *his* fault. Oh, no, of course not. Why would it be? There was always someone else to blame. He was insane. But then so was my mum to stay with him and put up with it. Me, I had no choice back then, and Mum wasn't the only one Dad liked to punish.

Maybe some of the things I've done are wrong. Bad. But the thing is, if you grow up without love, you don't know what it is. I don't have the same kinds of feelings as other people. I don't feel guilty. I don't feel much, most of the time. Not about humans, anyway. From what I've seen, they're all a waste of oxygen. Give me an animal over a human any day. They're much more worthy. They're uncomplicated, transparent. What you see is what you get. They nurture their babies. Do everything they can to keep them safe, unlike humans. Everything animals do is about survival, not about ugliness or viciousness. Not about making you suffer. They only attack to protect their young or territory or food. They don't attack for the hell of it.

So you can't judge me. Not unless you were there. Not unless you know what that does to a person. And to be honest, I'm way past caring what anyone else thinks, anyway. It's how I survived it all.

My earliest memory was when I was about four. The cows were continually pregnant, of course, to make them produce milk, but I didn't understand any of that back then. All I knew was that one of them was about to give birth. Dad didn't name the cows. They weren't important enough for names. They were just things to him. A commodity to exploit – a bit like me and Mum. They had an ear tag to identify them and that was it. But I named the pregnant one Jennifer. I have no idea why. When Jennifer was just about to calve, she was separated from the others and put into a concrete pen where she duly gave birth.

I stood watching with amazement as this new little life entered the world. Apart from the bloody bits, the calf was beautiful. And he was going to be my new pet. I pictured myself feeding him. He would contentedly follow me around the farm everywhere I went. The nearest neighbour was ten miles away, and I had no friends. I didn't even go to school then. But the calf would be my new friend. Maybe I could even sleep with him in my bed. And whenever the shouty arguments started between Mum and Dad, I could press my head against his warm hide for comfort and listen to his heartbeat instead to block everything out, and that would make everything OK. I'd love the calf and he would love me.

I listened to Jennifer calling out to her newborn baby. Watched her nuzzling him on the ground where he lay, unsteady and bewildered. I felt her happiness in the air like something fizzing on the breeze. I slid my fingers through the metal bars and touched the calf, deciding on what to call him.

My wonder was broken quickly by Dad flinging open the metal door to the enclosure and dragging the calf by his legs into a wheelbarrow. His face was an angry blob of fire, muttering swear words as he wheeled the calf out and yanked the enclosure door closed.

Jennifer bolted towards the bars, body-slamming against them, crying for her baby. The calf strained his wobbly little head back towards her calls, trying to search for his mum.

'Daddy, what are you doing? Jennifer wants her baby!' I cried.

'It's no use to me. It's a boy,' he snapped.

I hurried to keep up with him as he walked away. 'But where are you taking him?'

'Never you mind.'

'Can't *I* have him instead?'

'They're not pets!'

'But . . . why not?' My little legs pumped harder next to him as I tried to keep up. I reached out a hand to stroke and comfort the calf as he made desperate little noises. 'Daddy, *please* let me have him. I'll look after him, I promise.'

He grabbed my arm and flung me away so hard that I fell down on to the concrete path and grazed my elbow.

I burst into tears.

He stopped pushing the wheelbarrow and looked down at me, eyes screwed up with hatred. 'Great! I've got another bloody crier to put up with. You're just like your useless bitch of a mother!' He left me there and wheeled the calf away.

Jennifer's screams echoed in my ears. I can still hear them now. And all the other screams afterwards that came to mingle with my own.

That was just the start of all the shit to come.

THE DETECTIVE
Chapter 2

I wasn't asleep when the call came at 1.25 a.m. Sleep was elusive enough since Denise, but even more so now that Spencer was gone. Add a dose of Richard Wilmott into the mix and that was enough to keep any self-respecting copper awake. *Acting Detective Inspector Richard Wilmott,* I heard the detective superintendent announce in my head from our meeting on Friday. Acting bloody DI indeed. It should've been me that was promoted. Not that I was bitter and twisted or anything, but, well . . . ADI Wilmott was a twat. Maybe I shouldn't have been surprised. Wilmott was an arse-kisser who'd made a career of perfecting police politics and doing very little else, whereas I questioned things I probably shouldn't. Even so, I had more experience, more service in the job, more dedication. The only dedication Wilmott had was to his mirror.

It was the Mackenzie case that had tipped things in Wilmott's favour. I knew that. I was still mulling over the injustice of it all when I picked up my mobile. 'DS Carter,' I announced, even though it should've been *Acting DI Carter!*

'Hi, it's the control room. You're the on-call CID tonight, aren't you?'

'Yeah.' I sat up.

'Inspector Pritchard is at the scene of a suspicious death in Waverly and is requesting CID, Sarge.'

'Right. What's happened?' I swung my legs out of bed.

'An intruder broke into a house and stabbed one of the occupants to death.'

I scribbled the address down on a pad by the side of my bed as she carried on talking.

'The deceased is the owner of the house, Max Burbeck. His wife, Alissa, managed to flee the scene and is currently at the hospital. She's given a brief account but she was hysterical and in shock, so she's been sedated.'

'Did she know the offender?'

'No. He wore a balaclava. She caught a brief glimpse of him before she locked herself in the bathroom and escaped through the window.'

'Who's at the hospital?'

'PC Glover.'

'Right, tell him I want him to keep a close guard on her while she's there.'

I heard her typing on her keyboard, recording every instruction for the incident log.

'Will do.'

I stood up. 'Have SOCO been called?'

'Yeah, they've just arrived at the scene. One of them has gone straight to the hospital, though, to collect any evidence from Mrs Burbeck. The Home Office pathologist is en route, too.'

'Good. I'll be on scene in about half an hour.' I hung up and dressed hastily before brushing my teeth and heading out the door.

Waverly was a small Hertfordshire country village. There was a mixture of terraced cottages at one end, before the streets opened up to reveal bigger plots and large mansions set back from the road, hidden from prying eyes behind the privacy of high walls and fences. It had a village pub called the Cross Keys, a small shop, and not much else. As I drove through the deserted lanes, lightning lit up the sky and thunder rumbled loudly overhead. Wind blasted through the trees on either side of me and a plastic bag flew across the road, attaching itself to the windscreen wiper. The storm that weather forecasters had predicted was here a day early. So much for the Indian summer they'd promised at the beginning of the year.

The Burbecks' property, called The Orchard, was slap bang in the middle of the village, but you couldn't see any of it from the main road. I drove up the long, winding tarmac driveway and the house stood before me, large and imposing and smacking of money. The front garden was laid to lawn, with a roundabout in front of the house covered with topiaries sculpted from green bushes in various intricate shapes. In the centre was a fountain. There were two uniformed cars parked up, along with the scene-of-crime van, and a lone police constable stood outside the front steps.

I called the control room on my radio to log my arrival at the scene and opened the car door, the wind instantly slamming it back against my arm. I tried again, heaving my shoulder against the door, and managed to get out. I donned a protective white jumpsuit – a forensic onesie – from a box inside the boot, and was sliding a mask over my face when I noticed Inspector Pritchard exiting the house and heading my way with a grave expression on his face.

'Sir.' I nodded, walking towards him.

'Hi, Warren,' he said, dispensing with any further greeting and getting straight into the nitty-gritty. 'The owner of the house, Max Burbeck, was found in an upstairs bedroom used as an office. It appears he's been stabbed in the back of the neck. We were called by the next-door neighbour after Max's wife, Alissa, fled the house and banged on her door for help. From the little PC Glover could ascertain before Mrs Burbeck was sedated at the hospital, she was in the bath at the time the attack happened. She didn't hear anything because Mr Burbeck was playing music and she'd fallen asleep, but when she woke up, she went through the master bedroom and saw an intruder wearing a balaclava and brandishing a knife. She managed to retreat back into the en-suite bathroom and lock the door before climbing out of the window and running to her neighbour's house.'

I scribbled a few notes in my pocketbook.

'SOCO have filmed the scene and they're just photographing now. Forensic pathologist is on the way. The office is upstairs on the left.'

'Good. Thanks, sir.' I made my way inside.

The house was a Georgian mansion with a chimney at either end of the building, covered with a trailing of ivy, and there were two white pillars above the front door that held up a balcony on the second storey.

I walked up the elegant sweeping staircase in the centre of the entrance hall. The top floor branched off via a hallway to the left and right. I glanced to my right, counting one open door on either side and another straight ahead of me that must've led to the master bedroom. From where I stood, I could see the edge of a large bed, and past that an en-suite bathroom. The impressions of what looked like damp footprints were darker smudges on the cream hall carpet, coming from the bedroom and stopping just before where I stood. Yellow numbered markers had been placed next to the prints where they'd been photographed for evidence.

A scene-of-crime officer who was bent over a claw-foot bath in the centre of the en-suite glanced over at me. Even though she was suited and masked, too, I knew it was Emma Bolton, the senior SOCO. There was no mistaking the dyed red hair peeking out from underneath her hood.

'Body's that way, Sarge.' She jerked her head back down the corridor.

'Is the bath full, Emma?' I approached through the bedroom, taking care to step around the wet footprints.

'No. Empty.'

I stood just inside the doorway, taking in the scene. A walk-in shower took up the whole wall to my right. I swung my gaze left to the toilet and double sink with a creamy marble top.

Emma stood and pointed to the window above the bath. A gold-coloured blind was in the down position but ripped from its roller at the top along one edge. 'Looks like the blind was yanked down in her haste to get away.' She pulled it out further, creating a gap behind it for me to see the large picture window, which in daylight must've afforded views to the vast acres of woods that butted up to the rear of the property. The window housed two openings in white PVC Georgian style, easily big enough for someone to climb through. The one on the right side was opened wide, a brown towel snagged on the bottom of the frame, hanging over it.

'She was naked when she arrived at the neighbour's house. Looks like she lost the towel as she crawled out.'

I leaned out the window, the wind blasting me with frigid air, and looked below me, spotting a flat roof about three metres down.

'That's the orangery down there,' Emma said.

'Orangery?'

Her eyes creased at the corners behind her mask as she smiled. 'A posh name for a conservatory.'

'So, Mrs Burbeck escaped through the window, jumped down to the orangery, then down to the ground?'

'Looks that way so far. It's about another four metres' drop from the orangery roof.'

The heavens opened then, fat pellets of rain battering down from the sky, drumming out a heavy beat on the roof, the wind blasting them towards my face. I pulled away from the window.

'Great!' Emma sighed. 'The weather's not going to help when we do the outside.'

I walked back to the bathroom door and examined it. It was splintered where it met the frame, and from the damage it was clear that it had been forced from the bedroom side. 'Was this done by uniform or the intruder?'

'Uniform. It was locked from the inside when they arrived so they forced it open.'

I left her to it and dodged around the footprints again, heading down the corridor, taking a quick look in the two rooms on this side of the house, which looked like unused guest rooms.

The first door past the stairs I'd just walked up was a room decked out as an office. A male body was seated in a leather chair, slumped over the antique mahogany desk in front as if he was asleep, exposing the knife wound at the back of his neck. There was very little blood from the wound, and no spatter that I could see. No signs of a struggle. Another SOCO stood over the body, taking photographs.

I stepped closer, scanning the scene. A pile of paperwork sat neatly on the surface of the desk next to an open laptop, showing a screensaver photo of a couple on their wedding day. There was also a printer, a mobile phone, a pen tidy, and a calculator. 'Was the laptop found like that?'

'Everything's the same apart from I turned the "Mute" button on. It was playing music which was really loud. You couldn't hear yourself think over it.'

I peered at the photo on the screen. The woman was stunning – long, wavy dark hair entwined with delicate white flowers, hanging loosely over one shoulder. Huge oval brown eyes, long lashes – eyes you could easily get lost in. A fine nose and full lips. She was holding hands with a man dressed in a perfectly tailored white suit. He had blond hair, his contrasting brown eyes dancing with happiness, speaking of a wonderful future as he looked at his bride.

I glanced back at the body. Looked like that future was gone now.

THE DETECTIVE
Chapter 3

I sat on the edge of my desk in the CID office as the briefing began. Detective Superintendent Greene stood at the front of the room, sipping coffee. Next to him stood *Acting* Detective Inspector Wilmott, perfectly primped in a purple shirt and navy blue suit that looked every bit as tailored as Max Burbeck's wedding outfit from the photo. He reminded me of a preening peacock, strutting around with a superior look on his face. Even his tie was a peacock two-tone purpley blue. Yeah, I know I should let it go.

DC Becky Harris sat at her desk in the corner. Her gaze met mine and I caught the slight eye-roll she gave me, aimed at Wilmott as he examined his manicured nails. DC Ronnie Pickering sat up straight in his chair, fingers laced in front of him, ready and waiting, eager as always, like a puppy seeking approval.

'Right.' Greene put his cup down and addressed us all. 'As you know, we're very short-staffed at the moment. DCI Tiller is heading up an in-depth fraud investigation, and until DI Nash returns, Acting DI Wilmott will be the senior investigating officer on this case.'

Wilmott looked up from his nails and aimed a smug grin in my direction. 'Thank you, sir.'

Greene stood back, letting Wilmott take the stage.

'Right, people. Uniform arrived on scene at 1.20 this morning following a phone call to us from a Mrs . . .' he peered at a printout of the incident log, 'Mrs Downes at 12.58 a.m. Her next-door neighbour, Alissa Burbeck, awoke her by banging on the rear door in a hysterical state, saying there was an armed intruder in the house. Mrs Burbeck had managed to escape through a bathroom window and run, naked and barefoot, into the woods that border the rear of her property. Those woods also run the length of the back of the village. On arrival at the scene, PC Brightman and PC Summers checked the house, but no intruder was found.' Wilmott went through the rest of the details we knew so far, finishing up with, 'Alissa Burbeck was taken to hospital and a uniform has been stationed outside her door for her safety. She was in deep shock, and after hearing her husband had been killed, she had to be sedated.' He glanced at his expensive watch. 'She should hopefully be awake enough soon to be able to give us further details.'

'Was it a burglary, guv?' Ronnie asked.

'DS Carter, you were at the scene, maybe you'd like to take this,' ADI Wilmott said.

'There were no signs of forced entry at the property,' I said. 'There was a good alarm system on the house, but it hadn't been set. Either the offender had a key or got in through an unlocked door. It seems unlikely the offender was let in by Max Burbeck because he appears to have been working at his desk with the door to his office open. He was listening to loud music at the time, so it seems he didn't hear the attacker approach him from behind. There are also no signs of a burglary at this stage, although we'll need to confirm whether anything is missing with Mrs Burbeck when she's able to, and we're obviously still awaiting forensics, which will take a while. It was a big house, and due to the torrential rain and hail we've just had, SOCO might not be able to find any useful evidence from the grounds. I doubt very much this was a random attack, though. No murder weapon has been recovered at the scene so far. We don't know yet if any knives are missing from the house, so it's unclear if the offender brought it with them, but going on the assumption this isn't a burglary, then it's likely they did, which would suggest a planned attack.'

'Do we have any reasons to suggest why Mr and Mrs Burbeck were targeted?' Detective Superintendent Greene asked.

'Not at this stage,' Wilmott said. 'There are no previous incidents logged at the address, and a check of our databases hasn't turned up anything. But the scene would suggest the offender was not interested in the vast amount of expensive items in the house.' He turned to Becky. 'DC Harris, I want you to check whether any neighbouring properties have CCTV cameras. There are no council-run cameras in the village, but this is an affluent area; the surrounding houses to the Burbecks' are exclusive and expensive, so I wouldn't be surprised if any owners have their own security.'

Becky scribbled that down on her notepad.

'SOCO have recovered two laptops: one that Max appeared to be working on before the incident happened, and another one, believed to be Alissa's, from the kitchen. A mobile phone on Max's office desk has also been recovered, along with another mobile phone on the bedside table in the master suite, also believed to belong to Mrs Burbeck. The technical forensic team will work through them and see if they can find anything relevant. SOCO will get the documents from Max's desk to you to check out this morning, along with anything else they discover.' Wilmott nodded at Becky. 'Also, dig into the background of Mr and Mrs Burbeck and see what you come up with.'

More scribbling by Becky. 'Do we know what they do for a living?'

'I believe DS Carter has made some preliminary enquiries on that.' Wilmott gave way to me again.

'I found a few online articles about them. Max Burbeck owned a large property development company, Burbeck Developments, which is listed as one of the top six developers in the country, but I'm not sure if that's relevant in any way at this stage.' I circulated a printout of an article with a photo of the happy couple on it, announcing their engagement six months previously.

'Must be worth a fortune!' Ronnie piped up, taking his copy.

'This is Alissa Burbeck?' Becky stared at the photo. 'Is she a model?'

'Not as far as I can tell. She took a creative writing course and is apparently working on her first novel,' I added.

'What's the age gap between them?' ADI Wilmott asked, not taking his eyes from the photo.

'Alissa is twenty-four, and Max is thirty-five.'

'Lucky bugger,' ADI Wilmott said.

'Not so lucky now, though, eh?' I said. 'It seems they were married two months ago in Australia, and had a big reception at the house a couple of weeks ago on their return, so the forensic evidence is likely to be a mess up there. That's all I really know about them so far.'

'Married two months ago and he's worth a fortune?' Ronnie said. 'I bet it's the wife.'

'We're not making any assumptions at the moment. We'll follow the evidence and see where it leads us,' Detective Superintendent Greene said sternly, looking at me when he said it.

A prickle of annoyance itched under my skin, and I had to hold back a sarcastic snort. I'd been stopped from following the evidence in the Mackenzie case by Greene. He should've rephrased his instruction: we follow the evidence, as long as it doesn't lead to someone rich and powerful and we're forced to shut down an investigation.

'No, sir, of course not, sir.' Ronnie shuffled in his seat like a chastised schoolboy.

I glanced at ADI Wilmott, who seemed to still be staring at the picture of Alissa Burbeck. There was a brief pause in the air, broken by Detective Superintendent Greene clearing his throat, jerking ADI Wilmott's attention away from the photo.

'DC Pickering, I want you to get a statement from Mrs Downes. Then do house-to-house enquiries and see if any of the other neighbours saw anything suspicious,' ADI Wilmott said.

Ronnie nodded vigorously. Bless him. He'd been promoted to detective constable six months ago and was what I'd affectionately call a jobsworth. Keen to make an impression. He was as excited as I'd been twenty-five years ago after I'd become a DC. A lot had happened along the way to dampen that excitement for me. Maybe I was getting too old and cynical for all the crap that went with the role, especially since it now wasn't looking likely that I'd ever make DI before I retired.

'Becky, I also want you to put in the usual requests for phones and financial records.' ADI Wilmott glanced at her.

'Yes, guv.'

'DS Carter and I will be heading to the hospital to see Alissa Burbeck.' ADI Wilmott paused, his gaze flitting to each of us in turn. 'That's it for now. Keep me updated.'

~

In real life, Alissa Burbeck was every bit as beautiful as her photo. Maybe 'beautiful' didn't even do her justice. She was the kind of woman you'd describe as hypnotising. Every little feature had been perfectly designed to make you unable to look away, to make you think, *Is she really real?* Surely, no one who looked like that could be. In some ways, she reminded me of a doll – a manufacturer's idea of flawless perfection. Wide eyed, long lashed, cupid-bow lips, glossy chocolate-brown hair, all wrapped up in a delicate and fine-boned package. The kind of woman men wanted and women wanted to be like.

She lay on her side, facing the door to the single, private hospital room we'd just entered, clutching the bedsheet in her hands. Even though it was obvious she'd been crying, she still looked stunning.

'Mrs Burbeck, I'm Detective Inspector Wilmott and this is Detective Sergeant Carter.'

I fought the urge to say *Acting*!

Alissa forced herself into a sitting position on the bed, still clutching the sheet. Fresh tears snaked down her high cheek bones. 'They told me . . . last night . . . that policeman on the door out there . . .' She gasped in a deep breath. 'Max is dead, isn't he? He's really dead?' She blinked rapidly, her lashes glistening wet under the sickly lighting.

Wilmott pulled out a plastic chair next to her bed and sat down. I stood at the end of the bed.

'I'm very sorry for your loss,' Wilmott said.

I half expected him to take her hand in his and stroke it. He had a look on his face usually reserved for when he caught glimpses of his reflection in mirrors or windows.

She drew her knees up underneath the sheet and flopped her head on to them, wailing. Her shoulders heaved up and down as she struggled for breath.

'I know this is very difficult, but we really need to ask some questions about last night,' I said. 'The quicker we can ascertain what happened, the quicker we can find the person responsible.'

'Oh, God.' She lifted her head and swiped at her cheeks with her fingers. She swallowed hard, the cleft in her slender throat rising and falling. 'I just . . .' She shook her head. 'I . . .' She gulped in some more air.

DI Wilmott tilted his head. 'Would you like me to get a doctor?' He leaned in closer, watching her somewhat protectively.

She closed her eyes and bit her lower lip. 'I'm sorry.' Her voice was a quivering whisper as she opened her eyes and blinked at Wilmott. 'I . . . I want to help, but . . . this is so awful. I can't believe anyone would do this.' Her face seemed to crumple.

'Can I get you something? Some water, perhaps?' DI Wilmott asked. Before she could answer, Wilmott's phone rang. He glanced at it, then said, 'Sorry, I have to take this.' He stood up and headed towards the door, looking over his shoulder to me, saying, 'Get Mrs Burbeck some water.'

'Thank you.' Alissa held out an empty jug that had been on her bedside locker.

Wilmott left the room, walking down the corridor, and I filled the jug from a sink in the small en-suite bathroom in the corner of the room. When I walked back to her bed, Alissa was sitting up, reaching for a tissue from a pack on top of the cabinet next to an empty glass, and wiping her eyes.

'Here you go.' I poured some water into the glass.

She took a sip and I stood at the end of the bed again.

'Thank you.' She replaced the glass and clutched the bedsheet in one dainty dolly hand while wiping her cheeks again with the other. 'Ask me whatever you need to know. I want you to catch them, too. That policeman who was on my door outside . . . he said Max had been . . .' She trailed off again, then blinked, composing herself.

Wilmott walked back in and sat down. 'That was the forensic pathologist on the phone,' he told Alissa. 'The post-mortem is being carried out shortly so we're still waiting for the results, but it would appear at this stage that your husband died from a stab wound to the base of the neck.'

Alissa sucked in a deep breath and fell back against the pillows. Her head wobbled slightly, as if she was shaking it in defence against the words.

I pulled a digital recorder out of my pocket. 'We need to record this conversation, Mrs Burbeck.'

'Yes,' she said, not looking at me, vaguely indicating her agreement with a hand.

I pressed 'Record', then announced who was in the room and the date, time, and location.

'Can you tell us what happened?' DI Wilmott asked.

THE OTHER ONE
Chapter 4

It had been established from the start of school that I was the weird kid. When the teacher asked the class to do drawings of what they did at the weekend, the others scribbled colourful pictures of mums and dads and skippy little children with oversized smiles on their faces. Pictures of ice creams and shiny bright days where a huge sun shone down on perfect happy families.

Mine depicted angry red faces, fangs, blood. A mum and dad whose mouths were slashes of black. Dark skies with thunderbolts raining down.

Our teacher, Mrs Fuller, was ancient. At least she seemed so to me. Looking back, she was probably in her late forties. She would coo at the other kids' drawings, but when it came to mine, her frowny face appeared, the one that she liked using on me. She told me I needed to brighten things up, that my pictures were too dramatic and nonsensical. I wanted to tell her that that was real life, but, of course, I didn't. Mum said I could never tell anyone what happened at home. The things that went on behind closed doors were private, she said. All the times I was awoken at night with screams and bangs from my parents' room were just 'Mummy and Daddy having a disagreement.' All the times I'd run into their room and shout and cry, just to make my voice heard over the noise, trying to tell my dad not to hurt Mummy any more. All the times I clung on to my dad's legs to stop him getting near her, only to be flung aside roughly like one of the baby cows. When he marched me downstairs, gripping my arm so tight I thought it would snap, my feet barely touching the floor as he deposited me in the cupboard under the stairs and slid the bolt across with a sickening *click*! He said it was my fault. I was being disrespectful. I was wicked. I never listened. And he was going to drum some discipline into me because God said I was a nasty little bastard and needed to be taught a lesson. I didn't know who this God person was, but Dad talked about him a lot, especially when Mum or I didn't do something right and needed to be punished.

At first, I was scared of the cupboard. I banged on the wooden doors with my feet and hands, screamed, cried, broke fingernails trying to scrape away at the hinges, but it didn't make any difference. Dad wouldn't let me out until he was ready, and Mum would never dare to defy him. I didn't understand a lot about what was really happening then, but I knew that much. Mum defended Dad all the time: 'He's just exhausted,' 'He's just stressed,' 'The pressure of looking after us is a lot,' 'He worries about having enough money.' Blah, blah, blah. Looking back now, it was none of those things. He was just a horrible man who enjoyed inflicting pain and suffering on us, like he did with the animals. A weak, self-centred, psychopathic bully. An ignorant, evil man. He was the bastard, not me.

After it became a regular thing, I began to welcome the darkness and solitude of the cupboard. It was my friend, my silence in all the madness, my little haven. I even had a pet spider in there I called Freddie. Freddie was small and black, and the first time he scuttled across my foot, I shrieked and screamed and backed into a corner, not knowing what it was. But then one time, when Dad opened the door, I saw him in the corner as the light from the hall hit the interior wall of the cupboard. So, Freddie was my company in there. I talked to him a lot, and he was a great listener. I'd fall asleep in there, just chatting with my mate, the only one in the world I could actually talk to, because the kids at school avoided me like a dose of chicken pox. I didn't know how to talk to those other kids. I'd never been to nursery, and we didn't live near anyone else, so I'd never been around other kids. I thought shouting at people was the right way to communicate, but the others didn't seem to like it. It made the girls cry and the boys want to punch me, which they did. A lot. They thought it hurt me but it didn't. They couldn't hit like Dad could. The raggedy second-hand clothes I wore made me look so different from the other kids, too, and I had holes in the soles of my shoes where my big toe popped out. I didn't look right. I didn't feel right, either.

The number of times I was told to stop shouting by Mrs Fuller was too numerous to count. But I couldn't stop. I know she phoned my parents to tell them about my aggressive behaviour, which, of course, had a knock-on effect in that Dad would tell me I was an ungrateful, nasty little bastard, and God needed to knock some sense into me. So then I had Dad *and* God *and* Mrs Fuller to contend with.

But, despite that, I still thought of school as being like the cupboard. It was safe, my own space where I could get away from the black days at home. I stood in the playground alone, on the fringes of the other kids, while they giggled about me and called out rude names, like always. They thought it would upset me, but it didn't, because that was nothing. What they could do to me was *nothing* like being at home. They thought they were clever, but they didn't have a clue. School was my holiday. So, there I was, tuning out the taunts, laughing to myself because they thought they were getting to me, and I noticed a new little boy about to start his first day. I watched him cling to his mum's legs, like I tried to do to Dad when I wanted to stop that God person ranting and raving, spewing nastiness from Dad's mouth, and when

I was trying to stop his hitting and kicking. I thought that little boy was stupid. Why *wouldn't* he want to get away from home and spend a few hours without all *that* going on? Why *wouldn't* he want to draw pictures and be free? But the more I watched, the more I realised that his mum wasn't like my mum. She wasn't telling him to 'Stop that right now or Daddy will be angry!' There was no 'Just do as your dad tells you,' or 'If you'd only behave, he wouldn't be so annoyed! It's all your fault!' No, this mum crouched down in front of her teary little boy and wiped the crying away. She hugged his body tight towards her and kissed his cheeks, ruffled his hair. There was a twinge of something hot and pulsating as a thought rammed its way into my skull: *I want to be him. I want that mum.*

He was called George, and he was put in my class. I'd watch him all the time, copying what he did. How he held his pencil. How he ate his packed lunch. How he talked. The way he tilted his head to the left and poked his tongue out of his mouth slightly when he concentrated on spelling words. The way he laughed from his belly. If I could actually *be* George, his mum would take me away and I could have a new home. So I watched and learned some more.

I was the first kid to rush out of school one day, and I ran through the playground pretending to be a plane, like George did, with an excited grin on my face. The picture I'd drawn earlier flapped in my hand, one I'd copied from George by looking over his shoulder. I think the picture was supposed to be George, but he had a big round head and no hair and eyes that took up most of his face. Next to him was lovely Mum, with bright red lips in a smiley curve, and his dad, holding George's hand and carrying a briefcase. I ran towards George's mum and threw myself at her, hugging her legs, looking up into her surprised face and telling her how much I'd missed her.

'Well, now.' She crouched down in front of me. 'What have you got there?' She looked at my picture as I thrust it towards her, pride swelling inside my chest.

'It's a picture of you and Daddy and me!'

Her face wobbled a little bit, but the smile was still in place. 'And who are you?'

'I'm your new George!' I declared brightly.

Her smile faltered then.

They found George locked in the cupboard at the back of one of the classrooms a little while later. No matter how much I swore it wasn't me that did it, they didn't believe me.

THE DETECTIVE
Chapter 5

'It was about midnight,' Alissa said. 'Max was doing some work in his office while he listened to music on his laptop, and I went to have a bath in the en-suite in our bedroom.'

'Did he often listen to music when working?' I asked.

She sniffed and nodded. 'Yes, all the time. I fell asleep in the bath and then, when I woke up, the water was cold, so I don't know how long I'd been in there for, but . . .' She took another shaky breath. 'I got out and dried off, wrapped a towel round me, and went into the bedroom, but Max still wasn't in bed, so I . . .' She clutched at the bedsheet.

'It's OK. Take your time,' DI Wilmott said.

'I . . . I wanted to pop my head in the office and tell him it was late and that I was going to bed, but as I walked out into the corridor, I saw . . .' Her eyes widened, dark lashes flashing against tanned skin. Her face contorted with sadness.

'What did you see?' I asked.

'It was a man. He was coming out of Max's office and heading right . . . right towards me! I screamed and ran back to the bathroom and locked the door. Then I climbed through the bathroom window and down on to the roof of the orangery and jumped to the ground. Then I just ran. Through the garden into the woods, along to our nearest neighbours so they could call the police.' She ran shaky fingertips down her cheeks to bat away the tears. 'If I'd stayed . . . if only I'd . . . maybe Max would still be . . .' She inhaled a hiccupping breath.

'You did the right thing to ensure your safety.' DI Wilmott lifted his hand as if to place it on hers, before changing his mind at the last moment and running it through his hair instead.

'Did you get a good look at the intruder?' I asked.

She swallowed, blinking rapidly. 'He wore black. And he had this . . .' she pointed to her face, 'this balaclava on, which covered all of his face apart from his eyes. I thought I was going to d . . . die. I thought . . . he had a knife in his hand, you see.'

'Did you have time to recognise whether the knife came from your house?' DI Wilmott asked.

She shook her head. 'No, it was too quick.'

'Did you notice anything else about him?' I asked. 'Height, build, eye colour? Did he say anything?'

'Um . . . it was all so quick, but I think he was about my height . . . maybe five foot nine or ten. I don't know what kind of build . . . it's hard to say because he had a puffy black jacket on. He didn't speak.'

'So, he was average height?' I suggested.

She bit her lower lip and nodded. She squeezed her eyes shut, as if to block out the picture that would be forever burned in her mind.

'Did you notice anything else?' I asked.

'Um . . . yes. He wore gloves. Black ones. And he had these things on his feet, like plastic covers. They were dark blue. They rustled when he walked.'

'Plastic shoe covers?' I asked.

She nodded.

'Anything else?' DI Wilmott asked, wearing a sympathetic frown.

Her eyes flashed open and I was hit again by her beauty.

'No. Like I said, it was too quick, and I was trying to get away from him.'

'We think the offender entered the house through the kitchen door at the rear, which was unlocked when police arrived on scene,' Willmott said. 'The alarm hadn't been set. Was it unusual to leave that door unlocked?'

'No. Max smoked outside. I didn't like him smoking in the house, and now . . . well, now it's all just . . . maybe I should've let him. Maybe then that man wouldn't have got in! Max didn't usually lock the door until he was going to bed.' She paused for a moment. 'Nothing ever happens in our little village. It's quiet and . . . well, it *was* quiet.'

'And what about the alarm? When was that usually set?' I asked.

'Again, when Max was going to bed, he'd set the alarm after he locked up.'

'At this stage, it doesn't look like a burglary, although I'll need you to accompany me to the house when our scene-of-crime officers have finished to confirm whether anything has been stolen,' DI Wilmott said. 'It would appear that Max was attacked while seated at his desk and so wasn't a threat of any kind to the intruder. And none of the other rooms appear to have been disturbed. If he was listening to music at the time, it's most likely that he didn't know someone was in the house until it was too late.'

She gasped. 'Do I have to . . . I don't think I could go back there!'

'I know it's going to be very difficult, but we need to explore all avenues, and we need to do it as soon as possible. Don't worry, I'll be with you,' DI Wilmott assured her.

She bit her lip again. 'Of course you do. I'm sorry, it's just that . . .' She reached for another tissue from the box on the cabinet by her bed and blew her nose, balling it up in her hand and clutching it afterwards. 'It's really hard.' Her voice cracked.

'We know, Mrs Burbeck,' I said. 'You're doing great.'

'Alissa. Please, just call me Alissa.' She looked at DI Wilmott. 'If it wasn't a burglary, then what . . . why . . .' She trailed off, as if unsure of how to phrase the question.

'It's possible you and Max could've been targeted specifically. Is there any reason you could think of as to why this might be? Any enemies or disgruntled employees?'

'God, no!' Her mouth fell open.

'Have you received any threats recently?' I asked. 'Have you noticed anyone hanging around the property? Have you had any disagreements with people?'

'Oh, no.' She collapsed forward, her face falling into her hands.

'What is it?' DI Wilmott asked.

'There were a couple of things, but . . .' She shook her head. 'I found out about something that was going on at Max's company just after we got back from Australia.'

'Australia?' Wilmott said.

'Yes. It was kind of a working holiday and honeymoon rolled into one. We only . . .' She stared down at her wedding and engagement rings and swallowed hard. 'We only got married eight weeks ago, in Australia. We wanted it to be a quiet ceremony, just the two of us. We didn't want the fuss of arranging a big wedding, or the stress. So we had the idea of just going away on our own and doing it in Australia. Max wanted to get into property development over there, too, so it was the perfect solution. We got married first, then travelled around, and he had some business meetings in between, which left me free to soak up the sun and have some pampering. We were there for a month, and two weeks after we returned, we had a party, a celebration at the house.'

'Your husband owns Burbeck Developments, is that right?' I asked.

'Yes. His dad owned it first, but his parents died a couple of years ago in a boating accident and left the company to Max. He'd worked for them ever since he left uni and . . . well, anyway, I guess that's not really important right now.'

'So what was going on at the company?' DI Wilmott asked.

'I'm not really sure. He didn't go into details with me. He didn't want me to worry about anything, and I probably wouldn't have understood it anyway. I'm not great with finances and planning things. And it was . . . you know, it was his business, and I've never been involved in it. But he said some customers weren't happy about a development he'd built quite a few years ago. They were complaining about something. He said it wasn't anything major, but he seemed quite stressed about it.'

I noted that down. 'And you're a writer?'

'Yes.'

'Have you written anything that someone could've taken offence to, or that attracted unwanted attention?'

'No. I'm working on my debut novel at the moment. I haven't written anything else.'

DI Wilmott ran a hand through his sandy-blond hair again, the solid gel parting briefly before springing back into place. 'You mentioned there might be a couple of things? What else can you think of?'

'Well, my ex-boyfriend, but he . . . God, there's no way he could do something like this.' She took a sip of water and cradled the glass to her chest.

'Tell us about him,' DI Wilmott said.

'Um . . . Russell was my first boyfriend. We met at primary school, and then we lost touch when we went to different secondary schools, but we met up again at a party when I was seventeen and started seeing each other. He was at college doing horticulture, and I went on to do my creative writing course.

'We dated for four years, but then . . . I don't know . . . it was just young love, I suppose, and it fizzled out. At least on my part it did. I . . . um . . . I met Max one night at a club and, well, nothing happened between us then, but Max was persistent and he . . .' Her lips lifted in a smile, as if remembering her husband. Despite her grief, it was a dazzling smile. 'He kept asking me out and sending me flowers and things, and the short story is I ended things with Russell and started seeing Max. Russell had become more of a friend to me than a boyfriend by that stage. I didn't want to hurt him, but I knew it was over between us.'

'How did Russell take it?' DI Wilmott asked.

'Not too well, at first. He couldn't accept things were over. He kept turning up at my mum's house where I lived at the time before she went into a nursing home. And he kept texting me and sending me letters, wanting us to get back together. It got a bit, um . . . awkward for a while. But then we met up one day and I told him it had to stop. I was with Max now and, you know, I was sorry about ending things with him, but we'd kind of outgrown each other. He seemed to be OK about it then, and the texts stopped when he decided to go travelling – backpacking round Australia for a year.'

'How long ago was this?'

She tilted her head, thinking. 'I've been with Max for three years now. Russell carried on with the pleading texts for about six months after we'd split up. He lives in the same village now, though, at the other end, so I'd see him occasionally out and about. If we were in the village pub at the same time, we'd say hello, but I never really heard from him properly again until recently. He knew Max and I were getting married and started texting me again, asking if I was OK, was I sure I was doing the right thing and all that.' She looked at me, a trace of guilt etched on her face. 'I wanted to be friends with Russell. He'd been a big part of my life growing up, and I didn't mind him texting again, really. I thought it was innocent, friendly stuff at first, but . . .'

'But?' DI Wilmott asked.

'He turned up at our wedding celebration uninvited. He was really drunk and he made a bit of a scene.' She paused and fiddled with the bedsheet again. 'He cornered me outside on the lawn and told me I was making a big mistake and that he still loved me and still wanted me back.' She looked up at DI Wilmott. 'I asked him to leave, but he wouldn't stop talking and pleading, and then Max spotted him and came over. Russell got very emotional and shouted at Max that he wasn't good enough for me and that it wouldn't last and . . . God, the last thing Russell said was that Max deserved everything he got and that he should watch his back.'

'What did you think he meant by that?' I asked.

'I don't know. At the time, I thought it was just words in the heat of the moment, but now . . . with what's happened, maybe he meant he was—' She hiccupped in some air. 'It could've been a veiled threat to kill Max.'

'Was Russell ever violent?' I asked.

'Yes,' she said quietly. 'Only once. He punched a man in a pub one night because the man was making rude comments to me. But he was never violent with me. Max asked him to leave after he said that, and Russell did. I thought that was the end of it, and I haven't heard from Russell since. But it seems crazy. Russell can't have done this, can he?' And then something seemed to spark behind her eyes. 'Or do you think . . .' She threw her head back, her chocolatey hair fanning against the pillow, eyes wild with terror. 'Was that man after both of us?'

'We're not sure,' DI Wilmott said. 'It could be that Max was the target and you disturbed him, but I have to be honest with you: until we catch this person, your safety is of great importance. I'm told that you'll be released later this morning and we'll need to move you somewhere that no one knows about for the time being.'

Her lips trembled and she looked like a lost, frightened child you wanted to wrap your arms around. 'But where? I don't have anywhere to go now.'

THE DETECTIVE
Chapter 6

DC Becky Harris was the only one in the office when I got back. She was poring over her laptop with a phone tucked in the crook of her neck, talking and typing at the same time.

I ran a hand over my face, fighting the tiredness. I'd only been up for six hours, but it was more if you counted the sleepless night beforehand. Or the many before that.

Coffee. I needed some caffeine to jolt through my bloodstream.

I switched on the kettle in the corner of the room and looked at the whiteboard that had been erected in my absence. A photo of Max and Alissa took centre stage. Underneath was a map of the Burbecks' house and surrounding area, and in Becky's handwriting was a list of the salient points we knew so far. Alissa's eyes seemed to follow my every movement as I made the drinks.

I took a mug of coffee to Becky's desk and then sat at mine, taking a sip.

She put the phone down and looked at me. 'Do you want a Kit Kat with that?'

'How can I refuse an offer like that? You're going to make someone a great wife one day.'

'You can't say stuff like that any more. It's not politically correct.'

'Bollocks,' I said. 'I'm old school.' I rolled my shoulders and moved my neck from side to side as if I was a boxer limbering up. 'That's just how I roll.'

She smirked and delved into her drawer. 'I'll report you to *Acting DI* Wilmott.' She wagged a Kit Kat at me.

I shrugged.

'You should be acting DI, you know.'

You see? It wasn't just me who thought that. I shrugged again, this time shrugging off the issue. I'd deal with it later, or just put it in a box in my head with the rest of the stuff I tried to have selective denial about. Not that it seemed to be working. 'No one should be acting DI. Spencer shouldn't have been killed and DI Nash should still be here.' I'd worked with Ellie Nash for eight years. She wasn't just an outstanding DI; she was a good person. One of the few you could rely on in a crisis. One of those friends who would always drop everything and come running if you needed them. She was solid. Until now. Now she was shattered.

'You're right. Sorry. Where is DI Wilmott anyway?'

'He's taken Alissa back to the house to check for anything missing, and for her to get some personal items. Then he's taking her to a hotel.'

'Yeah, I bet he's going to *love* babysitting her.'

Everyone knew Wilmott was a sleaze when it came to women. Maybe sleaze was too harsh. Perhaps smarmy was better. Trouble was, he loved himself too much to ever fall in love with someone else. It was all about the conquest for him. And the shag.

Becky opened her mouth as if to say something else but closed it again, throwing the chocolate bar at me instead.

I caught it and began unwrapping it. 'How are you getting on?'

'Not much to report at the moment, I'm afraid.' She dunked a finger of chocolate in her coffee and swallowed half of it in one bite. 'There's no CCTV in the village. I've managed to contact some of the property owners nearby to see if they have private camera systems, but so far nothing helpful. Ronnie's doing house-to-house.' She demolished the rest of the finger and said, 'The Burbecks' phone and financial records should be coming in soon. I've just been down to the tech team to see if they've found anything interesting to go on yet on the laptops or phones. It's going to take them a while, but they gave me a heads up that there are a lot of recent texts on Alissa's phone from a guy called Russell, who seemed to be stalking her.'

I filled her in on what Alissa had said about Russell. 'What did the texts say?'

'I only saw a few, they're going to print them off for us. But what I did see backed up what you've just told me. He wanted her back after they split up. Didn't seem to take no for an answer.'

'That tallies up with what Alissa told us. She said he made a veiled threat to Max at their wedding reception.'

'Interesting.' She raised an eyebrow.

'And according to Alissa, there were some customers of Max's company that were complaining about something to do with a development he built. I'll need to take a trip up to their head office to find out more. Apart from that, there are no recent threats or suspicious people making a nuisance of themselves. Can you check out whether Max and Alissa used social media – Facebook, Twitter, Instagram, et cetera. See if you can build up a picture of them or if there's anything of interest on there.'

'Will do.'

I took another swig of coffee and clicked my mouse to wake up the laptop on my desk, entering Russell Stiles' name in our databases.

There were no incidents logged to his address, but he was known to the police. He'd been charged with affray when he was eighteen, following a fight in a pub with another man, as Alissa had said. He'd been given a twelve-month community service order, so he hadn't served any time. Five years later, he was caught poaching rabbits and given a three-hundred-pound fine.

I chewed on my pen, watching Stiles' name jump even higher up my mental persons of interest list. He had a history of violence. Because of the poaching, it was likely he knew how to skin and dissect game, which would make him handy with a knife. He'd harassed Alissa following their breakup, and had started again when he'd found out about their wedding. He appeared to still be in love with her, and seemed to harbour a grudge against Max Burbeck. But was it big enough for Russell to kill him over?

THE OTHER ONE
Chapter 7

There were two Dads. The one who thought I was the devil, and the one who was friendly and jokey with the customers and suppliers, who went to church on Sundays, smiled and sang hymns and held tight on to Mum's hand while chatting to the vicar like he wasn't really a raving lunatic.

But as soon as we got back to the farm, the nasty Dad would appear again, like an invisible button in his head had been pressed. I'd have to help him with the animals while Mum made his favourite roast dinner. I had no free time myself. Not that it mattered much. I didn't have any friends, and even if I did, I wouldn't have been allowed to have them at the house. Dad hated children. And he would never have let me play at their houses because every spare minute I had to work with Dad, whose favourite saying was *The Devil finds work for idle hands*.

At first, I liked stroking the cows and helping Dad with the milking machines. But as time went on, I saw how he kicked them and hit them and forced them into tiny stalls for most of their lives, living in their shit and piss and stink, barely able to move. And I'd look into their huge, watery brown eyes and see my own eyes looking back at me. They were trapped. They were scared. They were in pain. Just like me.

I'd talk to them, kiss the fur between their eyes, rub their backs – try to let them know they weren't alone. Even at that age I understood what they felt and thought because I felt it, too. If I cried about the cows, Dad laughed at me, calling me a 'Useless, snivelling bastard.'

When I was locked in the cupboard, I'd dream up ways to let them all out. They'd be free to escape then. Free from all the horribleness and misery my dad inflicted on them. Free from his poisonous mind that lashed out at the weak, the ones who couldn't answer him back.

If Dad caught me talking to the cows, he'd silence me with a look or threaten me with his fists, so we worked in silence, even though I'd chatter away to them in my head. I knew they could secretly hear me, and it was my private act of defiance.

One time, after the cows were milked, we went back into the house, and I caught a waft of burning smells, which became more pungent with each step we took towards the kitchen. Mum looked harassed and anxious, the bun she'd worn at church now loose and hair plastered to her forehead with sweat. She pulled a very crispy-looking piece of meat from the oven, wafting smoke all over the place, which set Dad off.

'What have you bloody done?' he boomed at her as she set the roasting tray on the worktop. 'Money doesn't grow on trees, you know, and you've just ruined a perfectly good bit of meat! How am I supposed to eat that rubbish? It's burnt to a crisp!'

Mum blinked away the tears in her eyes, cowering in front of him. 'I'm sorry, love, I . . . I don't know what happened. I got distracted making the apple pie.'

'Why can't you do anything right?' He sneered in her face, a fleck of spittle flying on to her cheek and making her flinch.

I hid under the table, crouching into a ball, knowing something bad was going to happen.

I saw the roasting tin skitter across the floor, bouncing meat and juice everywhere. Heard the slaps and the crying and pleading and whimpering. Then I saw Dad pick up a bottle of cooking oil from the worktop and pour it all over Mum's head.

THE DETECTIVE
Chapter 8

I sat in the interview room across the desk from Russell Stiles. He had short brown hair, a stud in his right ear, tattooed sleeves on both arms, and broody dark eyes. He wore ripped beige combats and an old, faded T-shirt. He was probably as different from Max as you could get.

'Thank you for coming in to see me, Mr Stiles.'

He frowned, and leaned his elbows on the desk. 'Look, I know I've got a couple of speeding tickets, but this is a bit much, isn't it? I just haven't got round to paying them yet.'

'Firstly, I need to inform you that this interview is being recorded and videoed. Present are Russell Stiles and DS Carter. The time is . . .' I glanced at the clock, then added the time and date for the benefit of the tape . . .

RUSSELL STILES: What's going on?

DS CARTER: There was a serious incident last night at The Orchard, and we think you may be able to help us with our enquiries.

RUSSELL STILES: What? That's . . . Is Alissa OK?

DS CARTER: An intruder broke into Max and Alissa Burbeck's house and stabbed Max to death.

RUSSELL STILES: *What?!*

DS CARTER: Sit down, please, Mr Stiles.

RUSSELL STILES: Shit . . . I . . . Is Alissa alright? Where is she? I have to see her!

DS CARTER: Alissa mentioned you'd had an altercation at their wedding reception two weeks ago. Is that correct?

RUSSELL STILES: (Inaudible)

DS CARTER: For the benefit of the tape, Mr Stiles, is that correct?

RUSSELL STILES: Well, yes, but that was . . . What's going on? Is she OK?

DS CARTER: Can you tell me what happened that day?

RUSSELL STILES: I haven't done anything! Why are you asking me? Please, just tell me if she's OK.

DS CARTER: Just answer the questions, please.

RUSSELL STILES: Am I under arrest or something?

DS CARTER: No. You're here voluntarily and you can leave at any time. But we believe you may have information that might help us.

RUSSELL STILES: Umm . . . I don't know what to say.

DS CARTER: Just start by telling me what happened at the party. Did you threaten Max or Alissa?

RUSSELL STILES: Of course not! I . . . look, I was a bit pissed. Well, more than a bit. I don't remember a lot of it. I was . . . upset that she'd married him. And, it was a stupid thing to do, but I turned up at their house and then . . . Shit, is he really dead? I can't believe this. (Inaudible)

DS CARTER: What happened at the party?

RUSSELL STILES: I just went to their house and . . . this is way out of proportion. It was nothing. I admit I shouldn't have gone there, but I just wanted to make sure she knew what she was doing.

DS CARTER: How did you get on to the premises?

RUSSELL STILES: Their house backs on to the woods, like most of them in the village, and they've only got a post-and-rail fence. I was . . . this is going to sound . . .

DS CARTER: Sound like what?

RUSSELL STILES: Well, it sounds like I'm some kind of stalker, but I'm not. I'm definitely not!

DS CARTER: OK, go on.

RUSSELL STILES: Well, I sat up in the woods and I was drinking a bottle of Jack Daniel's, just . . . um . . . watching. I saw the marquee in the garden and everything and I . . . look, it was a stupid snap decision. I just wanted to make sure she was OK. He's not as squeaky clean as he looks, you know.

DS CARTER: Who? Max Burbeck?

RUSSELL STILES: Yeah.

DS CARTER: What do you mean by that? Is there something we should know about Max Burbeck?

RUSSELL STILES: Just something I heard.

DS CARTER: And what was that?

RUSSELL STILES: Apparently, Max bought some land quite a few years ago and developed it with houses, but recently the owners have found out it's contaminated with asbestos from industrial waste. And that stuff causes cancer, you know!

DS CARTER: And where did you hear this from?

RUSSELL STILES: I don't remember. But Max knew all along it was contaminated, but it would've cost too much to get it decontaminated, so he buried the findings of a report and paid some company to do a fake report that hid everything. And now the owners are obviously seriously pissed off and worried about it, and he's refusing to compensate them. So he's not exactly Mr Nice Guy. I bet he's made a few enemies doing stuff like that.

DS CARTER: Where is this land?

RUSSELL STILES: I don't know.

DS CARTER: Do you know which companies were involved in making these reports?

RUSSELL STILES: No. I think it's up north somewhere.

DS CARTER: Do you remember anything else about it?

RUSSELL STILES: No.

DS CARTER: But you just suddenly happened to find out this information?

RUSSELL STILES: Look, I was worried Alissa didn't know what he was really like. I wanted to warn her what a nasty bastard he was underneath all that charm.

DS CARTER: And you thought she'd be better off without him, is that right? So you started digging up things about Max to convince Alissa to leave him?

RUSSELL STILES: (Inaudible)

DS CARTER: So what happened when you didn't manage to convince her? Did you think about getting Max out of the picture some other way?

RUSSELL STILES: I didn't do anything to him! I didn't kill him!

DS CARTER: For someone who's not a stalker, you seem to know a lot about Max Burbeck.

RUSSELL STILES: I'm not a stalker!

DS CARTER: OK, let's get back to the wedding reception. So, you watched them from the woods and you were drinking. Then what happened?

RUSSELL STILES: I could see Alissa, in the garden. She was drinking champagne or something at the edge of the pond. As I was climbing over the fence, I fell over it. I was pretty far gone by that stage. Then I got back up again and . . . well, I just asked her if she was OK and everything, and . . . I just wanted to make sure she was happy.

DS CARTER: Then what happened?

RUSSELL STILES: Max came over and asked me to leave.

DS CARTER: And what did you do?

RUSSELL STILES: I left.

DS CARTER: Did you say anything to Max?'

RUSSELL STILES: I said something, but I can't remember what. I was really drunk.

DS CARTER: So you don't remember saying he'd get everything he deserved and he should watch his back?

RUSSELL STILES: No! I'm sure I never said that.

DS CARTER: You just said you can't remember because you were drunk, so how can you be sure you didn't say that?

RUSSELL STILES: (Inaudible)

DS CARTER: Did anyone else witness this exchange?

RUSSELL STILES: I don't know. Maybe. I wasn't interested in anyone else.

DS CARTER: Did the conversation get heated?

RUSSELL STILES: Well, maybe.

DS CARTER: Maybe? What's that supposed to mean? Were you angry? Shouting?

RUSSELL STILES: OK, I might've raised my voice. I don't know what I said exactly. I know how it looks now, but I didn't mean anything like . . .

DS CARTER: Like what?

RUSSELL STILES: I didn't mean I'd come back and kill him, because I know that's what you're thinking.

DS CARTER: So what did you mean?

RUSSELL STILES: I don't know. It was just heat of the moment stuff. I was angry, yeah, and upset. I shouldn't have gone there at all. I know that now. If I did say that, I was probably thinking of that development site I told you about. I heard the owners were going to have to sue his company. And I hope they win, too. You can't go round messing with people's lives like that.

DS CARTER: But you thought you'd mess around with Max and Alissa Burbeck's lives, though, right? You stalked her and you threatened him. Have a look at these text messages. For the benefit of the tape, please note I'm showing Russell Stiles copies of text messages recovered from Alissa Burbeck's phone. Please read out the messages, Mr Stiles.

RUSSELL STILES: Do I have to?

DS CARTER: I'll read them, shall I? 'I heard you're marrying him. You don't know what he's really like! He's a lying bastard.' Here's another one: 'What are you doing with someone like that? I know I messed up, but I'll always love you.' And another: 'I'm just trying to make sure you're OK and you know what you're doing. He's not good for you. Come back to me. We can talk.' And then they get a bit more pleading, don't they? 'Please just meet me for a chat.' And, 'Why won't you meet me? Just five minutes. Just a coffee. I know we can make things work again.' And, 'I love you. Please just meet up with me!' There are a lot more of a similar nature.

RUSSELL STILES: So what?

DS CARTER: This is harassment. Her replies are very polite, but basically saying the same thing – that she's happy and she's not coming back to you – but you repeatedly carried on. You stalked her at her wedding reception. You threatened Max Burbeck. You can see how this looks, can't you?

RUSSELL STILES: I didn't do anything wrong.

DS CARTER: But you do have a history of violence. You were convicted of affray six years ago.

RUSSELL STILES: Oh, for fuck's sake! It was a pub fight. It wasn't anything serious.

DS CARTER: Tell me about it.

RUSSELL STILES: There was some drunk guy in the pub when I was with Alissa. He was making all kinds of inappropriate comments to her and I got angry with him and told him to shut up. He wouldn't, so I hit him. That was it.

DS CARTER: So you were protecting her?

RUSSELL STILES: Yeah.

DS CARTER: And were you protecting her again now by killing someone you didn't think she should be married to?

RUSSELL STILES: No!

DS CARTER: You were also charged with poaching.

RUSSELL STILES: I don't do that any more.

DS CARTER: What did you do with the rabbits you took?

RUSSELL STILES: I gave them to my parents to sell.

DS CARTER: Your parents?

RUSSELL STILES: They've got a farm shop that sells meat and stuff.

DS CARTER: How long have they had that?

RUSSELL STILES: Since I was a kid.

DS CARTER: Did you ever work there?

RUSSELL STILES: When I was younger I helped out. Before I went to college. Just weekends and school holidays and stuff.

DS CARTER: Did you butcher the meat?

RUSSELL STILES: Yeah, Dad taught me.

DS CARTER: So you know your way around a knife, and Max Burbeck was stabbed in the back of the neck.

RUSSELL STILES: Jointing a slab of meat is a bit different from killing a person!

DS CARTER: Did Alissa Burbeck ask you to murder her husband for her?

RUSSELL STILES: That's bloody ridiculous. Of course not! Why would she do that? And I didn't kill him. How many times do I have to tell you?

DS CARTER: After the threats you made to Max Burbeck at the party, did you contact either of them again?

RUSSELL STILES: I don't know that I did make any threats. I can't remember what I said.

DS CARTER: It's very convenient that you can't remember.

RUSSELL STILES: Not from where I'm sitting.

DS CARTER: Did you contact them again?

RUSSELL STILES: Umm . . . I texted Alissa to apologise for making a scene. That text's not there in your pile. Why not?

DS CARTER: Did she text you back?

RUSSELL STILES: No.

DS CARTER: Did you go to the house after that incident?

RUSSELL STILES: No.

DS CARTER: But you were still in love with Alissa Burbeck?

RUSSELL STILES: (Inaudible)

DS CARTER: Mr Stiles?

RUSSELL STILES: *Yes!* But it doesn't mean I'd do anything like . . . like this! It's ridiculous!

DS CARTER: You were angry and upset that Alissa had married Max?

RUSSELL STILES: I was . . . upset. And worried about her.

DS CARTER: Were you angry and upset enough to kill Max? Or to try to kill Alissa?

RUSSELL STILES: Of course I bloody wasn't! How can you even say something like that?

DS CARTER: Will you consent to being fingerprinted and have a DNA swab taken?

RUSSELL STILES: Well, yeah, if it will help clear me.

DS CARTER: Good. We'll sort that out after the interview. So, where were you late last night and early this morning?

RUSSELL STILES: What?! You can't seriously think I killed him.

DS CARTER: Please answer the question.

RUSSELL STILES: I . . . um . . . I was night fishing.

DS CARTER: Night fishing?

RUSSELL STILES: Yeah. I go every Sunday night because it's quieter then. It gets annoying when there are too many other night anglers there. I like it peaceful.

DS CARTER: Where?

RUSSELL STILES: Twyford Lakes. I was there from about 10 p.m. 'til about 4 a.m.

DS CARTER: Was anyone with you?

RUSSELL STILES: No.

DS CARTER: Did you see anyone else there?

RUSSELL STILES: No. The place was empty. But I haven't done anything! Can you just tell me how Alissa is?

THE DETECTIVE
Chapter 9

The offices of Burbeck Developments were every bit as exclusive and flashy as you'd imagine. A glass-fronted building letting in lots of light. A glass lift in the centre. And a wide open, minimalist reception area.

A polished, thirty-something receptionist was busy dealing with calls as I approached her. She gave me a practised smile and asked if she could help me.

'I'd like to talk to Adam Gillmore, please.' I flashed my warrant card at her.

Two perfectly arched eyebrows inched up with surprise. 'Can I ask what it's about?'

'There's been a serious incident I need to speak with him about.'

'Oh. OK.' She picked up the phone and murmured into it before replacing the receiver. 'He won't be long. Please have a seat.' She swept her hand towards some velvet sofas.

'Thanks.' I ignored the sofas. If I sat down, I probably wouldn't get up again. Instead, I walked towards some A4-sized photos along one wall that showed previous developments by the company. There were modern apartment buildings that I thought looked ugly, large executive houses, a shopping mall. I picked up a glossy brochure and flicked through it. Burbeck Developments' mission statement was *We build it better!* That remained to be seen.

'Hello? You wanted to see me?' A suited man in his early fifties appeared behind me, square glasses perched on the end of his nose.

'You're Adam Gillmore?' I asked.

'Yes.' He wore a pinched, confused frown.

'I'm Detective Sergeant Carter. Is there somewhere we could speak in private?'

The frown shifted, and he began to look intrigued. 'Yes, my office. Follow me.'

We got into a lift and headed to the top floor. Adam Gillmore's office was more like the size of a one-bedroom apartment, and the office desk was dwarfed by all of the space. He sat down and indicated me to follow suit in the chair opposite.

'I'm sorry to have to tell you this, but last night, Max Burbeck was murdered in his home.'

His mouth gaped open. 'Max? What? Oh . . . how terrible. What happened? Is Alissa OK?'

'It appears someone broke in and stabbed him to death. Alissa managed to escape from the house and is in a safe location.'

'I thought it was very strange that he wasn't answering my calls. I've been leaving messages for him. He was due in today for a meeting and it's very unlike him not to keep in touch.' He removed his glasses and rubbed his hands across his face, shaking his head. 'Sorry, I just need a moment.'

'Take your time.' I glanced around the room while Adam composed himself, looking at several model-sized buildings on a table in the corner.

'I don't know how I can help you, Detective Sergeant. I last saw Max yesterday afternoon, about five-thirty, before he left for home.'

'Do you always work on Sundays, then?'

'No, not usually. But some things have cropped up that we needed to discuss.'

'Was he here all day yesterday?'

'Yes, from about ten in the morning.'

'You're the projects manager for Burbeck Developments, is that right?'

'Yes I am.'

'At the moment, we're not sure if Max was attacked for a specific reason, but we think he was targeted by someone, rather than it being a random attack. Were there any disgruntled employees here?'

'No.'

'Do you know if he'd received any threats in conjunction with his work? I've heard there was some kind of problem with one of your developments, and we found this document in his office.' I slid a copy of a letter across the desk. It was from a law firm called Browning & Co., confirming they were being retained to act on behalf of Burbeck Developments in any future litigation regarding a site called The Goldings.

'Ah.' He pushed his glasses further up his nose and pursed his lips, his frown lines furrowing deeper. 'Yes, we've had a few . . . issues with an old site of ours. That's what we were discussing yesterday, actually, but I can't believe anyone would . . . would *kill* him because of it.'

'What kind of issues?'

'About twelve years ago, we built a development – twenty executive houses. Now, it would appear that the site was contaminated with asbestos from the previous industrial units there.' He swallowed, his Adam's apple bobbing up and down.

'Did you know the land was contaminated when the houses were being built?'

'Well I certainly didn't. I joined the company shortly after it was completed.'

'But Max was working here at the time?'

'Yes. His father started the company and Max began working here when he finished university. The Goldings development was Max's first big project. I've tried to check the files to look at the environmental reports which should've been done, but they appeared to be . . . er . . . missing. In fact, I was due to have another meeting with Max about it today because he said he had the reports at home and would bring them in. He told me the reports cleared us of any knowledge, that they apparently said the land wasn't contaminated.'

'How serious is the contamination?'

'The site has significant amounts of raw asbestos waste from an asbestos manufacturing plant that was there previously.'

'So, let me get this straight. The soil could cause cancer and other diseases?' I shook my head, aghast.

'Yes.' He looked down at his desk, avoiding my gaze. 'It's very tragic.'

'When did you find out about this?'

'About four weeks ago, when Max was still in Australia. Apparently, some of the owners had arranged for soil samples to be taken after several of them became ill. Max and I had a difference of opinion about it all.'

'What does that mean?'

'I felt that the properties should be razed to the ground to ensure the owners' safety, and the land decontaminated at our expense. Legally, the first person to bear responsibility of cleaning up contaminated land is the person who caused it, so Max was passing the buck on to the company whose factory was on the site before we bought it. He said he wasn't aware that the factory had ever produced asbestos. I was trying to trace them, but apparently they no longer exist, and the director is deceased.'

'So whose responsibility is it to bear the cost in those circumstances?'

'Well, if the person can't be found or isn't in a position to clean up, then the person who currently owns or occupies the land is responsible. I felt ethically that we should do it, though, but Max disagreed, citing that he was unaware of it at the time of development, and his environmental reports put us in the clear. He'd instructed his lawyer to vigorously defend any actions brought against the company holding us responsible.' He frowned. 'But these people won't be able to sell their properties, and to ensure their health, they should really move out. Some of these owners are elderly or have children. Not surprisingly, we have indeed received some very strong complaints from the homeowners.'

'Weren't the council aware of the previous factory before they granted planning?'

He shuffled in his seat. 'Like I said, I wasn't here then, but it's a point I raised with Max. I think it's possible he may have . . .' He glanced at his office desk for a moment before looking back to me. 'It's possible he may have reached an agreement with them about it.'

'You mean he bribed someone in the planning department to turn a blind eye to it?'

'It's very likely. Although he denied it.'

I shook my head with disbelief. 'How did the complaints about the site come in? Via phone or letter or email?'

'A few calls, but mostly emails.'

'From all the homeowners?'

'Yes.'

'What are the properties worth?'

'In today's market, without any problems, they should be worth in the region of five hundred thousand. Now, obviously, they're worth nothing.'

I exhaled a breath, thinking about the chunk of money invested in those properties. Not just money – life savings.

'Max was adamant Burbeck Developments wouldn't pay for the demolition, decontamination, and reconstruction of the houses.'

'So, basically, that would mean these people had lost everything? They wouldn't be able to sell the properties, and presumably the cost of decontamination would be astronomical?'

'Yes,' he said sadly. 'It would cost several million to decontaminate, raze the buildings, and rebuild, and he wasn't prepared to . . .' He took a deep breath and glanced around, as if searching for the right words. 'Max didn't want to eat into the company profits.'

'Was the company having financial problems?'

'Well, things have been slower since the recession hit, obviously, but we had a pre-tax profit of 8.5 million last year.'

'8.5 million? And Mr Burbeck wasn't prepared to use any of that for compensation?' I pictured myself in the same position as those homeowners and felt like killing Max myself.

Adam swallowed again. 'No.'

'I'll need to see copies of these emails you received from the homeowners. And a list of all their names.'

~

DI Wilmott rang as I pulled into a petrol station, summoning me back to the station for a quick progress report. I grabbed a random sandwich from the fridge, which was supposed to be cheese and ham, but on closer inspection could've been made from plastic for all I could tell. Still, needs must. My stomach was growling and it didn't look like I'd be going home for a good few hours yet.

When I got back into the office, DI Wilmott was already there, sipping from a Starbucks cup, looking like he'd just stepped out of a *GQ* magazine ad as he read through a document. I glanced around the room, looking for any other Starbucks cups he might have graced his team with, but the room was sadly Starbucks-less. We'd have to make do with crappy instant. I sat at my desk and opened my sandwich, peering at it with suspicion before taking a bite. Yeah, probably plastic.

Ronnie bustled into the room, looking flustered.

'We've got the preliminary post-mortem results back, although we're still obviously waiting for any toxicology reports.' Wilmott waved his piece of paper in the air. 'Max Burbeck's cause of death was transection of the spinal cord from a sharp force injury. The single stab wound to the back of the neck was between two of the cervical vertebrae, which severed the spinal cord. Apparently, when the spinal cord is damaged in this area, the victim immediately goes into spinal shock. His blood pressure would've dropped to zero and his heart stopped very quickly, which explains why there was very little blood from the wound. He would've lost consciousness in a few seconds and died in a minute or so. There were no defensive wounds, and we know that there doesn't seem to have been any struggle, so it would appear he didn't hear the killer approach from behind. The pathologist believes the murder weapon was something very sharp with a narrow blade. Estimated time of death is between 11 p.m. and 1 a.m.' He glanced around the room. 'SOCO may not be finished at the scene until tomorrow, but so far it seems there's too much evidence *and* not enough.'

Ronnie frowned. 'What do you mean, guv?'

'There was a wedding reception at the house a couple of weeks ago. Prints everywhere. According to what they've found so far, and from Alissa's initial statement, the killer wore gloves and protective plastic shoe covers, so we don't have anything useful as yet. And, of course, the weather didn't help last night.' He paused. 'I walked Alissa through the property and she confirmed that nothing appears to have been taken from the house, so we'll work on the assumption this isn't a burglary, but was a specific attack where the killer brought the murder weapon with him. So, motives?' He glanced around the room.

I vigorously chewed my bite of sandwich and swilled it down with the dregs of cold coffee from earlier. 'Several,' I said. 'The ex-boyfriend Russell Stiles does seem to have been obsessed with Alissa. He harassed her with texts, gatecrashed their wedding reception, and when he was asked to leave by Max, he basically threatened him, although he says he can't remember much about the incident because he'd been drinking heavily. He does have a history of violence – was convicted of affray six years ago following a pub fight, where he was apparently defending Alissa's honour.'

I thought about how precise the knife wound was to slide in between two vertebrae like that. Either the killer knew what he was doing, or it was a lucky strike.

'Russell is also experienced with using knives. He was done for poaching rabbits before, and he worked in his parents' butcher shop.' I handed out copies of the texts Stiles had sent Alissa, and Stiles' antecedent history. 'He has no alibi for last night. Said he was night fishing. He's medium height, the same description as Alissa gave us.

'Secondly, Max Burbeck had received some threats from homeowners of a development he built twelve years ago.' I filled them in on the details. 'It's possible he bribed the council to overlook the previous asbestos factory on the site. Or maybe they turned a blind eye because they were under pressure from the government to provide more housing, or they were completely incompetent. But I don't think the council's actions have any relevance to Max's murder. I've got a list of homeowners who need talking to, though. And one in particular . . .' I glanced down at a copy of an email Adam Gillmore had provided. 'A Mr Porter. He said in an email to Max, "You deserve to die for what you've done to us!".'

'Those poor people were about to lose everything?' Becky asked.

'Seems like it, so big motive there, too,' I said. 'Also, let's not forget that Max was worth a lot of money. Alissa was his heir, so that's another huge motive.'

'I'm satisfied Alissa has nothing to do with this,' DI Wilmott said. 'She's clearly traumatised by what happened and only just managed to escape the house without being killed, too. We don't need to waste time on that angle. Are we clear on that, Detective *Sergeant*? I know you have a hard time following orders, and I don't want a repeat of the Lord Mackenzie saga on my watch.' He glared at me.

Anger bubbled up inside me. We'd been at Lord Mackenzie's vast estate following a call from him to report that his collection of classic cars had been stolen from an alarmed outbuilding. Thirty vehicles had been taken, worth in excess of twenty-five million quid, including Bentleys, Ferraris, Aston Martins, and Bugattis. The alarm system had been tampered with, and the offenders had got away with the lot while Mackenzie was conveniently at a charity dinner in London with politicians and royalty. From the start, I knew he was involved. He had increasing debts from bad investments and had been living way beyond his means for years. One of my informants had passed on information about a classic-car salesman who was rumoured to have met with Mackenzie in the weeks prior to the burglary in order to set up the fake theft. And if I'd been allowed to dig deeper, I would've proved my theory right. But as soon as Detective Superintendent Greene knew I was pursuing Mackenzie's involvement, I was dragged off the case and threatened with suspension. The inquiry into Mackenzie had been quashed, Mackenzie had made blustering noises about suing the force for harassment, and I'd been made to sit on the naughty step ever since.

What was the point of being a copper if you could only investigate certain crimes properly? When investigations into the rich and influential got swept under the carpet? It made a mockery of everything I'd joined the force for, and I was still reeling from it. It wasn't even about the fact that I'd been threatened with suspension unless I backed off, and was still paying the price by bloody Wilmott being promoted and not me. It was the injustice of it all that pissed me off, the corrupt police politics that let outside influences dictate how and when investigations were made. Lord Mackenzie was guilty – simple as that. If I'd had more time, I could've proved it, too. If he'd been Mr Average from a council estate, would the powers that be have scrapped the investigation? No answer necessary, really.

'Mackenzie was bloody guilty and you know it,' I said.

'*Lord* Mackenzie,' Wilmott corrected me.

'Exactly. Which is why he got away with it. Am I the only one who sees something wrong with that?'

Ronnie avoided my gaze and started doodling on his pad. Becky gave me a sympathetic smile.

'So what if he plays golf with the chief constable and has tea with members of the royal family! He's a crook. And a liar. And he should be in jail.'

'Sorry, team, but I think DS Carter and I should continue this conversation in private for a moment.' Wilmott jerked his head impatiently towards his office door in the corner of the room.

I stood up and followed him inside, shutting the door behind me.

Wilmott crossed his arms, treating me to a smirk. 'I think Detective Superintendent Greene made it very clear at the time, didn't he? I mean, you *were* almost suspended. You're on thin ice as it is, and I'm sure it won't take much to have your suspension finalised if you take one step out of line. Or even for you to be demoted.' His eyes twinkled with excitement. He would've loved that. 'I don't know what would be worse, actually – being made to walk the beat again in uniform or sitting at home twiddling your thumbs.' He raised sarcastic eyebrows at me. 'So stop wasting time and forget about the Lord Mackenzie case. It's over. And since I'm SIO on *this* case, get on with what you're tasked to do. Is that clear?'

'Perfectly.' I bit my tongue.

'Good. I'm glad we've got that cleared up.' Wilmott strutted back into the CID office again and sat on the edge of a desk.

I sat down at mine and bit into my sandwich, knowing it would take a while to get through the stodge, which would stop me blurting out something I shouldn't say.

'The Russell Stiles and Goldings development angles look promising,' Wilmott carried on. 'Until we can be sure that Alissa's safety isn't an issue, I've taken her to the Berkely Hotel. She's staying in a suite there and I'm sleeping on the couch, but that information doesn't leave this room. I'll be staying with her overnight until we can get a uniform stationed with her, but they're just as bloody short-staffed as us. So, anything else?'

Ronnie put his hand up, as if he was a schoolboy in class. 'Sir, house-to-house didn't reveal any suspicious sightings last night. I spoke with Mrs Downes, the neighbour Alissa ran to after the attack, and she said she didn't know them that well, but they seemed like a very sweet couple. She used to feed their cat for them if they were away. The other neighbours in the village said the Burbecks kept themselves to themselves, so they only knew them to say hello to.'

'Was there a cat at the house last night?' Becky asked.

'No,' I said. 'It may've been spooked and run away. I didn't see any cat bowls or litter trays, either. But I'll ring SOCO at the house to make sure there's some food left out in case it comes back.'

'Right. Any CCTV evidence of the surrounding area?' Wilmott asked Becky.

'No. The offender could've come in through the woods at the rear of the property and not been seen anyway. I've just been checking out any social media for the Burbecks.'

'Who told you to do that?' Wilmott frowned.

'Erm . . .'

'I did,' I said. 'You weren't here, so . . .' I shrugged. 'You can tell a lot about someone from their social media pages. We need to build up a picture of the Burbecks.'

'Yes, well, that was going to be my next order for you, Becky,' Wilmott muttered.

Order? Christ, the power's going to his head already.

'What did you find, then?' Wilmott asked Becky.

'Max Burbeck didn't use any of it. Alissa Burbeck is on Facebook only and has fifty-one friends on there. She doesn't post much, usually photos of her and Max, or cute animal photos, and has the highest privacy settings, so only friends can see her page. The last time she posted anything was before their trip to Australia, a status update of them checking in at the airport.'

'Is she friends with Stiles on there?' I asked.

'No.'

'OK.' Wilmott clapped his hands together. 'SOCO are also checking through the woods at the rear of the house, but it's going to get dark soon. Tomorrow morning, I'm doing a press conference, appealing for any witnesses to come forward. Alissa is obviously far too traumatised to sit in on the press appeal.' He handed me a photocopied list of names and addresses. 'This is a copy printed off Alissa's laptop of all the people invited to the wedding reception at The Orchard. It also includes the catering and marquee company who would've been there. We need to talk to everyone who attended and find out if any of them witnessed this incident with Russell Stiles.'

I glanced through the list, estimating about a hundred people. Next to the names was listed their relationship to Max or Alissa – friend, colleague, et cetera. 'There's no one listed as family.'

'Max Burbeck was an only child whose parents are dead. No living relatives, either. Alissa's mum is ill in a nursing home, so she couldn't make the wedding. Her dad died when she was young, and she also has no other family left,' Wilmott said.

I carried on flicking through the list. 'We should split this. There are a lot of people on here. Plus, I need to see the homeowners on that development.'

Wilmott waved a hand dismissively in the air. 'You can delegate. I need to get back to Alissa.'

So it was alright for me to delegate when it suited him. That was Wilmott all over – he was lazy, easily bored with minor details, and avoided doing any work himself, preferring just to butt in on the glory when there was a result.

'Anything else?' Wilmott asked.

Noes all round. Wilmott ran a hand through his hair, smoothed down his eyebrows with his fingertips, and rushed out.

I took another bite of my sandwich and wondered what it was doing to my insides. 'Right. Becky, start phoning these people and find out if they witnessed what happened between Russell Stiles, Alissa, and Max at the wedding reception. Ring the catering and marquee company and find out which employees worked at The Orchard that day – they'll need to be printed, too.' I handed her the photocopied list. 'I don't think we should disregard anything, so see if you can find out what Alissa's relationship with Max was like. I know they'd only been married a few months, presumably they were in the honeymoon stages, but it's worth checking to see if there were any problems between them. Alissa has a huge motive, too. Max was worth millions.'

'Um . . . Sarge,' Ronnie said. 'DI Wilmott said not to pursue that angle.'

'Well, DI Wilmott isn't here, and I'm delegating.' I smiled at him.

'Yes, Sarge,' he said hastily.

I turned back to Becky. 'OK?'

'Yep.'

'You're with me,' I said to Ronnie, throwing the rest of the unappetising sandwich in the bin.

THE OTHER ONE
Chapter 10

I think night-time was definitely the worst. Dad would sit and drink in the evenings in his favourite armchair. The one Mum and I weren't allowed to sit in. Whisky was his favourite thing. It didn't make sense to me that he told Mum she couldn't buy any new clothes for herself or me, when I knew how much a bottle of whisky cost because I saw it on the label. I added up one day how much he spent on it a year and knew that we could get loads of new things if he spent that money on us. Instead, we had to make do. Mum would darn socks, put patches on my jeans with threadbare knees, turn trousers into shorts. When I grew out of clothes I'd still have to wear them, even though my arms poked out the ends so I had three-quarter-length sleeves and my waistbands dug into my belly because they were too small.

Still, as long as Dad had his whisky, we couldn't complain.

But the drink made him even madder than usual. Sometimes I'd lie awake in my bedroom, unable to go to sleep because I was just waiting for the screaming and thumping to start.

It was winter then, and a storm had whipped up, torrential rain lashing at the house. The wind howled through the cracks around the windows in my bedroom, whispering things to me that I tried to make out but couldn't understand.

And then I heard it, as usual. The familiar sounds of Dad's anger and abuse.

I pulled the covers over my head, but it didn't block the noise out. Even when it wasn't happening, I could hear the echoes of it turning over in my mind. Even when I tried to drown it out with my own thoughts, it was there, pick, pick, picking at my brain.

By now, it made me angry, too. Why couldn't my mum take us away from him? Why didn't she stand up to him? Why did she put up with it? Why did she let me get punished for doing nothing wrong? And I realised then that she was just as mad as him. Even so, my instinct to stop him hurting her arose every time. So what if I ended up with a bruise or a kick or in the cupboard with no dinner? I didn't care about any of that by then.

I ran to their bedroom and banged on the door. 'Stop hurting her! Stop it!'

I heard another loud noise from inside, Mum's scream, then the door swung open and Dad towered over me. Before I knew what was happening I was in his clutches. He carried me downstairs, and I wriggled and strained to get away, but he was too strong for me. He opened the front door and dumped me outside on the freezing cold step. Then the door closed and the lock turned.

The wind nipped ferociously at my thin pyjamas, stinging rain pelted down, soaking me instantly as I banged on the door, begging to be let in. I hopped on my bare feet, trying to stop the cold from seeping into my skin, crying for my mum to let me inside again. Crying because I wished I'd never been born.

I don't know how long I pounded on the door for, but no one came. Tears sprang into my eyes, mingling with the rain, as I rubbed my hands up and down my arms, shivering, teeth chattering. I wasn't afraid of the darkness. I had the cupboard to thank for that. But the cold – that was something else.

I ran to the cow barn and stepped inside, my feet squishing on urine-covered hay, the stench burning into my nostrils and the back of my throat. It was warmer in here, the heat from the cows' bodies drifting through the building. The cow in the first stall was Lulabelle. At least, that's what I called her. I had names for all of them, even if Dad didn't. She had barely enough rope tying her to the metal bars at the front of her pen to lie down, which forced her to sleep in an uncomfortable position. I crept into her stall and lay down next to her, stroking her head as she nuzzled her wet nose into me and sucked on my pyjamas.

I fell asleep listening to her snorts and snuffles, knowing she was the only one who loved me, and I was the only one who loved her.

THE DETECTIVE
Chapter 11

I parked the car in The Goldings development and glanced around. The houses were set on large plots, but most of them had a shabby appearance. I stared at the front gardens and wondered about the asbestos hidden under the soil. A silent killer that none of them knew about when they'd been sold the dream.

Ronnie started on the opposite side of the close while I went to Mr and Mrs Porter's house first. They were both in their mid-sixties. Mrs Porter was all bones and sharp angles, her clothes practically hanging off her. She had sunken eyes and protruding cheekbones. Her white hair was thinning around the back of her scalp. Mr Porter didn't look much healthier, slumped in a floral armchair with an oxygen tank on the floor beside him attached to a mask resting on the arm of the chair. In contrast to her skeletal frame, he was very overweight, his stomach folding over the top of his belt.

'I'm sorry to bother you, but I have to ask some questions following a murder last night,' I said as I sat in their lounge.

'A murder?' Mrs Porter gasped.

'Max Burbeck was stabbed to death in his home.'

Mrs Porter snatched a glimpse at her husband.

'Good,' Mr Porter said.

'Good?' I repeated.

'He was—' He broke off into a coughing fit.

Mrs Porter shot up from her seat with amazing speed for someone so frail-looking and sat on the arm of his chair, rubbing his back.

Eventually, the coughing subsided into a wheezy breath.

'That man was a bastard.' Mrs Porter lifted her chin in the air, as if daring me to say otherwise. 'Do you know what he did to us? To all the other people in this close?'

'I heard that this site was built on contaminated land.'

'Yes, and he knew all about it!' she spat.

Mr Porter coughed again.

'Use the nebuliser,' Mrs Porter said to him, reaching out to get the mask.

Mr Porter pushed her hand away. 'No, not yet. I want to say something.'

I glanced at Mr Porter. When he spoke, his voice was gravelly and slow, with pauses between each word as he struggled for breath.

'We bought this house from new,' he said. 'It was supposed to be an investment. Our retirement fund. We were always going to sell it when we got too old and move into a little retirement flat with a nice bit of equity to subsidise our pension. But now, thanks to what that man did, we have nothing. We can't sell. We've got no inheritance to leave our kids or to fall back on as a nest egg in our old age. And look at me.' He reached for the oxygen mask and inhaled some breaths.

'My husband was a keen gardener,' Mrs Porter stepped in. 'Every chance he got, he was outside. He grew vegetables in a patch at the bottom that we've been eating for the last twelve years! And now we know . . . we just know that his health problems have been caused by the asbestos that was in the ground this whole time!' Tears sprang into her eyes.

'I'm very sorry to hear what's happened. Have you sought legal advice about it?'

'Yes. If we take Burbeck Developments to court we might lose. They say they've got documents absolving them of any prior knowledge of the contamination, and the company that dumped the waste doesn't exist any more. We could try to sue them, maybe, or even sue the council, but we probably wouldn't win, and we'd probably be dead by then anyway! They'd drag it out for years.'

Mr Porter sucked hard on the oxygen.

'You sent a threatening email to Max Burbeck saying he didn't deserve to live?' I asked Mr Porter.

'So?'

'Death threats are a serious offence.'

Mr Porter snorted. 'He gave us a death sentence, didn't he? Why aren't you doing anything about that?'

'Was the email as far as it went?' I asked.

Mr Porter's eyes widened incredulously, wheezing hard. 'Look at us both! Do we look like we could kill someone? I might've thought about it, but I'm in no fit state to do anything about it.'

~

A little girl of about seven opened the door to No. 5, closely followed by a woman in her late thirties.

'I've told you not to answer the door!' the woman said to her daughter, stepping in front of her.

'Mrs Cox?' I asked.

'Yes. Are you from the council? Because you were supposed to take more soil samples from my house, too, and we got missed last time.'

'Sorry, no. I'm Detective Sergeant Carter. Can I come in and ask you a few questions?'

'Oh.' She took her daughter's hand and stepped back. 'Yes.' She glanced down at her daughter and said, 'Go into the lounge and watch TV with your brother. And do not go outside again.'

Her daughter gave me a gap-toothed smile and skipped away.

Mrs Cox led me into a kitchen at the other end of the house that overlooked a large messy garden. Weeds were growing through what once would have been a neat lawn and were pushing up cracks in the path. The bushes were ratty and filled with dead flowers. 'Is it a police matter then? They told me it was a civil thing. But it should be a police matter! They're murdering us slowly.'

'I'm not here about the contamination. Well, not directly anyway.'

She put a hand on her hip. 'What's going on then?' And then she had a sudden thought and a hand went to her throat. 'It's not Jim, is it? Has something happened?'

'Jim's your husband, is that right?'

'Yes.'

'It's actually regarding Max Burbeck.'

Her eyes narrowed. 'What about him?'

'He was murdered last night in his home.'

'What? And you think I did it?' She barked out a laugh. 'Chance would be a fine thing.'

'I understand his company was responsible for building this site on contaminated land.'

'Not his company. *Him*. I'm holding him responsible.' She picked up a photo on the windowsill of her and three children and thrust it towards me. 'This is my family! My kids have been playing in that soil for years. And now we find out how toxic it is. We might not know for years whether they've got any kinds of illnesses. It can cause cancer, you know, all sorts of things. And that . . . *man* was responsible for it! The council have been absolutely useless, too! I'm sure they're trying to cover up their involvement in it all. Bloody corrupt is what they all are. This development should never have been allowed to happen. Have you spoken to Mr Porter yet? He's got emphysema and lung cancer from living here! We're all living under a death sentence now.'

'I'm very sorry about what's happened, Mrs Cox. I can understand how upset you are.'

'Upset?! *Upset?* I'm bloody livid. I'm so angry I could . . .'

'You could what?'

'Do you seriously think I could kill him? I'm not exactly sad that he's dead. It's called karma, you know. But I didn't have anything to do with it.'

'Where's Jim?'

'He's in Paris, on a conference to do with work.'

'And when did he go there?'

'Two days ago. He's due back tonight. Why?'

'I have to ask, Mrs Cox. Obviously, the situation you're in is very emotive.'

'Jim didn't kill Max, either, that's ridiculous!'

'I'm not saying he did, but I still need to eliminate him from our enquiries.'

'And when did it happen, then?'

'In the early hours of this morning.'

She put the photo down and scribbled a number on a Post-it note. 'Here, this is his mobile number. He wasn't even here when it happened.'

~

The front garden of No. 6 was overgrown and shabby, too, and I wasn't surprised that the owners had stopped caring for their gardens, given the circumstances. Who'd want to touch that soil, knowing there was a potential ticking time bomb in it?

Mr Knowles was older than the Porters, maybe in his early seventies. He had watery eyes and saggy, sallow skin. The stress of the situation had obviously taken its toll on him, too.

'I'm conducting an investigation and I have some routine questions for you,' I said after I'd introduced myself.

He sighed. 'Well, you'd better come in.' He shuffled down the hallway, which was just as shabby as the exterior. The once-pale apricot carpets were smudged in places with darker stains. Wallpaper curled at the edges of the walls.

'I'm here about Max Burbeck,' I said, perching on the end of a sofa. 'He was murdered in the early hours of this morning.'

'What? And I'm supposed to feel sorry for him?'

'I know about the situation with this site.'

He looked down at his thighs and rubbed arthritic, gnarled hands on them. Another sigh. 'It's a good job my wife's not alive to see what's going on. She died of bowel cancer, you know, a couple of years ago. Even though I can't prove it, I know, I just know that it's this house that caused it. And it was my idea to move here.' He pointed a finger at his chest. 'Me. She didn't even want to leave our old house. I thought it would be a nice place to retire. And now look. She's gone, and I'm stuck in this big house all alone and I can't even sell it.' He fixed his watery eyes on me. 'I've got nothing now. Nothing. So, no, I'm not going to feel sorry for that bastard after he's taken everything away from me.'

THE DETECTIVE
Chapter 12

It was 6 p.m. by the time Ronnie and I got back to the office. We'd compared notes on the way from the interviews we'd carried out. All the owners were angry, and rightly so, but none of them matched the description of the offender given by Alissa Burbeck, and most seemed to be in no fit state to kill anyone. There were a few more avenues to check: people who weren't home and children of the owners who might harbour a grudge, and there were some alibis to look into, which I asked Ronnie to deal with, but I thought these would be dead ends. In theory, one of them could've hired a hitman, but in my twenty-eight years on the job I'd never known anyone to have done so. In movies, yes. But in real life? No. And these were families or elderly people, not gang members or people involved in the criminal underworld. Plus, a hitman would cost money, and I very much doubted these people would want to spend their non-equity on killing Max Burbeck, when they'd need to use it for decontaminating their land (or maybe even buying a new property), a court case, or possible medical bills borne of the toxic chemicals in the soil. It's one thing to say you wished someone was dead, but acting on it – that was something different entirely. I was gutted for their seemingly hopeless situation, but none of them struck me as killers.

Becky was working the phone as I sat down. Ronnie busied himself making coffee, humming away enthusiastically. He presented me with my mug and a look of expectancy, as if waiting for a pat on the head.

'Thanks.' I examined my copy of the list of the Burbecks' wedding party guests on my desk, waiting for Becky to finish and cross-check who she'd already called. When there was no sign of the conversation ending, I mulled over the day so far and stared at the photos of Max and Alissa on the whiteboard.

'Sarge?' Becky's voice pulled me out of my thoughts a few minutes later. 'Some of the guests on this list couldn't attend the reception. Most of the ones I've spoken to so far didn't see the altercation happen in the rear garden because they were inside the marquee or in the lounge at the front of the house. They've all described the Burbecks as a happy couple; it was a beautiful ceremony; a lovely day – all the usual wedding reception stuff. But I did just speak to a Vicky Saunders, who's friends with Alissa, and she witnessed it.'

'Right, I'll go and speak to her,' I said. 'You and Ronnie can split the rest of the list. If you speak to anyone else who saw something, give me a ring.'

Ronnie walked to Becky's desk and she handed him a photocopy of the list.

'Which ones have you done?' Ronnie asked.

'Everyone on the last two pages. About half of the guests.'

'You're working backwards?'

She shrugged. 'Maybe it's the Chinese in me. They write backwards, don't they?'

'You're not even Chinese.' Ronnie frowned, confused.

'Well, talking of Chinese, who fancies one?' Becky grinned. She could eat for England and never put on weight. I'd piled on the pounds since Denise's death. As old-fashioned as it was, she was the one who'd cooked in our relationship. Now I made do with microwave meals and takeaways. I'd become a walking cliché. 'I'll get it delivered to the front desk. I'm starving and it looks like we're on overtime.'

'I'll have a chicken chow mein and barbecue sauce,' I said. 'I'll pick it up later. Actually, make that two.'

'Two?' Becky said, trying not to eye my stomach but making a bad job of it. 'They're massive!'

I sucked in my gut. 'I'll drop one round to DI Nash on my way home.'

'Ah. Nice thought.' Becky scribbled my order down. 'I'm sure she'll appreciate that.'

I doubted it. She hadn't even picked up or returned any of my calls. She was in a bad place. A place I'd been in for a long time after Denise died of breast cancer. A place I was still in most of the time. I missed my wife more than I could ever express in words.

'Ronnie? What do you want?' Becky shouted over to him.

'Boiled rice.'

Becky waited, pen poised, for the rest of his order. When he went back to his laptop she said, 'And what else?'

'That's it.'

'You just want boiled rice?!' She scrunched her face up as if swallowing a mouthful of vinegar.

Ronnie rubbed his stomach. 'Chinese is too greasy for me.'

'You can order something else, if you like.'

Typing away distractedly, he said, 'No, boiled rice is OK.'

I left the office and drove to Vicky Saunders' flat. It was a new build in a modern block in the Old Town area of Stevenage, six miles from Waverly, with an intercom entry system. She opened the door, red-faced and wet-eyed. Her hair was cut in an edgy style, chin length at the front on one side and shorter on the other. She reminded me of a horse, coltishly long limbs and a long nose.

I introduced myself and she started crying.

'It's terrible. I can't believe it! How's Alissa?'

'She's obviously very distressed. Can I come in?'

She sniffed and stood back. 'Sorry. I'm all in a daze since that policewoman told me on the phone.' She led me into a small but tidy lounge, the black sofa covered with pink fluffy scatter cushions. She slumped down on to the sofa, grabbed one of the cushions and held it to her stomach. 'Where's Alissa? And why didn't she call me? I've tried to ring her mobile, but it's just going to voicemail. I'm her best friend! She has to come and stay with me!'

'Don't worry, Alissa is safe, but we don't believe it was a random attack, so we're keeping her location under wraps until we know more. I'm sure she'll contact you as soon as she's able to.'

'Oh. God, I bet she's devastated. They were only married, like, two months! It's just awful. Awful!'

'That's actually what I wanted to talk to you about. You mentioned to DC Harris that you'd witnessed an altercation between Max and Alissa and Russell Stiles at the wedding reception?'

'Yes. I mean, they got married in Australia. They wanted a simple ceremony, just the two of them, barefoot on the beach – so romantic – and a couple of witnesses arranged for them. Alissa didn't like to be the centre of attention, although it's hard sometimes not to be when you look like her.' She said it without a trace of malice. 'But they'd organised the party for a couple of weeks after they got back.' She sucked in a breath, eyes wide. 'Do you think Russell killed Max, then?'

'We're not making any assumptions at this stage, but we have to follow all leads, and apparently there was some kind of argument between them.'

'I . . . I mean, Russell is a bit of a rough diamond, but . . . to kill someone! I've known Alissa and Russell since primary school. We all went to the same one, you see.' She picked at a long piece of fluff from the cushion, rolling it in between her forefinger and thumb as she looked at me.

'What's Russell like?'

'Um . . . he's a landscape gardener now. He's a bit intense. Kind of broody. A loner, he never really had many friends. But he was always nice to me and Alissa.'

'Can you tell me what happened at the reception?'

'Well, a couple of hours after it started, Alissa wanted to go out of the marquee to get some air in the garden. I got chatting with another friend, and when I looked around for her a while later she still wasn't back, so I went to find her to see if she needed me to help do anything. Anyway, she was standing by the fence at the bottom of the garden, talking to Russell. I stayed just outside the marquee, watching in case she needed any help.'

'Why? Did you think Russell might get violent?'

'No. No, nothing like that. He did hit someone once who was being rude to Alissa, but from what I heard, the guy deserved it. And Russell would never hurt her, I'm sure. But . . . well, Russell was a bit obsessed with her. They went out for four years and he was still in love with her. And . . . it's hard not to love Alissa. I mean, obviously she's gorgeous-looking, but she's just a really, really nice person, too. She's loyal and kind, funny, considerate, sweet. It's tragic what's happened.' The piece of fluff she was picking at came away from the cushion, falling on to the carpet. She smoothed the material of the cushion down with her fingers repeatedly as if it was giving her some comfort.

'Did you hear what they were talking about?'

'No. I was too far away. I saw Alissa smile a few times, so I didn't think it was anything too heavy. But he hadn't been invited, for obvious reasons, and Max would've been pissed off to find him there, so I was hoping it didn't escalate into something else. Anyway—' She broke off and sniffed loudly. 'I'm sorry. This is just a shock. Who would do something like this? I can't take it in.'

'I understand this is difficult, but we really need to find out as much as possible so we can catch who's responsible.'

She sniffed again. 'I know. Sorry.' She took a deep breath. 'Um . . . Russell was staggering a bit, he looked pretty drunk, and then he grabbed her arm and it looked like he was pleading with her. She tried to shrug him off but it didn't work, and then the next thing I knew, Max was storming down to the end of the garden from the kitchen, and I did hear a bit of what he said because he was shouting, telling Russell to fuck off and that he wasn't welcome and wasn't invited and if he didn't leave Alissa alone he'd get the police involved.'

'What happened then?'

'Max was waving his hands in the air and kind of motioning Russell to get off their property, and Russell said something I didn't hear, but whatever it was, it set Max off and Max made a move towards him, as if he was going to hit him. Alissa stepped in front of Max to try to diffuse the situation, and Russell climbed back over the fence and stumbled away into the woods. Then Max and Alissa were having a bit of a discussion about it and Leo came out from the house to speak to them. Then Leo climbed over the fence after Russell. I slipped back into the marquee then to give them some privacy since it was all under control.'

'Leo?' I took the guest list out of my pocket and scanned it, looking for the name.

'Leo Smithers. He's Max's best friend.'

'And how was Max and Alissa's relationship?'

Vicky seemed surprised by the question. 'What do you mean? They'd just got married.'

'Was he jealous of her, was she jealous of him?'

'No, they were really happy. And . . . and so in love.'

'Were there any money issues? Debts, maybe?'

I knew for a fact from the Mackenzie case that appearances could be deceptive. On the outside, people could seem flashy and rich, but they could be hiding loans or debts behind their leased cars and mortgaged-to-the-hilt property.

'No, absolutely not. Max was loaded.'

'Any other problems you can think of?'

'No, none at all.'

'How long had Max and Alissa been in a relationship?'

'About three years. I was there when they met each other. Alissa and I were in a club and Max sent over a bottle of champagne to us. Then he came over with Leo and we all started chatting.'

'But Alissa was still seeing Russell at the time?'

'Yeah. But I think Max just swept her off her feet. He was obviously a lot older than her, but she liked that. He made her feel protected, I think. She was very close to her dad, but he died when she was fourteen and I think she just . . . well, she thought Max was more mature than Russell. So she ended things with Russell before she started actually seeing Max.'

'And how did Russell take it?'

'He kept turning up at her house, where she lived with her mum before her mum went into a nursing home. And he kept texting and stuff. Sometimes he turned up at the same places she was, like he was following her, but eventually it all petered out when he went travelling for a year. Then, when he heard she was getting married, the texts started again. She showed me a few, but they weren't threatening or anything. More kind of pleading, really, wanting to meet her to talk, saying Max wasn't right for her, that she was doing the wrong thing and that he wanted her back and was still in love with her. Alissa is just a really sweet person and she didn't want Russell to be hurt or upset. She still wanted to be friends with him – he was her first love, after all. So she kept things polite and cool, but she didn't encourage Russell. Max wanted her to report Russell to the police, but she said no. She felt guilty about breaking Russell's heart.'

'So you think Alissa and Max were happy together?'

'Of course! They never even argued.'

I doubted that very much. Even the happiest couples argued. I could remember some humdingers between Denise and me over the years after which we didn't speak for days. You're never going to agree with your partner one hundred per cent of the time. Unless you're a Stepford wife or husband.

'Apart from Russell, do you know of anyone who might've been jealous of Alissa or Max? Or upset with them for some reason?'

There was silence as she thought about that. 'Maybe some people were envious. She's stunning, after all. You'd think it'd be easy being as pretty as her, but she had a hard time. All through school, groups of girls would be jealous of her because of how she looked. She got bullied a bit and became more introverted and shy, less confident. Because of that, she didn't really hang around with other women much, and I was her closest friend. They had a fairy-tale romance. They were totally in love. He was loaded. And some people don't like that, do they? Sasha was a bit strange with Alissa. I'm sure she was jealous of her.' She hugged the cushion tighter towards her.

'Who's Sasha?'

'Sasha Smithers. She's Leo's sister. Leo and Max have known each other since uni, so Sasha was friends with Max a long time before Alissa came on the scene. Sasha thinks she's better than everyone else, and she's got a bit of a nasty streak. She liked putting Alissa down, making snide comments and things, but Alissa was too soft to make a fuss over it. You never know what's going to come out of Sasha's mouth. Because Sasha was Max's friend, Alissa just put up with it, but it pissed me off, so of course I'd always stick up for Alissa. Sasha says things to purposely upset people, and when you call her up on it, she makes out like it's all a big joke. She loves being the centre of attention, even if she has to shock you with inappropriate comments.' She paused for a moment. 'I'm pretty sure Sasha fancied Max and hated it when Alissa started seeing him.'

'And what was Max like?'

'Charming. Generous. Good fun. He was a nice guy.'

I thought about the homeowners at The Goldings and doubted they'd describe him the same way. I wondered about the different sides of our personalities we show people. 'Did you know anything about Burbeck Developments? Or about any problems with it? Any complaints against the company?'

'No. Alissa didn't have anything to do with his business, so she never told me anything.'

'Did Alissa talk to you about any problems they were having?'

'No, she was completely happy, I told you. They didn't have any problems at all.'

Until now. Now there was a big problem.

~

I parked outside Leo Smithers' million-pound barn conversion in the village of Benington, not far from Waverly, noting the 1964 Aston Martin DB5 parked outside with the personal plate 'Money1'. He was obviously doing well for himself.

I knocked on the door and waited, looking at the car. It was one of the same models that Lord Mackenzie reckoned had been stolen from his mansion, with a price tag of about seven hundred grand. That familiar flash of anger rippled through me again at the thought of Mackenzie getting away with it all.

A tall guy in his thirties opened the door wearing neatly pressed pin-striped trousers, a white shirt undone at the neck, and shiny shoes.

'Leo Smithers?' I asked.

'Yes.'

'DS Warren Carter. You might've already heard on the news about an incident at The Orchard last night? I need to speak to you about it. You may be able to help us.'

'An incident? At Max and Alissa's house?' he said with a slight Australian accent. He raised concerned eyebrows at me. 'I've been up in London all day at meetings, so I haven't seen the news. What kind of incident? Is everything OK?'

'I think it's best if we speak inside.'

'Of course.' He led me through a large open-plan lounge with wooden beams everywhere into the kitchen area at the end with top-of-the-range appliances. A heavily made-up stocky woman with a black bob sat on a stool at an island in the middle of the room, swinging her purple pixie-booted foot back and forth and sipping red wine.

'This is my sister, Sasha.'

'Hi.' She raised a hand and looked quizzically at Leo.

'This is Detective . . . sorry, I've forgotten your name.'

'DS Carter.' I broke the news about what had happened to Max and Alissa the night before.

'Oh, my God! I travelled up to London with Leo today to see some art galleries and my phone ran out of juice so I haven't heard a thing.' Sasha's accent was a more pronounced Australian than her brother's. 'How awful.' Her mouth fell open.

Leo slumped on to a stool next to his sister, his eyes vacantly staring at the floor. 'Poor bloody Max.'

'I've just been speaking to Vicky Saunders and she said you were Max's best friend.'

'Yeah, yeah.' Leo rubbed his forehead, shock plastered all over his face. He stood up and grabbed a wineglass from one of the cupboards, then sat back down again, reaching for the open bottle of red on the island in front of Sasha. He poured himself a glass before speaking. 'We've, um . . . known each other since uni. He was doing architecture and I was doing business and economics.'

'I'm friends with Max, too. Well, and Alissa,' Sasha said. 'How is she?'

'Very traumatised, but she's safe.'

'Is she up to seeing anyone? I should go and check up on her, I suppose. She's not . . . Christ, she's not still at the house, is she?' Sasha screwed up her face. She had pointy features, a sharp nose and chin, cheekbones you could slice a loaf of bread with.

I explained that Alissa's location was being kept a secret for the time being, until we could ascertain whether she was still a target.

'Can either of you think of anyone who would want to harm Max and Alissa?' I asked.

Leo and Sasha exchanged a glance.

'Only that Russell character,' Leo said.

'Alissa's ex-boyfriend,' Sasha jumped in. 'He's a psycho.'

I looked at Leo, his face now pale despite the heat in the kitchen from something cooking in the oven. 'Apparently, he gatecrashed their wedding reception and threatened Max. Vicky said you went after Russell following the incident.'

'Yeah, I came into the kitchen and caught the tail end of it from the window. Russell tried to grab Max and Alissa stepped in between them. I rushed down to the end of the garden to see if they needed any help, but by the time I'd got there, Russell was walking off. I had a quick word with Alissa and Max, and then Max told me to follow him and make sure he'd really left and wasn't hanging around in the woods anywhere.'

'And had he left?'

'By the time I'd got into the woods, he'd scarpered.'

'So you didn't hear what Russell said to Max?'

'No. Max told me he'd said something like he should watch his back. He was livid that the guy had turned up, causing trouble.'

'Did Russell seem drunk?'

'God, yeah, he looked plastered. Staggering all over the place.'

'OK, so what happened afterwards? Did Max tell you he'd received any more threats from Russell? Or were there any further incidents between them that you knew of?'

Leo downed the rest of his wine and poured another glass before topping up Sasha's. 'Sorry, I've been rude. Do you want something to drink?'

'No, I'm fine, thanks.'

Leo drank more wine as if it was water. 'Max was hoping that was the end of it.'

'Did you know Russell was stalking Alissa again? Texting her and stuff?' Sasha asked. 'He was obsessed with her.'

'Yes.'

Sasha shook her head. 'I kept telling Alissa to make a formal complaint to the police and get an injunction against him or something, but she wouldn't. She thought it was harmless. She's too soft for her own good. Now look what's happened.' She raised her eyebrows in a *told-you-so* kind of gesture.

'Did Max know Russell was harassing Alissa with texts again after he found out they were getting married?' I asked.

'No. Alissa didn't tell him,' Sasha said. 'She didn't want to upset him. She thought Russell would stop it again like he did the last time.'

'Why didn't you tell me that was going on?' Leo's eyes flashed anger at his sister. 'I could've warned Max about it. Then maybe all this wouldn't have happened.'

'Because Alissa wanted it kept quiet. Us girls like to have our secrets, you know. And how was I supposed to know he'd go crazy?' she spat back, then turned to me. 'Do you think he did it, then? Killed Max? I wouldn't be at all surprised if he'd done it.' Sasha gasped, but there was something a bit gleeful sparkling in her eyes, as if she was relishing the drama of it all.

'Who else could it be?' Leo snapped. 'The bastard!'

I deflected the question with one of my own. 'You've both got Australian accents. Were you born there?'

'What's that got to do with anything?' Sasha asked.

'Just an observation.' I smiled at her.

'Ignore my sister. She can be bloody rude sometimes.' Leo glared at Sasha. She glared back.

'No,' Leo said. 'Our parents emigrated to Australia when we were little. They were out there for about twelve years, but then they died in a car accident so we came back here to live with our aunt. I was eighteen, then, and Sasha was sixteen. I got a place at uni and met Max there. We hit it off right away and—'

'We all used to hang round together, the three of us,' Sasha butted in. 'Then Max started seeing Alissa and . . . well, now Max is dead.' She shrugged.

'Sasha!' Leo gave her a thunderous look.

'What do you mean by that?' I asked her. 'Are you suggesting Alissa could've had something to do with Max's murder?'

'I'm not suggesting anything. I'm just stating a fact.'

Leo shook his head and stared at the island in front of him.

'Is there a Mrs Smithers who might've seen something at the party?' I asked Leo.

'No, I'm not in a relationship at the moment.'

'How about you, Sasha? Are you married?'

'Are you asking?' She tilted her head, a coy smile on her face.

The inappropriateness of her comment made it hard to stop my eyebrows rising in surprise. Hardly the kind of thing to say when reacting to the death of a friend, but then, everyone dealt with shock and grief in their own way. There was no standard reaction. I eyed her wineglass and wondered how many she'd had before I'd arrived. Was she drunk? On drugs?

'For fuck's sake, Sash! Max is dead, stop being so heartless,' Leo spat.

Sasha sat up in her seat, her coy expression morphing into an attempt to look chastised, but coming across as completely insincere. 'Sorry. I have a tendency to say thoughtless things when I'm stressed. It's a nervous condition. It must be the shock.'

I stared at Sasha for a moment as Vicky's description of her reverberated in my head, trying to work out if she was arrogant, an attention-seeker, immature, something more malicious, or had a mental health condition. I still hadn't made my mind up when I asked my next question. 'I heard Max wanted to expand his business to do some developing in Australia.'

Leo looked as if he hadn't heard me.

'Mr Smithers?' I prompted him.

'What?' He glanced up. 'Sorry, I'm still trying to take it all in. Can you repeat the question?'

I did so, keeping an eye on Sasha. She looked as if she was about to say something, but changed her mind.

'Yes, when Max became interested in some development in Australia, I put him in touch with one of my dad's old friends out there, who does the same thing. They were thinking of working together. They met up several times for business meetings when Alissa and Max were there.'

'Did Max tell you about any problems going on with Burbeck Developments?'

'You mean The Goldings site?' Leo rolled his eyes. 'They weren't liable for it. He wasn't doing anything wrong. He had evidence proving he didn't know about the contamination.'

'What's this about?' Sasha asked Leo.

'I'm sure the homeowners don't see it like that.' I quirked an eyebrow. 'Profit over lives?'

'Do you think that's why he was killed?' Leo frowned.

'He had received some threats over it, and we're still making enquiries, but it seems unlikely at this stage.'

'What? Tell me!' Sasha narrowed her eyes at Leo.

'I'll tell you later. It's not important.'

'How was Alissa and Max's relationship?'

'What kind of a question is that?' Leo said. 'You can't think Alissa had something to do with it, surely?'

'I'm trying to build up a picture of their life together.'

'But you said the killer came after her, too,' Leo said.

'I said Alissa escaped from the house. And if we're going to catch the offender, we need to know every little thing we can. Even if it seems inconsequential. So, how was their relationship? Were there any problems between them, any fights recently, disagreements about anything?'

Leo shot off his chair. 'That's an offensive question. Of course there were no fights or problems. They'd just got married! They had a great relationship. They were very happy and in love. I think it was love at first sight between those two. They had the perfect relationship. And there's no way Alissa would hurt Max. No way at all.' He started pacing the floor, knocking back more wine. 'In fact, after they got back from Australia, Max and I went for a drink, and he said they'd never been happier. He told me that getting married had added a new dimension to their relationship that he didn't even think was possible.'

I looked at Sasha. She seemed the type to relish a bit of gossip, or probably even start it.

'Well, there's no such thing as perfect, is there?' she said, and I'm sure I detected a hint of jealousy or bitterness in her voice. She glanced down into her glass and swirled the wine around. 'And they always say you never can tell what happens behind closed doors, don't they?' She glanced up at me through her fringe.

It was gone 10 p.m. when I left the office. Becky and Ronnie had been through all of the list of party guests, but no one else had anything useful to add to what Vicky, Leo, and Sasha had told me: Alissa and Max were very happy and in love. They couldn't think of any reason to target Max or Alissa. No one knew of any threats. No one knew about the Burbeck Developments issues. No one had heard first-hand what Russell had said to Max at the reception or seen the argument occur.

No one knew anything.

I took a detour to DI Nash's house. As usual, it was in darkness. I pictured her sitting in the lounge or the bedroom, staring into the void, crying, trying to make sense of it all, questioning everything. Been there, done that. Ellie Nash was there for me in all the dark days after Denise had gone; now it was my turn to repay the favour. I just wished I didn't have to.

I parked outside on the street and knocked on her door. No response. I didn't really expect one, but I was starting to get a bit worried now. It had been six weeks since her husband, Spencer, had been killed by a crazed husband taking out his psychotic frustrations on his wife and kid, keeping them prisoner in their own home. Mix together a police sergeant first on the scene with no knowledge that the man had a hunting rifle, a hostage situation going drastically wrong, and bang! Another copper dead. And Ellie was left to deal with the outcome. Except she wasn't dealing with it, but I knew all about that. She'd get there in her own time. I hoped. I wasn't there yet, and it had been a year for me. Wasn't sure I'd ever get there, actually. I still thought I heard Denise's voice. I still found myself thinking, *I must tell Denise this when I get home*, only to get hit with a fresh jolt of grief. I still found myself expecting her to walk round the corner with that amazing smile. Nighttime was the worst. I was afraid to go to sleep because I dreamed about her. But the dreams were never conjured up from good memories. They were all of her dying, skin melting away from her face, blood dripping from her nose, her bones forcing their way through the soft tissue. Her hair falling out in clumps from the poisonous chemo. They all ended the same: with her opening her mouth and screaming, vomiting up maggots and flies. That was usually the time I jerked awake, sweating, heart pounding, trying to force the image out of my head and replace it with another one. A happier one. God, there were so many to choose from. We'd met when we were both fifteen and working in the Co-op as a Saturday job. I knew all about love at first sight. I'd lived it with her. Thirty-six years we'd been together. We weren't just partners, lovers – we were best friends. And now all I had left were memories and nightmares.

I knocked on Ellie's door again and heard nothing. I rattled the letterbox and waited. Then I flipped it open and shouted into it.

'Ellie, it's me. I hope you're . . .' What? I paused and tried to think of the right word: OK? Alright? That sounded way too insignificant and banal. Not trying to slash your wrists? Not wanting to kill the person who killed Spencer? Not giving up hope? From my own experience, that was more like it. I wasn't that great at doing emotional stuff, and sometimes there are no right words to say. 'I brought you something to eat. Maybe you don't feel like it, but . . . well, it's here anyway. Call me, OK? When you're ready.'

I left the Chinese food in a bag on the doorstep and drove home. Another day to cross off the list of empty, endless days left of a life without my wife.

THE OTHER ONE
Chapter 13

I was ten years old when he made me commit murder. One of the cows had given birth to a male calf, and unlike that first time, when I wondered where Dad was taking it to, now I knew. The males were no good on a dairy farm, and there was no veal industry where we were, so the boys had to be killed immediately. It would cost Dad more to feed them than they were worth for sale as cheap meat, he said. And he didn't want to spend money sending them to a slaughterhouse, so he did it himself.

It was Lulabelle's baby. Lulabelle cried out frantically as Dad took the calf away, dumping it on to his red plastic wheelbarrow. He took it into a small shed he'd built with white tiles on the walls and a drain in the floor. The tiles weren't white any more, though, and the grouting was stained a dark browny-red.

'You can start doing this yourself now. You need to do something to make yourself useful,' Dad said as he lifted the end of the wheelbarrow and dumped the calf on the floor. It couldn't even walk yet. Its legs were weak and bent, unable to hold its weight.

I put my hands over my ears to block out its tiny cries and watched the poor thing that had never asked to be born looking at me with two dark, brown watery pools of hope, waiting for me to save it.

'Shut the fuck up!' Dad kicked the calf in its back legs, sending it skidding across the floor.

'No, please!' I yelled. 'Please don't do it.'

He laughed at me. 'You're pathetic. Pathetic and weak. What did I do to deserve you?'

I wiped away the snot dribbling down my chin and pleaded some more with Dad. I couldn't kill an innocent animal. But I couldn't stop him doing it. The only thing I could do was leave.

I ran towards the door of the shed. My fingers were on the latch when I felt myself being pulled back by my hair.

'Don't be such a cry baby. What do you think farming's all about? You'll have to do this when I'm not around any more. I'm teaching you a valuable lesson.'

I shook my head, my whimpers matching the calf's, knowing that if Dad wasn't around, I'd burn this place to the ground and rejoice.

'If you don't watch and learn, I'll just kill that one you call Lulabelle.'

My throat burned with the tears sliding down it and the bile rising up to meet them. 'I can't kill him. You shouldn't kill him. *Please*, Dad. *Please* don't do it.'

He laughed again. 'God put these animals on earth for us. It's *His* law. Who are you to question that? What's it going to be? You or the calf? Because this works just as well on kids, too.' He sneered at me, an icy, evil look in his eye. 'Your choice.'

But how could I make that decision? How could I do anything? I was as helpless as that calf. And I knew he'd kill him anyway.

He grabbed my hand, put the handle of the knife in it, and curled my fingers around it, his hand clutched over mine so I couldn't drop it. 'Come on!' He pulled me by the same hand towards the calf.

I squeezed my eyes shut and cried, a shuddering ball of fear and hate and hurt.

'One stab behind the neck into the spinal cord and it's all over. Much less messy than slitting their throats.'

'No.' I tried to pull my hand out of his strong grip.

He manoeuvred my hand up to my throat, the tip of the blade touching my skin. 'Shall I kill you then?'

I stared into his grotesque, demonic eyes, not recognising the person behind them. Saliva had pooled at the side of his mouth. How could anyone be so cruel?

He pressed the knife harder against my neck, and I felt hot pain and liquid running down my skin. Then he jerked my hand away in his and kneeled down next to the calf, pulling me along with him.

I tried to tug my hand away again, but he was too strong for me. Instead, he lifted my hand in the air and plunged the knife into the back of the calf's neck.

I pressed my eyelids together and screamed and screamed until I was thrown through the air, the knife clattering to the tiled floor. I landed against the side of the shed, banging my spine hard. Curling into a ball, I put my hands over my face, trying to ignore the pain, knowing I never wanted to open my eyes again and see the reality of my world. My pain was nothing compared to the calf's, and I couldn't bear to see its dead body.

That was around the time I first fantasised about killing my dad.

THE DETECTIVE
Chapter 14

I put off sleeping again. I knew it would catch up with me eventually, dragging me to somewhere I didn't want to go, tormenting me with vile images of Denise. Most of the time I'd sit in a chair in the lounge, watching the TV but not really seeing it, feeling the loneliness crushing me as I tried to put off the moment when it would suck me under. No wonder my back hurt when I woke up, wedged into the chair at an awkward angle. I was exhausted. I couldn't go on like this, but what was the alternative?

Tonight I had something better than the TV to stop me sleeping, and spent hours going through the texts from Max and Alissa's phones and the documents and emails from their laptops that the forensic technical department had recovered. The only documents on Alissa's laptop were her romance novel, a plot synopsis, some PDF files on creative writing lessons, and the same list of party guests that Wilmott had given us. Max's were more complex: there were company accounts spreadsheets, copies of planning files and applications, templates for land option agreements, various legal files, and scans of the environmental report Burbeck Developments had commissioned prior to building The Goldings site. It had been carried out by a company called DBT Engineers and did indeed say there was no contamination on that land. I checked out the company and they'd gone bankrupt several years ago. Barring that site, I found nothing that would give a motive for Max's murder. All the homeowners' alibis had checked out now, so I was pretty sure that was a dead end.

The emails for Alissa were few and far between – PayPal receipts for things she'd bought, a couple of exchanges between her and her tutor on the creative writing course asking for advice, and some junk mail. According to her phone records, she preferred to text her friends, but they were all benign: *Hi, how are things? . . . Do you fancy shopping on Saturday? . . . Shall we meet up for a coffee?* The ones between Alissa and Max were just as you'd expect for a newly married couple: *What time will you be home? I'm missing you already! Xx . . . If you're going into town can you pick up some squirty cream, LOL! . . . Can't wait to see you!* and the random *Love you! <3 xx.*

Apart from the texts sent by Russell to Alissa, nothing of interest had turned up.

The next morning, I was the first one in the office at 7 a.m. Wilmott was bringing Alissa to the nick for a more thorough, videoed statement while he managed the press conference and strutted around the place trying to look useful and impressive.

At ten to eight, Becky walked in, deposited her jacket on the back of her desk chair, and said, 'Have you been here all night?'

'I might as well have been.'

'You look awful,' she said with concern.

'Thanks. Now I know who to turn to when I need a confidence boost.'

'I didn't mean it like that and you know it.'

I sighed. 'Having trouble sleeping.'

'Still? Why don't you take some sleeping tablets?'

I shook my head. As if that could fix things.

A short while later, Ronnie bounced in, energetic and raring to go. 'Tea, anyone?'

'I'll have one.' DI Wilmott loomed in the doorway. His hair contained so much gel even a nuclear explosion wouldn't mess it up.

'Did you get any further information from Alissa yesterday?' I asked.

'Not much,' Wilmott said. 'She was far too upset. My primary role was to ensure her safety.'

And not be a detective? But that was Wilmott all over. He wasn't concerned with the nitty-gritty of detective work. He just wanted to look good for the camera, kiss arse, push pieces of paper around, and gloss over all the day-to-day shit that actually solved crimes.

'How is she today, sir?' Ronnie asked.

'Still very fragile, but she realises we need to get as much information from her as we can.'

'Any word about uniform taking over from you at the hotel?' I asked, which was code for, *In case you haven't noticed, we could do with an extra pair of hands.*

'They're too short-staffed,' he snapped.

'What about a family liaison officer?' I suggested.

'All of them are tied up on other jobs. Now, where are we? I want to tell Detective Superintendent Greene we're making progress.'

I gave him an update.

He put his two index fingers together and rested them on the tip of his nose. 'So, the Burbeck Developments angle doesn't look promising?'

'Doesn't look like it, no. Russell Stiles still looks like our main person of interest. I spent last night going through the information recovered from the phones and laptops. There's nothing of particular note apart from Russell's texts to Alissa. He didn't make any specific threats to her or Max, but they show a pattern of him having too much interest in her.'

'Did Alissa reply to Russell's texts?' Ronnie asked me.

'Yeah. Her replies were always friendly and polite. According to her friend, Vicky, Alissa wanted to stay friends with Russell and not upset things further. But her replies weren't encouraging, no can-you-kill-my-husband-for-me type messages.'

'As I said yesterday, Alissa Burbeck is *not* considered a suspect. She is a *victim*.' Wilmott glared at me. He seemed to be getting a bit too personal about Alissa for my liking.

'Sasha struck me as a bit strange, though, which is how Vicky Saunders described her, too,' I said. 'I'm not sure if she was pissed or on something, but I think she's possibly jealous of Alissa. It seemed like there was some gloating going on under the surface.'

'Most girls would be jealous of Alissa in some way,' Becky said. 'Looking the way she does, and marrying someone rich. Why should one woman get to have it all when they don't? Some people like seeing their so-called friends fail. Makes them feel better about their own lives.'

'True,' I said.

'What else do we know about Stiles' background?' Wilmott asked.

'He worked for a few landscape gardening companies before starting his own,' I said. 'He's rented a cottage in Waverly, not far from the Burbecks, for the last eighteen months following his return to the UK from backpacking round Australia.'

'All the better for keeping an eye on her,' Wilmott said, then looked at us all expectantly. 'Anything else I should know?'

Noes all round.

He glanced at me. 'You'll do Alissa's interview while I handle the press.'

I nodded. God forbid he should have to do some real work.

'She's waiting in interview room two at the moment, and I want to wrap this up as quickly as possible. I'd like to spare her the unnecessary trauma of a long investigation. Emma Bolton, the senior SOCO, should be here in a minute to tell us what evidence they've found so far. She's on her way back out to the scene to finish up afterwards. Now, where's that tea?' Wilmott raised one eyebrow at Ronnie, who shot up to oblige.

Wilmott moved to the whiteboard, staring at Alissa's photo, sipping tea, and generally doing nothing helpful until Emma appeared.

'Morning, sir.' She nodded at Wilmott.

He turned to face her and beamed a smile, running a hand through his hair. 'Thanks for coming in. Please tell me you've got something useful.'

Ronnie sat up straight in his chair, all ears.

I picked up a pen, ready to take notes.

'OK, the scene is consistent with what Alissa Burbeck described. There are a lot of fingerprints downstairs, most likely from the wedding reception, and we're still taking more. It will take some time to eliminate Max's. And obviously Alissa's prints and DNA will be all over the house. Upstairs in the office, we found four sets of prints. A fingerprint officer has confirmed one set belongs to Max. Another set matches Alissa's prints we took from her yesterday at the hospital. Two are unaccounted for and aren't a match to anyone on record. We're still taking prints from everyone who attended the wedding reception, including catering staff and those who set up the marquee, to see if they tie in with one of them.'

'So they didn't match Russell Stiles?' Ronnie asked her.

'No. But the offender was wearing gloves. We also recovered a couple of short black hairs on Max's body that don't appear to be consistent with either Max or Alissa. The follicles suggest they were shed recently.'

'What colour hair has Russell Stiles got?' Wilmott asked me.

'Black.'

He turned a charming smile on Emma and asked her to continue.

'I've asked for a rush on DNA testing, but . . .' She shrugged. 'Short-staffed and underpaid, like all of us, so I'm not sure how long it will take. We've found no helpful footprints in the house or the grounds. Alissa said the offender also wore plastic shoe coverings, so that's not surprising, plus the weather didn't work in our favour. The only ones of note we did find were the wet prints which are consistent with Alissa's from when she came out of the bathroom. We also found white hairs around the house which don't appear to be human. Possibly dog or cat.'

'I asked Alissa about a cat after Mrs Downes said she fed it when they were away,' Wilmott said. 'Alissa told me it went missing after they had the wedding reception at the house. Must've got spooked by all the people around and ran away.'

Typical. He asked her about a cat but not any more pertinent questions? What planet is he on?

'Well, when we extended the search to the wooded area behind the rear garden, we found a dead white cat. Looks like its neck was broken. Nearby we found an empty bottle of Jack Daniel's and some cigarette butts.'

'Maybe from the day of the wedding reception,' I suggested. 'Stiles was seen entering the garden from that wooded area, and apparently he was pretty drunk.'

'He would've had a good view of the house and garden from the spot where we found them, so he could've been sitting watching from that point.'

Ronnie raised his hand.

Wilmott rolled his eyes at him. 'You don't have to put your hand up. We're not five.'

Ronnie's cheeks flushed and he lowered his hand. 'If the murderer was wearing a balaclava, how would some of his hairs get on Max's body?'

'Balaclavas are generally reversible,' Emma said. 'If he'd worn it before, a hair could've snagged on the inside, then when it was used again it was worn inside out. Or it could've collected a hair on the outside of it as he was pulling it on and then it transferred to the body.'

Ronnie put his hand up again.

'What?' Wilmott asked him in a bored voice.

'Killers often start by abusing animals. So . . . um . . . maybe Stiles killed the cat first.'

Wilmott glared at Ronnie. 'I was just about to get to that. It's highly likely that killing the cat was a precursor to Stiles' escalating violence.' Wilmott gave Emma his full attention again. 'Anything else?'

'Nothing of note at this stage. We're still looking. It's a big house.'

Wilmott slapped his hands together. 'Right. Let's get to it, people!'

THE DETECTIVE
Chapter 15

I gave Alissa my condolences again as I sat down in the interview room across the desk from her, taking in her blotchy cheeks and swollen, red-rimmed eyes.

She glanced down at her hands balled in her lap and bit her lip, shaking her head. 'I still can't believe all this.'

'I know it's very difficult going over things again, but we need to get a more detailed statement from you so we can try to piece together what happened.'

She lifted her chin and looked me in the eye. 'I know. I know you have to ask things. I want to help you catch him.'

'Do you need anything before we start? Tea? Coffee? Water?'

'No, thanks.'

I switched on the tape recorder and video and gave the preliminaries – date, time, who was present.

'I want to get some more background information first, Alissa. It may give us more insight into the case. Some of my questions might seem strange, but every little thing helps in a case like this.'

She nodded.

'Can you give audible replies for the benefit of the tape, please?'

'Sorry. Yes.'

'How long have you lived at The Orchard?'

'Just over a year. It was Max's parents' house. He moved back there when they died several years ago, and then . . . yes, I moved in with him.'

'Who has access to the office?'

'Um . . . M . . . Max does.' She paused. 'Did.' She blinked back tears. 'And me, of course. And the cleaner.'

'Who is the cleaner?'

'Brenda Johnson.'

'How long has she been cleaning for you?'

'She worked for Max before I moved in, and for his parents before. Years, really.'

'Does anyone else have access to the office?'

She clenched her hands together, wringing them. 'No. No one else has access to the upstairs. No one else has a need to.'

'So no one else has been in that office apart from you and Max and Brenda Johnson?'

'Not that I know of.'

'Are there any other staff who work for you?'

'Yes, there's Malcolm Briggs, the gardener. He's also worked for Max's family for years.'

'Do you have a white cat?'

'I've had her for five years. I thought it might be good for Mum when she was ill, you know, after her first stroke. They say animals are therapeutic. She was a really friendly cat and would go to anyone for affection. I love her to bits. When I moved into The Orchard, she really liked it there, exploring the woods at the back. But she went missing a couple of weeks ago.'

'So around the time of the wedding reception?'

'Yes. Why? Did she come back to the house?'

'I'm afraid the cat was found in the woods at the rear of the property. Her neck appears to have been broken.'

Her hands flew to her mouth. 'Oh, no! What happened to her?'

'It's impossible to tell. Did she ever climb trees?'

'I never saw her do that, but she might've. Or . . .' Her eyes widened. 'Do you think this has something to do with Max? Was she killed by the same person?'

'We're not sure at this stage. The cat was found in an area that we believe Russell Stiles was watching the wedding reception from. We also found a bottle of Jack Daniel's and some cigarette butts in the same place.'

She gasped. 'You think Russell killed Buttons?'

'It's possible. He's no stranger to killing animals. Did you know about his arrest for poaching?'

'Poaching?! Oh, God, no. He never told me about that. I knew he liked to eat game, but I didn't know he did that.' She stared off into space, her face pale. 'Max loved Buttons, too. And now they're both gone.' Fresh tears snaked down her cheeks.

I pushed a box of tissues towards her. She took one and dabbed them away daintily.

I glanced down at my notes. 'OK. You'd been in a relationship with Max for three years, is that right?'

She didn't answer, just stared at a spot on the floor, her lower lip trembling.

'Are you OK to carry on?'

She fanned her face. 'I'm feeling a bit hot. There's no air in here.' She fanned herself a little more, then covered her face with her hands. 'Sorry,' she squeaked. 'I just need a minute.'

'It's alright. I know how difficult this is.'

When she'd sat upright and composed herself again, she said, 'Sorry.'

'When did you decide to get married?'

Her cheeks lifted in the ghost of a smile, as if remembering her husband. 'He kept asking me. I think the first time he asked was about six months after we'd started seeing each other. But my mum was ill, she'd had the stroke and I was looking after her, and . . . it was a difficult time, so I said no. Then he just carried on asking, every six months or so. My mum wasn't getting better. She had another stroke and went into a nursing home where they could care for her properly. And then . . . well, I still wasn't ready. I was only twenty-two at the time, I'd spent time looking after Mum and I was still finishing off my creative writing course that had been put on hold when Mum was still at home. I wanted to be sure about him.'

'You weren't sure?'

'No, I was, but I was still young and he was older and . . . he was only the second guy I'd been out with. I knew I loved him, but . . . I thought we should live together first, so I moved in with him. Like I said, I lived there for a year. Then, the last time he asked, I said yes.'

'Where did you get married?'

'In Sydney. On Bondi Beach.' She blinked rapidly and looked at the floor.

'Were you specifically going to Australia to get married or was it a holiday?'

'Max was thinking of starting some developments out there, so it was an existing business trip for him, and we just decided to combine it with a holiday and then . . . a wedding. Leo, Max's friend, used to live out there, you see, and there was an old family friend of Leo's dad in Australia who's a developer. He put them in touch with each other and they had a lot of business meetings while we were there.'

'Did anything strange happen in Australia?'

'Strange?'

'Anything that might've attracted attention. Did anyone seem upset with Max? Did you notice anyone suspicious? Did you receive any threats?'

'No. I didn't go to his business meetings, but he told me everything was going to plan. The rest of the time was our honeymoon. We travelled up the east coast, going to various different places, but we didn't run into anyone strange.'

'OK. So, when you got back, you had the reception?'

'I'm sorry, can I have some water? I feel a bit . . . faint.' Her voice hitched.

'Of course.'

The interview was suspended while I fetched some water. Alissa's complexion beneath her recent tan had turned pale.

'You're doing really well, Alissa.'

She brought the glass to her lips with a shaky hand, spilling some water on the desk, although she didn't seem to notice. 'I want to do everything I can to help.'

'Can you describe your relationship with Max? Were there any problems between you?'

'No! Of course not. I wouldn't have married him if there were problems. We were very happy.'

'You said Russell Stiles gatecrashed the reception. Can you go through in detail again what happened?'

She told me how she'd been standing by the pond at the bottom of the garden, getting some air because she was hot, stealing a quick moment alone in the hubbub of the party, when Stiles appeared. By the time she'd noticed him, he'd already climbed over the post-and-rail fence and was walking towards her.

'What was he wearing that day?'

She gave a slight shake of her head. 'Um . . . I think he had jeans and a T-shirt on.'

'Do you remember the exact conversation between you?'

She took another sip of water. 'He asked if I was sure I knew what I was doing. He said Max couldn't be trusted. He asked if I was happy and said it wasn't too late for us to get back together. He told me he still loved me, and he wouldn't stop loving me.'

'Did he give a reason why he thought Max couldn't be trusted?'

'No. I was a bit . . . well, shocked, I suppose. We were just supposed to be friends now. He kept sending texts asking how I was and that he wanted me back, and I replied, but I didn't encourage him. I just wanted him to be as happy as I was.' She sucked in a deep breath, waited a moment, then continued. 'Then Max appeared and told Russell to leave and said he wasn't welcome.'

'What did Russell say to that? How did he react? Did he get angry?'

'Um . . . he was angry and emotional and he was slurring his words because he was drunk. Then he looked at me and said, "Are you staying?" Which was just a weird thing to say.'

'How did you respond?'

'Of course, I said I was staying. I kind of laughed with disbelief and told him it was my wedding reception. Max was furious. Then he said to Max that he deserved everything he got and he should watch his back. Max tried to go for Russell. I stepped in between them, and then Russell climbed back over the fence. We watched him go into the woods, and then Leo came out and asked us what had happened. Leo went into the woods to make sure Russell had gone, and when he came back, he said there was no sign of him.'

'What did Max do after that?'

'He was fuming, but he didn't want it to spoil our celebrations. He put his arm around me and said, "Let's forget about this for the rest of the day and enjoy it." He also mentioned something about getting an injunction against Russell to stop him contacting me.'

'Did you ever pursue an injunction?'

'No. Max was stressed about something going on at work and he was busy with that, and I suppose I didn't take it that seriously. I'd known Russell for years and I didn't think he would do anything to hurt . . .' She let the sentence drift into thin air, as if unsure how to finish it. Her eyes shone with tears. 'Do you think he did this? Murdered Max?'

'Do you?'

'I wouldn't have ever thought so, but . . . now I've had time to go over what happened that night, what I saw, there *was* something familiar about the way the man moved, and his height and build. Although he was wearing the balaclava, I think . . . I think it could've been Russell.'

'Can you walk me through again exactly what happened that night?'

She closed her eyes, lashes fluttering against her skin. Then she took a deep breath. 'It was about midnight. Max was working in his office, and I ran a bath. While I was waiting for it to fill, I popped in to the office and Max was studying a document on his laptop, listening to music. We had a quick chat. He said he would be working for a bit longer and then going to bed. I gave him a kiss on the cheek, then I went into the en-suite and got in the bath.'

'Did you leave the door to his office open or did you shut it?'

'It was open.'

'What about the door to your bedroom and the en-suite. Were they open or closed?'

'The door to our bedroom was open. I shut the bathroom door to stop the steam going into the bedroom.'

'So could you hear the music coming from Max's laptop when you were in the bath?'

'Yes, it was quite loud. He turned it up after I went out.'

'OK, so what happened next?'

'I got in the bath and fell asleep. When I woke up it was cold.'

'Do you often fall asleep in the bath?'

'Yes, all the time.'

'Do you always take a bath at that time or does it vary?'

'It varies. Sometimes it's earlier if I'm tired. But I always have one before I go to bed.'

'Who would know that was part of your nightly routine?'

'I don't know. I probably mentioned it to Vicky in the past, maybe Sasha, too. Russell knew I always used to do that when we were together.'

'OK, what next?'

'Um . . . I let the water out of the bath, dried myself and wrapped a towel around me, and walked into the bedroom, but Max still wasn't in bed, so I walked through the bedroom and into the hall, intending to go into the office to check on him.'

'Check on him?'

'Well, to see if he'd finished and was coming to bed. And . . .' Her hands shot up and cupped her mouth, eyes wide with fear, as if reliving the moment.

'Take your time. You're doing great.'

She bunched her fists together under her chin. 'I . . . I got almost as far as the stairs. Then I saw a man coming out of the office with a knife in his hand.'

'It couldn't have been a woman you saw that night?'

'Um . . . I don't know. It's possible. They were wearing a bulky black jacket. Probably the same height as me. I just assumed it was a man.'

'Can you describe the person again for me, please?

'Yes, they were average height, average build, I suppose, and dressed in black, with a balaclava on, wearing gloves and blue plastic shoe covers. And now . . . now I do think it could've been Russell. He had the same colour eyes.'

'He had brown eyes?'

'Yes, I saw them through the—' She motioned around her eyes in a circular movement. 'The bit that was cut out for the eyes. I froze for a second and then ran back through the bedroom and into the bathroom. I locked the door and climbed out the window, on to the roof of the orangery. I must've lost my towel as I got through. Then I ran into the woods at the back of the house and towards the nearest neighbour. Gloria, Mrs Downes, she has the same post-and-rail type fence as most of the properties there, so it's quite low. I climbed over it into her back garden and banged on the door that leads to the kitchen. She let me in and called the police.'

'While you were climbing through the window, did you notice whether the intruder tried to open the bathroom door?'

'I don't think so. But I was so scared, and it all happened so quickly. They might've done.'

'What happened earlier in the day?'

She took another sip of water before she answered. 'Max went into Burbeck Developments for a meeting. He left about nine-thirty and got back about six. I cooked some pasta and we ate at about eight. Then we . . .' Her cheeks flushed. 'We had sex. In the kitchen. And afterwards, we watched a DVD in the lounge. It finished about eleven, then Max went upstairs to the office to work. He said he had a few more things to prepare for another meeting, and I watched the TV until about midnight, before going to have a bath.'

'The curtains in the office were open when the police arrived. Are they usually left open at night?'

'Yes. Apart from our bedroom, we often leave most of the curtains open at night. We only overlook the woods.'

'What were you doing that day when Max was at work?'

'I was working on my novel.'

'Do you remember anything else that might be helpful?'

'No, I don't think so.'

I wrote out her statement and passed it to her to read through. As she perused it, I observed her carefully. She seemed every inch the genuine grieving widow. But there was something about her, a gut impression that made me question whether she was telling the truth. She was saying all the right things in the right way, but it didn't feel exactly genuine, like she was trying too hard.

She finished reading, glanced up, and nodded.

I slid a pen across the desk and pointed to everywhere she needed to sign.

Her right hand lifted slightly, hovering in the air for a second before fluttering towards the box of tissues. She took one, wiped her nose delicately with it, and balled it in her fist, then picked up the pen with her left hand and signed it.

~

I checked out Malcolm Briggs, the gardener, on our databases. He'd been convicted of drink-driving twenty years before, and according to his details, he was sixty-five, short, and had blue eyes – as far away from Alissa's description of the intruder as you could get. Not only that, he had a solid alibi. On the afternoon of the murder, he'd been rushed into the same hospital Alissa had been taken to for an emergency appendectomy, but had suffered a heart attack on the operating table. After a quick visit to the ICU, I discovered he was too weak to speak to us, so I left a message with his wife, asking for him to contact us when he'd recovered. That just left the other member of staff, Brenda Johnson, although as a cleaner she had a legitimate reason to have been in all areas of the house.

She sat in the same interview room three hours later. She was fifty-two, but looked much older. Her hair was dyed jet black with silvery roots poking through. She had the lines of a smoker around her mouth, giving her a harsh look, but when she spoke her voice was soft and friendly, her eyes sad pools of blue. She'd already given her fingerprints, and a DNA swab had been taken when she arrived at the station.

'Anything I can do to help,' she said. 'It's just horrific. You don't think something like that's going to happen to someone you know.'

'I believe you worked for Max and his family for a long time as a cleaner, is that correct?'

'Yes. I started working for Max's parents ten years ago, cleaning twice a week. They were a lovely couple. Rich, you know, but they weren't snobby with it. They'd always give me little gifts. They were very thoughtful. Then, when they died a few years ago, Max decided to move back into the family home and he kept me on.'

'And when did Alissa move into the house?'

'About a year ago.'

'Being a cleaner means you often get to witness things behind closed doors no one else sees.'

'Yes. I suppose so.' She gave me a grim smile. 'You wouldn't believe some of the things I've had to clear up, or seen, or heard over the years! People often think cleaners are invisible, I swear.'

'So how would you describe Max and Alissa's relationship?'

Her forehead crinkled. 'What do you mean?'

'Well, how did they get on? Did you notice any arguments between them lately? Hear anything or see anything out of the ordinary?'

She inhaled a puff of air. 'Are you saying you think Alissa had something to do with Max's death?'

'No. But we need to ask these questions. Build up a picture, you know.'

'Oh, right. I suppose the partner is always the most likely suspect, aren't they? But Max and Alissa were head over heels for each other. Doted on each other. Alissa worked from home, writing her novel, and Max did, too, occasionally, so I got to see them quite a bit at the house when I was there. I never saw them argue. They were . . .' She shrugged. 'Well, they were just happy and in love. I don't know what else I can tell you.'

'How would you describe Max?'

'I was his cleaner, not his friend.'

'I know, but what were your impressions of him?'

'He could be a little bit arrogant, I suppose, but he was always kind to me. Always friendly and jokey.'

'And Alissa?'

Her face brightened into a smile. 'She's a real sweetie. You know those few genuinely lovely people? That's Alissa. Always kind and smiling and polite. She looked after her mum single-handedly for a long time after the stroke. Put her studies on hold. That's the kind of person she was. Warm-hearted.'

'Did you notice anyone suspicious hanging around the house?'

'No.'

'How about anything odd that happened with Max or Alissa recently? Anything that seemed out of character? It doesn't matter how small or inconsequential you think it might be.'

She pursed her lips, thinking. 'Well, Max seemed a bit stressed about work. When I went into the office to clean last week and he was in there working, he told me not to bother. He actually snapped at me, which is something he'd never done before.'

'Right. And anything with Alissa?'

She shook her head. 'No. Oh, wait, there was something, but it's not really odd, I suppose. She always used to make me lunch when I was working there and we'd sit down together and have a little chat. But she stopped doing that when they came back from Australia. I mean, she was still lovely and friendly, but . . . she was just busy, organising the finishing touches for the reception, settling into married life, writing her book. But I missed that. Missed our little chats.'

'Is there anything else you can think of?'

'No. Sorry.'

'Well, thanks very much for your time.'

She clutched my arm. 'You will find out who did this, won't you?'

I smiled reassuringly. 'We're doing everything we can.'

THE OTHER ONE
Chapter 16

The only thing I was any good at was art. It was the only way I could express everything bad inside. I hardly talked to the other kids at school, but I'd learned by then not to shout at everyone. I'd learned by watching and listening to all the others. How they ate in the canteen. How they laughed. What they talked about. I could probably hold a conversation and pass for normal, but it didn't interest me. I was just keeping to myself, biding my time, waiting for some way to escape everything.

But art was my way of talking. It was something *I* was in control of. I'd tried to stop eating meat at home after Lulabelle's calf was killed, but Dad forced me to. Even though I threw up every time. He made me clear up the sick and sent me to the cupboard. It was a constant battle that I knew I wouldn't win. He seemed to take great delight in sitting at the table, making me force every mouthful down my closed-up throat, watching me retch, knowing it wouldn't be long before it came back up again. But it didn't stop me trying to refuse every day, and sometimes he'd shove the food in my mouth himself, holding my jaw open with one strong hand, shovelling in meat with the other, until I choked and spluttered. The thought of eating animal flesh after what I'd seen was unbearable, and the only satisfaction I had was when I vomited on him.

So even though I couldn't control what went inside my body, through my eyes and ears and mouth, I could control what came out of my head. Mostly.

My art teacher at secondary school was called Mrs Tucker. She looked at me differently from the other teachers. They just saw a sullen, uncommunicative kid who'd never amount to anything, so they'd stopped trying. If you weren't in the boffin brigade, they weren't interested. And they didn't bother to root around to find the cause of my weirdness. But Mrs Tucker smiled at me, put her arm around me in class as she examined my work, gave me words of encouragement, and slipped me chocolate bars for my undernourished body in the canteen during lunch. She tried to get me to talk, to open up about my home life, but what would I say? And my mum's voice still echoed in my head: *Never talk about what goes on behind closed doors!* I'd grown to hate Mum as much as him, for her weakness, for letting the badness in, for not caring.

There was an art competition at school and Mrs Tucker announced with excitement that we could work on our entries as part of our homework and to submit them to her by the end of the week. The prize was a voucher for an art supply shop.

I hadn't gone past what I call my 'dark art' stage – the drawings of people with no faces, self-portraits with me as the devil, couples screaming as they were devoured in flames – but I knew by then that interpreting the boring still life of a fruit bowl as something warped would attract more unwanted attention. And I didn't need that, thanks. The school calling my parents again and complaining about my antisocial behaviour was the last thing I wanted. The punishment at home wasn't worth it.

I wanted to win. For once in my life, I wanted to achieve something more than just simply surviving each day. Even if I won, though, Dad would never let me spend the voucher on something I actually wanted. He'd think it was frivolous. *Good money thrown down the drain on things that don't matter!* (Hello? What about all the whisky?!) I could get away with never telling him, but how would I get into the nearest town to spend the voucher? The only time I left the house was with Mum, when she made me help her with grocery shopping. Or to school, when the bus picked me up at the end of the road and deposited me back at that madhouse at the end of the day. Still, if I could win, at least I would've beaten him somehow. And that was all the incentive I needed.

I worked on my project in my bedroom at night when they thought I was asleep. I no longer interrupted their fights. They were both as bad as each other, feeding on the other's insecurities. Both looking for someone to blame and usually coming up with me as the No. 1 reason. Never doing anything to end the constant violent loop. So they were welcome to each other. It wasn't my problem any more, and I wasn't going to intervene and get stuffed in the cupboard again. Or worse. Fuck that! You shouldn't go round having kids if you didn't even want them in the first place, so there was no loyalty left inside me. If they were on a game show, there'd be a loud buzzer squawking over their heads constantly, saying *Loser! Loser! Loser!*

I drew through the shouting and screaming and holes being punched through doors, and Mum crying and appearing in the mornings with yet another bruise or black eye or barely able to stand up properly, and Dad drinking himself to boiling point. I ignored it all, and immersed myself in the lines taking shape on the page and the colouring and shading and getting the perspective just right.

But I didn't win. A girl called Trisha did. One of those popular kids who had all the latest clothes and was always immaculately dressed. Whose hair wasn't butchered into a pudding bowl shape by her mum. Who giggled a lot and always did her homework on time. I shouldn't have been surprised, but my entry was way better than hers. That night, I went into my room after all the chores were done to work on a new art project. Not winning would just make me more determined for next time. I hummed to myself as I etched charcoal across the page, rubbing with my finger, sitting back to study it from different angles, leaning in and drawing more. I couldn't bring myself to care about what was going on in the room next door. Screams, shouts, chairs scraping against the floor, things being smashed. It had become like background noise now, so normal that it barely registered.

Sometimes I look back and feel guilty that I didn't do something else to prevent it. That I'd stopped listening to them. I'd stopped caring that Mum wasn't going to save me. Stopped feeling. I was just numb. Emotionally frozen.

So, yeah, maybe I am partly to blame for what happened that night. What if I'd gone into their room like all those other hundreds of times over the years? If I'd tried to break it up? If I'd turned Dad's anger on me instead?

Then maybe he would never have stabbed her to death.

THE DETECTIVE
Chapter 17

'Did anything come out of the press conference? Have we had any witnesses come forward? Anyone with information?' Wilmott perched on the edge of a desk and picked a bit of fluff from his trousers, staring at it with distaste before he flicked it on the floor.

Poor Becky and Ronnie had been manning the phone lines following Wilmott's moment of fame in front of the cameras, as well as trying to follow other lines of enquiry.

'Just the usual nutters coming out of the woodwork,' Becky said.

Ronnie nodded his agreement.

'Shame. I looked good on TV.'

Becky rolled her eyes.

'Anyway, we've had some more fingerprint and DNA results back,' Wilmott carried on. 'The long strands of hair found on Max's body were from Alissa – no surprise there – and were most likely transferred during their last conversation and kiss in his office. The other two black hairs found on Max's body are a match to Russell Stiles.'

Ronnie whistled.

'Any more updates on the two unknown fingerprints in the office?' I asked.

'One set matched Brenda Johnson, the cleaner. Everyone who attended the wedding reception has given their prints now and none match the other set that was recovered. But that doesn't matter, because Stiles is our prime suspect.' Wilmott grinned proudly, as if he'd personally solved everything. 'He was clearly obsessed with Alissa and stalked her, wanting them to get back together. He threatened Max, and according to Alissa's more detailed account, she believes he had similarities to the man in the house.'

I folded my arms and leaned back in my chair, chewing on the end of a pen.

'He has no alibi for the night in question,' Wilmott carried on. 'He also has a previous record for assault and for killing animals, hence the fate of Alissa's cat. DNA taken from the Jack Daniel's bottle and cigarette butts in the woods also matches Stiles. He was most likely unable to stand the thought of her with someone else, so he murdered Max Burbeck to get him out of the way, hoping to rekindle his relationship with Alissa.'

'I'm not entirely convinced.' I removed the pen from my mouth and twiddled it between my forefinger and middle finger.

'Why?' Wilmott raised a sceptical eyebrow.

'You keep saying Alissa was lucky to escape the house that night without being killed herself, that she's a victim. But it was around midnight, so the killer must've been reasonably sure that she'd be in the house at the time if he knew Max and Alissa. Why take the risk of her being there? Why not do it when Max was alone in the house? If it was Stiles, who seems to be ultra-protective of Alissa and completely in love with her, what would've happened if Alissa had come to Max's aid? How could Stiles be sure he wouldn't have had to hurt her to stop her sounding the alarm?'

'You can't second-guess a psychopath. Sometimes there's no rhyme or reason to what they do. He was most likely worried about being caught and didn't want to hang around any more when he was spotted by Alissa in case she raised the alarm. Do you have any other suggestions?' Wilmott tilted his head. 'If you do, I'm all ears.' But his tone indicated he didn't give a toss what I thought.

'I think Alissa and Stiles were working together,' I said. 'Alissa and Max had only just got married, therefore she was the heir to millions. It's very convenient she managed to get away from a crazed, knife-wielding man who'd just killed her husband. A man who made no attempt to break down the bathroom door to get to her when she spotted him, or to wait outside to get her when she climbed through the window. He just killed Max and vanished into thin air, which is weird. If he'd already killed once, then why not try to kill the only witness? Because the killer was just after Max and let her get away. And the way she says it played out gives her an alibi.'

'It's not convenient; it's damned bloody lucky that she survived.'

'And she seems to remember a hell of a lot of descriptive details about the killer during the highly stressful, frightening, and adrenaline-fuelled situation of running for her life, away from an armed man. In my experience, I've never known any witness in a similar situation to give as much information as she did.'

'She's a writer. She's used to describing things in detail. Look, I read all the witness statements and notes on this case, *Detective Sergeant* Carter.' I noted the little dig he couldn't resist. 'They all say the same thing about Alissa. That it was her who put off getting engaged, despite Max's constant proposals. That they were very happy together. She was very much in love with him. That she is a very nice, very sweet girl, who looked after her mother when she was severely ill. That doesn't sound like someone plotting to kill her husband. Plus, there's the towel.'

'Huh?' Becky said.

'If she was working with Stiles, how many women would voluntarily run around naked when they didn't have to? In my experience with women, most of them are never happy with their bodies.'

'That's a bit of an assumption, sir,' Becky snapped.

113

Wilmott shrugged. 'Not really. If Alissa and Stiles planned this, she would've been in a bathrobe or something similar at the time.'

I snorted. 'Unless she's an exhibitionist? Or one of the few women you've never met in your vast conquests who actually *are* happy with their bodies?'

Wilmott glared at me.

'I think something is a little off with Alissa,' I said.

Wilmott gave me his best sarcastic *Really? Do tell* look. 'Of course something's off with her – she's severely traumatised. Her husband's just been murdered!' He folded his arms and looked pointedly at me. 'Do you have anything else, other than a *feeling*?'

'Not yet, no.'

'Right, well, as *SIO* on this case, I want Stiles arrested and brought in again. We have DNA placing him at the scene on the night of the murder with a strong motive. And this time *I'll* be interviewing him.' He rubbed his hands together. 'My first case as DI, and I've got a result in record time! Looks like they picked the best man for the job, eh?' He winked at me.

I fought the urge to punch him.

'If you're lucky, I'll buy you all a drink later. It's the least I can do for helping me clear this one up so quickly.'

I would rather suddenly develop a case of Ebola than have a drink with him.

~

After arresting Russell, I brought him back to the station for questioning. Now that Wilmott had a prime suspect, he wanted to swoop in and take over, banishing me to the sidelines. But I didn't want to miss out on what Russell had to say, so I sat in the office and watched the live feed of Wilmott's interview with him.

DI WILMOTT: We have some more questions for you about the night of Max Burbeck's murder.

RUSSELL STILES: Why am I under arrest? I haven't done anything! I told you last time. Should I have a lawyer?

DI WILMOTT: You are entitled to a lawyer if you want one. Do you *need* a lawyer, Russell?

RUSSELL STILES: No, of course not! I haven't done anything wrong. How's Alissa?

DI WILMOTT: She's very fragile and distraught, as you can imagine. Her husband has just been brutally murdered. Now, let's go back to that night.

RUSSELL STILES: I keep telling you, I don't know anything!

DI WILMOTT: We've spoken to a number of people about the incident when you trespassed on Max and Alissa's property during their wedding reception.

RUSSELL STILES: (Inaudible)

DI WILMOTT: Can you repeat that for the tape, please, Russell?

RUSSELL STILES: I've already told you about that. I just wanted to check that Alissa was happy.

DI WILMOTT: But your relationship with Alissa had ended three years ago, before she began a relationship with Max. So why did you think you were entitled to go on to the property, in the middle of their wedding reception, and speak to Alissa?'

RUSSELL STILES: I don't know. Because we were friends. And Max was bad news for her.

DI WILMOTT: In what way was he bad news?

RUSSELL STILES: Because of that development I told you about. Did you check it out? Those people have lost everything and he wouldn't even compensate them, despite the amount of money he's got. That's not the kind of person Alissa should be with.

DI WILMOTT: And who should she be with? You?

RUSSELL STILES: Look, I just wanted her to be with someone who deserved her.

DI WILMOTT: And you think that person is you, don't you? You think no one else should be with her. Isn't that why you killed Max?

RUSSELL STILES: No! I didn't do anything! How many times do I have to say it?

DI WILMOTT: You said you watched the reception from the wooded area at the rear of the property?

RUSSELL STILES: Yeah.

DI WILMOTT: You'd been drinking that day, hadn't you?

RUSSELL STILES: Yeah.

DI WILMOTT: Had you watched Max or Alissa from that spot before?

RUSSELL STILES: No.

DI WILMOTT: We found a bottle of Jack Daniel's with your prints on it in those woods, along with some of your cigarette butts.

RUSSELL STILES: Yeah, they're mine.

DI WILMOTT: In the same spot, we also found the body of Alissa's cat, which had gone missing. It had a broken neck. Did you kill her cat?

RUSSELL STILES: What?! No, of course not.

DI WILMOTT: Did you see the cat when you were sitting there drinking and watching Alissa's house? When you were stalking her?

RUSSELL STILES: No, I never saw the cat. Is this about the cat? I didn't touch it! I couldn't hurt an animal. That's . . . horrible.

DI WILMOTT: But you have hurt animals before. You were fined for poaching. And how about hurting a human? You have a previous record for affray.

RUSSELL STILES: That was a misunderstanding.

DI WILMOTT: What kind of misunderstanding?

RUSSELL STILES: I was eighteen, I got involved in a scuffle in a pub with this guy.

DI WILMOTT: Over Alissa?

RUSSELL STILES: I was trying to protect her. The guy said some horrible stuff about her. Called her names.

DI WILMOTT: And you're still trying to protect her now, aren't you? You thought if you got Max out of the way you'd protect her from someone you didn't think was worthy of her, isn't that right?

RUSSELL STILES: I never touched him.

DI WILMOTT: But you do have a temper. The affray proves that.

RUSSELL STILES: No, I don't.

DI WILMOTT: You lost your temper in the pub.

RUSSELL STILES: That was different. I would never hurt Alissa.

DI WILMOTT: How about Max? Would you hurt him?

RUSSELL STILES: No way! You've got the wrong person.

DI WILMOTT: But you did stalk Alissa. You did watch her. You did send texts to her, even though you knew she was in a relationship with Max. You threatened Max at their wedding reception, told him to watch his back. Then, lo and behold, he's stabbed in the back of the neck! Wouldn't it have been better for you if Max was out of the picture?

RUSSELL STILES: I was worried about her. I just wanted her to be happy.

DI WILMOTT: But she was happy. In her text replies to you, she told you she was. She didn't want you harassing her, did she?

RUSSELL STILES: I wasn't harassing her.

DI WILMOTT: She was going to get an injunction out against you because she was worried about your attention.

RUSSELL STILES: I don't believe you.

DI WILMOTT: I think we've established a pattern of harassment here, don't you?

RUSSELL STILES: (Inaudible)

DI WILMOTT: On the night of Max's murder, you said you were night fishing, is that correct?

RUSSELL STILES: Yes.

DI WILMOTT: But no one saw you?

RUSSELL STILES: No, I don't think so.

DI WILMOTT: You live approximately a mile away from Max and Alissa's house in the same village. It would've been quite easy for you to slip out of the house after killing Max and return home through the woods, unseen.

RUSSELL STILES: I didn't kill Max!

DI WILMOTT: Well, you can see my predicament, can't you? You had a motive. You had the opportunity. And you have no one to corroborate your whereabouts that night. You match the physical characteristics of the man described by Alissa as being in the house. You were so obsessed with Alissa that you wanted to get rid of Max, didn't you?

RUSSELL STILES: It wasn't me. What about Leo? I saw the way he looked at Alissa. He was in love with her, too. I bet he wouldn't have minded Max out of the way.

DI WILMOTT: And when did you see the way Leo looked at her? When you were stalking her?

RUSSELL STILES: (Inaudible)

DI WILMOTT: Did you ever go inside Max and Alissa's house?'

RUSSELL STILES: No.

DI WILMOTT: No?

RUSSELL STILES: That's what I said.

DI WILMOTT: You're absolutely sure about that?

RUSSELL STILES: I just said so, didn't I?

DI WILMOTT: We also found a hair at the scene, on Max's body, which is a DNA match to yours. How do you explain that, then, if you never went inside the house?

RUSSELL STILES: *What?*

DI WILMOTT: Go on, just tell me what happened that night. You were upset and angry Alissa had married Max. You watched the house from the woods, didn't you?

RUSSELL STILES: *No!*

DI WILMOTT: You saw Max working in his office because the curtains weren't closed. You saw the bathroom light on and knew Alissa would be in there, out of the way. You entered the house from the unlocked kitchen door.

RUSSELL STILES: No, I didn't!

DI WILMOTT: You stabbed Max from behind before he could hear you. Before he knew what hit him. Didn't you, Russell?

RUSSELL STILES: I think I want a lawyer now.

I sat back and removed my headphones, watching Russell's face on the screen, studying his body language for signs of lying. Something wasn't right about this whole thing. It seemed too neat, too convenient. And something about it all didn't ring true.

I scrubbed my hands over my face, thinking, until my mobile rang. It was Emma Bolton.

'Hi, I just thought you'd want to know that there's been another fingerprint match found on the bottle of Jack Daniel's.'

I sat forward, intrigued. 'Go on.'

'Leo Smithers' prints were on the bottle, too.'

'OK, great, thanks.' I hung up, stretched my twinging back, and headed off to pay Leo another visit.

He was the manager of a local branch of one of the biggest international banks. Judging by his house and car, I bet he was still lapping up a huge expense account and mega bonuses while Mr and Mrs Unfortunate lived in Shit Street. It reminded me of the Mackenzie case all over again – the rich and influential getting away with everything and the rest of us being stitched up. But they were protected, and where was the justice in that? I was rapidly coming to the conclusion that there was no justice any more. Instead of bailing out the banks that caused the global financial crisis and letting them get away with the biggest fraud in history, we should've done what Iceland had done: prosecuted their dirty, scheming, lying arses.

I was shown into Leo's lavish office, trying to push down my contempt for his kind. Despite my personal feelings, I still had to be objective.

He was on the phone, leaning back in his leather desk chair. When he saw me he held up his finger, indicating he wouldn't be long. He wore an expensively cut black suit, a pale yellow shirt and an orange tie. He was talking to someone about shorting gold to manipulate the market, his brown eyes darting at me every now and then uncomfortably. I didn't really understand what he was talking about, and that's what the financial sector relied on – us not really having a clue how our banking and economic system worked. One day, when I had a minute, I'd have to do some research.

He wrapped up the conversation and put the phone down. Leaning forward in the chair, he held out a hand for me to shake, his gold cufflinks sparkling in the light. 'I would say it's nice to see you again, but it's not, for obvious reasons.'

I smiled. The feeling was mutual. 'I have a few more questions for you.'

'Do you want coffee? I've got some kopi luwak.'

I bet he did. It was the most expensive coffee in the world, costing around £25–£70 per cup, and produced from the faeces of civets kept in cages and force-fed the coffee beans. What was the world coming to? 'Thanks, but I don't much go in for drinking cat shit.'

He gave me a tight smile and looked at his watch. 'I've got a meeting shortly, so if we could get to it . . . ?'

'It's about the altercation between Russell and Max at the wedding reception.'

'I've already told you about that.'

'Yes, I know. You said you caught the tail end of it. You saw Alissa step in between Russell and Max when it looked as if it was getting heated, and by the time you got to the bottom of the garden, Russell had left.'

'Yes, that's right.'

'And then you went into the woods to check that Russell had really gone.'

He crossed one leg over the other and leaned an elbow casually on the arm of his chair. 'Yes.'

'What happened when you went into the woods?'

'Just what I told you previously. I walked in and looked around for him in the immediate area. I couldn't see him, so I went back to The Orchard.'

'We found a bottle of Jack Daniel's near a large oak tree with Russell's prints on it.'

'Well, I'm not surprised. He was wrecked.'

'And your fingerprints were on it, too. Why was that?'

He shrugged. 'I picked it up.'

'Why?'

He tilted his head. 'I'm not sure, really. I saw it there and just picked it up to see how much was gone. He'd drunk almost the whole bottle while he'd been watching the house. Bloody psycho.'

'But you didn't mention that before.'

'I just forgot about it until you asked. It's not important, is it?'

'Did you see Buttons, Alissa's cat, near the tree and bottle?'

'No.'

So Russell hadn't killed the cat. Unless he'd come back again another day, but why? I could understand it if the cat had been Max's, but it was Alissa's cat, so surely if Russell was in love with her, would he really have harmed it? And was the death of the cat even relevant to the rest of the case, or had it died accidentally?

'What was Russell wearing that day?'

He tapped a fingertip on his chin, thinking. 'Blue jeans and a white T-shirt with some kind of logo on it.'

'Anything else?'

'Well, shoes, obviously.' He gave me a mocking smile. 'I don't know what kind they were, though.'

'How did you feel about Alissa?'

His nostrils flared slightly. 'What do you mean?'

He wasn't stupid. He knew exactly what I meant. 'Did you like her? Were you happy she was marrying your best friend?'

'They were very happy together, and if you're insinuating that Alissa was involved in this, then you're completely mistaken. I won't be answering any further inappropriate questions without my lawyer present. And I'm seriously thinking about putting in a complaint about your inappropriate questioning! Now, I'm extremely busy and I'll have to ask you to leave.' He turned to his desk and started shuffling papers.

But I noticed he hadn't answered my question.

THE DETECTIVE
Chapter 18

Ronnie and I were still executing the search warrant for Stiles' house while Wilmott was basking in the glory of his arrest. It was a rented two-bedroomed terraced cottage at the edge of Waverly – neat and tidy from the outside, with a postage-stamp-sized front garden. A far cry from The Orchard, and Alissa had definitely landed on her feet in choosing Max over Russell. Still, there was no accounting for love. Or was there? I still had doubts about her story.

Ronnie was in the tiny lounge, looking under sofa cushions. I glanced around, getting a feel for the place, for the person who lived there. There was a log burner along one wall. Under the window was a battered wooden TV cabinet. The stairs were set in one back corner of the room. In the other corner was a doorway that led to a kitchen overlooking the larger rear garden.

I climbed the stairs. The first door I came to was a spare room turned into a gym. The only things in it were a weight bench with a metal barbell resting on the rack, two metal dumb-bells, and a stack of free weights. On the wall opposite the bench was a huge, blown-up picture of Alissa. I stepped closer and studied the black-and-white image. It had been taken in a field full of wheat, but the background had been softened. She wore a pale-coloured, short sundress that accentuated the curve of her hips, the outline of her breasts, her long, toned legs. Her head was tilted slightly and she held a bunch of flowers in one hand, hanging loosely by her side. The smile on her face was inviting, sensual. Her big, brown eyes held a hint of sex. The word gorgeous didn't do her justice. She was more than that. Way more. I pictured Russell working out in the room and watching her, unable to let her go. I felt the same about Denise. I couldn't let her go, either. Part of me actually felt sorry for Russell. Love can be the most amazing feeling in the world – it can make you ecstatic, free, peaceful, content, make you want to do the impossible. But on the flip side, it can also cause pain, or make you hopeless, angry, bitter, fixated, jealous, like Russell seemed to be. He was stuck in limbo, unable to move on with his life without her. Unable to accept she was no longer there for him. And it struck me that I wasn't really that much different from him in that respect.

I looked under the bench and between the weights and felt for loose wooden floorboards in the bare room, but found nothing hidden.

I searched his bathroom, finding a few bottles of toiletries, a razor, some cleaning products, and a sponge. There was no cabinet in there to look through. The cistern was empty. A large plastic bin stood under the sink for dirty laundry. I poked around, found a damp towel, a flannel, two pairs of faded blue jeans, a ripped pair of camouflage combats, socks, and boxers. Alissa had said the intruder was wearing all black, but we only had her word to go on that this was the truth. I put the washing back and went into his bedroom.

There was a single pine wardrobe in one corner, a pine double bed, two matching bedside drawers, one of which had another photo of Alissa on it, and not much else. I searched the bed first, under the mattress and inside pillow cases, before turning my attention to the drawers. Boxers, socks, an old personal CD player, a packet of condoms past their sell-by date, a biro, a tube of antiseptic cream, some Olbas Oil. There was nothing taped underneath them or behind them.

The cupboard held clothing, footwear, a holdall bag, and a couple of beanie hats. I slid clothes along the rack, searching for something black, but there was nothing. He seemed to prefer grey or blue or camo. I checked pockets and inside boots, shoes, and trainers, but SOCO hadn't recovered any footprints from the scene – maybe due to the offender wearing shoe covers. Or maybe there was another reason. I didn't find a black, puffy jacket anywhere, nor a balaclava or gloves.

I went back downstairs and found Ronnie poking about in the back of a cupboard under the sink in the kitchen. 'Anything?' I asked.

'Nothing incriminating.'

I opened the back door and looked out into the garden. There were six-foot hawthorn hedges that separated his property from the neighbouring ones. At the far end, it backed on to the same woods as The Orchard did further up the village. The only thing between Russell's property and those woods was a four-foot wooden fence. It would've been easy for him to leave home that night, make his way to The Orchard through the cover of the trees without being spotted, and come back the same way under the blanket of darkness. But it was still bothering me *why* he'd done it when he knew Alissa would be in the house, unless Alissa and Stiles were really in on it together and he knew she wouldn't intervene. Had she let Russell into the house that night?

In the corner of the garden was an old shed, the timber rotting in some places. I walked down the flagstone path and tried the door. Unlocked.

It was full, but reasonably tidy. There was a rack along one wall with various fishing equipment hanging on it – nets, rods, flies. An old petrol strimmer stood in the corner, next to a couple of spades and forks and a branch lopper. There were several tins of wood stain, weed killer, a large plastic garden sprayer, and a big bag of fertiliser and mulch.

I heaved the bag of fertiliser away from the wall, and that's when I spotted it.

A plastic bag, wrapped around something. I opened the bag and found a knife. It was about five inches long, with a black handle and a very sharp, pointed blade.

And it was encrusted with what looked like dried blood.

THE OTHER ONE
Chapter 19

The farm was sold when Dad went to prison, and the money was put in trust for me for when I turned sixteen. I was placed with a foster family in a house that was as far away from my old one in terms of geography as it was in experience. I went from the middle of the country to the big city. My foster parents were David and Caroline, and they had a daughter who was two years older than me and a son who was four years older. A nice, normal, regular family. It took me a while to find out what normal meant in the real world. The unisolated world, where families ate dinner together without it getting thrown around the room or forced down their throat. Where parents spoke civilly to each other and had real conversations that didn't involve one of them shouting and the other being made to listen with their jaw clutched tight in the other's hand. Without being slapped or punched. Where you didn't have to walk on eggshells, afraid to say the wrong thing. Where kids had friends who did happy, fun things together, and their only job was to enjoy a protected childhood, instead of torturing and murdering poor, defenceless, sentient animals and laughing about their suffering.

Where touches and kissed cheeks and comforting cuddles replaced fists and lashing-out feet.

Their house had all mod cons. A TV in the lounge and one in each of the kid's rooms so they could watch what they wanted. We'd never had one at home. The TV was *God's way of talking the devil into us!* We had the Internet, mobile phones, video games, DVD players. That house had the lot.

I still don't think I know for certain what normal is. But I had a lot to learn in those days, and that thing with George was my starting point. Instinctively, I'd known even at that early age that to get by, to pass as normal, I had to be someone else. Because, of course, the *real* me would never be normal. There was something wrong deep inside. I couldn't feel anything for people. The only things I had strong emotions for were animals. Don't get me wrong, my foster family were lovely. It's just that maybe I was more like my dad than I realised. And if I couldn't get rid of that Dad-ness in me, then I had to blot it out.

There's a *lot* to concentrate on when trying to be normal if you've had a fucked-up childhood. A lot to remember. It's a constant battle. In that house was where my real education started.

I studied the daughter all the time. How she walked, her mannerisms, her accent, tone of voice, what she wore, how she laughed, how she swam, how she interacted with her friends, what make-up she wore, how she did her hair. I followed her around and took notes in my head. *Today, she threw her head back when she laughed at a joke her dad said, but why was that different to yesterday when she didn't laugh at one her brother told and glared at him instead?*

It was *exhausting*! The constant questioning in my head, the subtle changes in her from one day to the next, trying to figure out why, what it meant, was it important?

In my bedroom at night, I'd run through the days spent with her as she introduced me to her friends, her boyfriend, her life, scribbling manic notes, trying to keep up. I'd practise her voice in front of the mirror, her laugh, her hair, her expressions, until I knew I had it just right. But the practice needed an audience, so I'd steal some of her clothes and head into the city and force myself to talk to people I didn't know. To *be* her.

I'd sit in a coffee shop and smile at everyone, which was a no-no. People thought you were weird if you smiled at *anyone*. I scribbled that down as a reference and observed the place, sipping a black coffee. It seemed like it was OK to smile at the barista or people in line, but a permanent smile on your face as you glanced around the room was wrong. *Check!*

I'd wander around aimlessly, looking for people to talk to, so I could try out being her. Gradually, it began to come easily. Instead of *my* eyes looking out at the world, I really felt that they were *hers*.

Of course, I wasn't stupid enough to let on as to what I was doing. At home, I had to be me, just a changed version of me from when they'd first taken me in. Someone who actually talked to people now. Who laughed. Who'd filled out from her skinny body to a young woman with curves and boobs and arse. Who had long, glossy hair. Who actually looked pretty. Turned heads, even. The daughter loved me. She'd always wanted a younger sister and treated me as if I was a doll, or a little pet project. She taught me how to style my hair, which was previously just a tangled mess. How to apply make-up, which music was cool and which was crap. No matter how nice she was to me, I couldn't love her back, though. There was something missing in my heart. Something cold and dark. I think the son loved me, too. I'd see the way he looked at me, like he wanted to touch me, kiss me, fuck me. And I saw it was getting harder and harder for him to contain himself as time went on, but I managed to keep him at a distance. I had more important things to do.

When I'd perfected my emulation of the daughter, I studied TV programmes. Actresses in the teen series she watched or from films. I studied everyone. Everyone had something to teach me; they just didn't know it.

I became someone who worked hard at school, who had her own friends, went to the mall, the cinema, who learned to surf, who worked part-time at the local animal shelter, but it was all an act. I spent hours perfecting my artwork. Gone was the dark art. In its place was something real. Something you could feel through the canvas or pages lined with charcoal and watercolours. Mostly, I worked on animal images, because I could see into their souls and that shone through. We shared an understanding. I won competitions and awards. But the main thing was, I got through it. I got through it all with a fake smile plastered on my face and the personality and traits of hundreds of people itching beneath my skin.

On my sixteenth birthday, I found out Dad had hanged himself in prison. Good fucking riddance. What had my parents ever taught me? How to kill something with my bare hands? How to die a million times? How to go mad? How to hate and be hated? How to have something you love snatched away from you? How to be weak and pathetic?

I'm free now, and I need a new challenge, I thought, as I read through the balance of my trust fund. I wanted to go from the girl who had nothing to the girl who had it all. And this time *I'd* be the one in control. So I looked at the map of Australia and picked out a place.

Yeah. Sydney.

You see, the thing I'd really learned in my life above everything was that I could be anyone I wanted. And now it was time to reinvent myself.

PART TWO
REVENGE

THE OTHER ONE
Chapter 20

I have a real name, of course – the name on my birth certificate. The name *they* gave me. But I was Anita in Sydney, Jane in Byron Bay, and Alice in Brisbane, plus many others over the years. I was a chameleon, adapting to her surroundings, changing my personality at the drop of a hat. In the hostels I stayed in as I travelled up the east coast of Australia, there were so many people to meet. To watch. To copy. To steal their very selves from without them even realising. Travellers backpacking around the country, oblivious to the truth of the world. It was easy to get lost amongst them. To blend in or stand out, depending on my mood. Sunglasses, a big floppy hat, an unflattering tent dress – they hide you away. Make-up, hair, short skirts, and vest tops make you stand out. *Now you see me, now you don't!* A sleight of hand. My fabulous party trick.

I was getting bored, though. Men were easy. I don't want to sound big-headed, but they noticed me whenever I was in my 'standing out', shining-my-light mood. Noticed me a lot. I had anyone I wanted, but it didn't mean anything. I approached them the same way I approached all my *projects*. They were a learning curve. It was all a lesson, and they were just homework.

I liked my own company too much – I was used to it by now. Liked locking myself away in my head. Being 'normal' was fucking hard work sometimes, and after years of travelling, I wanted to settle in one place for a while and concentrate on my art while I worked out the next plan for my life.

Noosa was the town I'd felt the most connection to when I was doing my east-coast jaunt, so I headed back there, rented a little apartment, and set up a stall selling my artwork. One of the arty boutiques there also asked if I could transfer some of my animal pictures on to postcards that they'd sell for me. *Yes, of course, I can do anything!* I'd spent half of my trust fund travelling over the years, so the art paid my bills while I saved up some more cash to go . . . well, I didn't know where yet. Somewhere. My feet were constantly itching to head somewhere. Experience something new. Or maybe I was just trying to outrun my own thoughts and the voices that sometimes shouted annoyingly inside my brain. I'd been in Noosa nine months, trying out my new life, and after a while it grew pretty dull and repetitive. How did people get through years and years of it?

I'd survived everything for . . . *this*?

But things always change when you least expect it, and, of course, that's what happened on that sunny day at the end of August.

I had a stack of new postcards I'd just produced for the boutique and I was dropping them off before setting up my stall.

'Hi, Sam!' the owner said as I breezed through the door.

'Hi!' I smiled and placed a cardboard box on the counter. 'New supplies for you.'

'Great, thanks. Your stuff always sells fast.' She picked up a couple of postcards from the top and looked through them.

I put on another smile – a grateful, humble one – as she counted out some dollars and handed them to me. 'I'll call you for a top-up when we're getting low again.'

I stuffed the bills into my purse. Another smile. Breezy, fun. 'Fantastic! Shall I put them on the rack for you on my way out?'

'Oh, yeah, that would be great, thanks.'

I took the cardboard box to the postcard rack outside and picked out a batch, banging them on the windowsill to order them into a perfect oblong so they'd fit in the wire holders. I stood back to admire them, humming to myself, because that's what happy people did. When I turned to leave, my gaze strayed further up the road, towards a couple strolling along, hand in hand, heading my way. They hadn't noticed me yet, as I was hidden by the postcards, and I froze – eyes wide, heart almost stopping, a flash of confusion detonating in my head.

He wasn't bad looking. A bit preppy, maybe. Tall. Floppy blond hair. Designer clothes. But it wasn't him I was concentrating on. Instead, I stared at the woman.

Someone who looked exactly like another me.

THE OTHER ONE
Chapter 21

We weren't just similar. It wasn't simply a slight resemblance going on. We were *identical!* I recognised those lips, the top one just slightly fuller than the bottom, the arching sweep of those eyebrows over brown oval pools framed by long, dark lashes. The chocolate-brown hair, loose in long waves, the slender nose. High cheekbones.

As they approached, I backed into the shop again, hidden, watching with the corner of my eye through a display in the window, trying to make sense of what I was seeing. My forehead scrunched up as I delved into the dark years inside my head, searching for something that would explain how this was possible. If we were identical, then that could only mean we were twins, which meant . . . I was *adopted!* What the fucking fuck!

I had to find out more about them. About her. Who was she? How did I never know I had a sister out there? Did she know about me? Had she been laughing at me behind my unknowing back *all* this time?

I watched them walk past the shop, him saying something to her, her throwing her head back and laughing. They looked happy. In love. Casually strolling along as if they didn't have a care in the world. Oblivious to the turmoil building up inside me.

I delved into my bag and pulled out a pair of sunglasses and a big floppy hat that covered most of my face. I always kept them in there in case I wanted to blend into the background at any time. Old habits die hard, and I couldn't risk being spotted without a disguise.

I followed them to a plush hotel, watched them enter a lift. There was a complimentary newspaper stand by the bar to one side, so I grabbed a paper and sat inside the lobby with it open on my lap, as if I was a guest leisurely whiling away a few hours, but really I was watching, waiting, wondering what the hell was going on here, my brain scrambling and fizzing away.

Three hours later, they re-emerged from the lift. They'd changed clothes and had that happy post-coital glow about them. As they walked past me, totally wrapped up in each other, I took in his clothes, his watch, his shoes, her engagement and wedding rings, her handbag. They looked like the type who had money. Had everything, probably. I wanted some of that. This was an opportunity I couldn't miss.

I left the paper on a coffee table and followed at a discreet distance until they went inside a small clothing boutique. I couldn't follow them forever, and I knew that if I asked at the hotel about them, they'd never divulge any information on the guests. I didn't know if they were Australian or foreign tourists, but if they were staying in a hotel then they wouldn't be here forever. At some point they'd move on and they would slip away to their normal non-vacation lives. I had to find out who she was *right now* before that happened. Whoever said patience is a virtue was an arsehole. Patience is just a massive waste of time.

It was time to meet the other me.

I removed my sun hat and sunglasses, stuffed them in my bag, and shook out my hair. Then I calmly entered the shop. I spied them in the corner. She was sliding dresses along a rack with him patiently standing beside her with a look of adoration. She pulled out a dress and held it in front of her.

'What do you think?' she asked him. Even our voices were similar, despite her English accent and the Australian twang I was using at that time.

I kept my head down and moved closer towards them, as if I was browsing.

I heard her gasp and say, 'Oh, my God!'

I glanced up then, as if I'd only just noticed her. My lips fell open with fake shocked surprise as the woman walked closer, studying me as carefully as I studied her.

She was too busy staring at me to notice Mr Preppy looking from one of us to the other, like an umpire at a tennis match.

'What the . . .' he said.

I quickly ran through my 'normal' checklist in my head, wondering what was appropriate in a situation like this. *Meeting someone who is identical to you . . . do you gasp, laugh nervously, smile with a mix of uncertainty, run away?*

I settled for laughing nervously. 'Who are you?'

She grinned widely. I recognised those teeth, too. She pointed a tapered finger to her chest. 'Me? I was about to ask you the same question.'

'Sam,' I said, adding an uncertain smile to my performance.

'I don't believe it.' The guy, who I assumed was her husband, was still pumping his umpire act for all it was worth. 'You're identical! You look like you could be . . .'

'Twins!' the other me and I said in unison.

I stepped closer to her, drinking her in. I hadn't been mistaken. She was the same. 'Identical twins. How is that possible?'

An elderly woman huffed at us, trying to get past while we blocked the aisle.

'Look, why don't we all go somewhere more private, have a coffee, and find out what's happening here.' Mr Preppy interrupted our mutual staring-fest.

'Good idea.' The other me smiled, unable to turn her face away from me.

'I know a place, just down the road.' I indicated further along the street to a coffee shop with tables spilling out on to the pedestrian area and umbrellas dotted around.

The woman spoke to me as we walked, but her words didn't penetrate. I was too busy trying to stop the roiling anger surfacing. Because if we were twins, if I'd been adopted, then . . .

'What would you like to drink?' Mr Preppy asked me, his voice tearing me back to the present. He chose a table for four in a secluded corner and pulled out chairs for the woman and me.

'Um . . . an iced soya latte, please.'

'Usual for you, darling?' he asked her.

She nodded at him and sat down. 'This is so weird.'

I followed her lead, sitting opposite her, both of us unable to tear our eyes away from our duplicate faces. 'That's an understatement.'

She held her hand out for me to shake. 'I'm Alissa. Alissa Stanhope – oops, I mean, Alissa Burbeck now. We just got married.' Her shoulders scrunched up to her ears and she gave me a goofy, happy grin.

I took her hand in mine. Even the shapes of our hands, our fingers, were the same. 'Sam. Sam Folds.'

She held on to my hand, mirroring my own stare. 'We've got to be twins. Identical twins, right? I mean, I know people say everyone's got a doppelganger and all that, but . . . we don't just look similar. We look *exactly* the same.' Her eyes widened. 'But I don't understand. I mean, that would mean . . .' Her face paled as the thought hit her. 'Oh, my God, what does your birth certificate say?'

'Um . . .' I shook my head, trying to think, confused with shock and something else I couldn't analyse yet. 'It says my name's Sam Folds. I was born on the nineteenth of February, 1992, in England. My parents were . . .' I fought the bubbling anger at the mention of their names, wondering whether to lie. I wanted to get a look at her birth certificate, so no doubt she'd want to look at mine and then she'd find out. 'They were called John and Elizabeth. Apparently, they emigrated here from England when I was a baby.'

'My birth date is the same! But my parents were Rita and Bernard Stanhope.'

Her husband came back, carrying a tray of coffees. He dished them out, then put the tray on the next empty table and squeezed Alissa's hand, doing the umpire thing again, which was beginning to get annoying. 'I'm Max, by the way.' He hastily shook my hand. 'This is a bit bizarre.'

I sucked in some coffee through the straw to bring moisture back to my throat. Bizarre didn't even cut it. 'Have you lived in England all your life?' I asked.

'Well, yeah. I mean, my earliest memory is of the house I grew up in. How about you? Where did you live?'

The coffee threatened to climb back up my throat. I swallowed hard. 'Here in Australia. In the middle of nowhere, on a rural farm. My parents had a farm.' I forced the word 'parents' to sound calm, loving. 'Like you, I remember living there from an early age.' *Unfortunately! The place was called Hell, have you heard of it?*

'So, how did this happen? Who are we?' She clutched Max's hand.

I forced out a laugh, confused, intrigued, *check*! 'I've got no idea.'

Max leaned forward, repositioning the hand holding Alissa's on to his thigh. 'You both must've been adopted, obviously by different people.'

Duh! Really, Max?

I dug my fingernails into my palms to stop the unhelpful, nasty thoughts. They wouldn't help me extract information.

'My parents never said a word,' Alissa muttered, staring off into space. 'My dad died when I was fourteen, and my mum . . . well, she's had a couple of strokes. She can't speak now – she's in a nursing home. I couldn't even ask her about this if I wanted to. How about your parents? Are they still alive? Can you ask them about all . . .' She waved her hand in a circle in the air, as if searching for the right word. 'This?'

'Sorry to hear about your mum.' My eyebrows furrowed together, concerned, like a prospective, new, out-of-the-blue sister's would. 'Yes, they're still alive, but they're not in great health, either,' the lie rolled off my tongue without missing a beat, like a million others I'd had practice at. 'My dad had a heart bypass operation six months ago and he's not supposed to get stressed. And Mum . . .' I fluttered a hand to my chest, devastated with daughterly love, *check*! 'Well, she's just discovered she has bowel cancer. I wouldn't want to put a strain on them by getting them upset about all this. Can we keep this just between us, until we know what's going on, what's happened?'

Alissa looked to her husband, as if for guidance, and I tried to gauge what I saw in her face. Apart from the obvious prettiness, there was something sweet and wholesome there – something weak, too, as if she needed him to take care of her. There was love and admiration there, definitely. Happy, gooey, sickly, just-got-married love.

Alissa nodded her agreement. 'My mum hasn't got long left, and I don't really want this kind of thing out in the open before she goes in case it tips her over the edge. My parents obviously had their own reasons for not telling me the truth before.'

'I totally agree,' I said, not too breathy or overly anxious. I didn't want anyone knowing about this. Not until I could work out how it would benefit me, because even then, before I knew the whole story, before I knew what I could do with it, a new plan was growing from a little spark of an idea. It was like some mystical alignment of the universe was happening. *Crash, bang, slam!* I could see it all clearly now, for the first time. Everything had always been leading to this point. There had always been a purpose to the life I'd had before. And all this was happening right here. Right now. I'd been steadily moulding myself all along, working hard to get the right skills needed for the job. My opportunity to put everything I'd learned into action was here! Everything suddenly made complete sense.

THE OTHER ONE
Chapter 22

I listened to Alissa tell me about her wonderful childhood. How she was a daddy's girl who'd follow him around as soon as he got back from work, climbing on to his knee as he read her a story, giving her mum a break from looking after her all day. Alissa's mum and dad had 'date nights' once a week to keep their marriage fresh.

'It's hard work having kids, isn't it?' Alissa said. 'I definitely want to start trying now we're married, but a couple needs to still work at their marriage to keep things alive, don't they?'

'Absolutely,' I agreed. What the hell did I know with my parents as an example? Theirs wasn't a marriage – it was a death sentence.

So, a storybook childhood it was for Alissa, as she recounted family holidays to Devon and Cornwall as a kid, trips abroad, birthdays, so much fun and laughter and happiness.

'My parents weren't *rich*,' she said. 'But they were comfortable. Dad had a good job and earned enough for Mum to be a stay-at-home mum. They couldn't buy everything they wanted, but it didn't matter. They had each other and me, and that was enough richness for them.'

How sweet. I mentally shoved my fingers down my throat and chucked up.

'Being an only child, they spoiled me.' She said it with a touch of embarrassment — or maybe modesty — as she tucked her hair behind her ear for the third time, which I made a note of. She glanced down at the floor sadly. 'I still miss Dad, though.'

I expressed my condolences, the way you do, and she told me more.

Alissa didn't have a lot of friends growing up. She'd been bullied a bit by some kids at school who were jealous of her. *Awwww, what a shame.* But she had one best friend she'd known since primary school called Vicky, who she told me all about. Alissa had got good grades, though, was well behaved, excelled at English, and she was going to be an author, don't you know? Working on her debut romantic novel *and* already had the interest of a prospective agent. Spiffing!

'How amazing!' I gushed. 'I'm creative, too. An artist.'

'I wonder who we got those genes from,' she said wistfully, studying my face without blinking.

Max looked at his watch. 'Sorry to interrupt you, ladies, but I've got a business meeting I need to get to.'

'Oh, right, I completely forgot!' Alissa said.

'Well, I'm sure you've both got much to talk about, anyway. Why don't I meet up with you later?' He looked between his darling wife and her lovely new sister.

'We *definitely* do,' I said.

'Will you be staying here?' Max stood and kissed Alissa on the cheek.

'Actually, I could do with something stronger than coffee.' Alissa grinned at me. 'What do you think?'

'Oh, God, yeah! Look, I've got an apartment not far from here, why don't we go back there, crack open a bottle, and carry on talking? Looks like we've got a *lot* to find out.'

She took my hand in hers again, squeezing it gently. 'That would be lovely.'

I gave Max the address and directions, and he said he'd meet us there later.

'What does Max do?' I asked casually as we walked to my place.

'He builds things.' She laughed. 'He owns Burbeck Developments. They do houses, apartments, shopping malls. He wants to start up some developments over here, too, which is one of the reasons we got married in Australia. We're having a working holiday-slash-honeymoon.'

'He must be doing really well, then.'

'Yeah. His dad owned the company before him, so it's well established. And even with the recession, things have been going *really* well.'

How nice not to have to worry about money. I made a mental note of the company name in my head to research later.

'Here we are.' I let her into my one-bedroom apartment. 'It's small, but it's home.' I stood back and did a fun *ta-da*!

'It's cute.' She glanced around and walked towards a finished canvas of an elephant hanging on one wall. 'Wow, this is amazing! It looks like a photo, not a painting.' She stared at it, drinking it in. 'Really beautiful.' Her gaze swept over some more of the pictures hanging up. 'Did you do these?'

'Yes.' I magicked up a humble blush from nowhere.

'They're fantastic. You're really talented.'

'Thanks.' I walked into the galley-style kitchen. I could stand in the middle and touch the walls, it was so tiny. I opened the fridge and peered inside. 'Sorry, we could've stopped at the shop, but I didn't think. I've only got white wine, is that OK?'

'White's my favourite.' She beamed.

'I wonder what else we've got in common.' I giggled.

'Well, I'm here for another two weeks, so we've got plenty of time to find out.'

We sat on the tiny balcony, drinking chilled wine.

She took my cold hand in her warm one, blinking at me with misty eyes. 'I always wanted a sister.'

'Me too. You have no idea!' I willed my own tears to suddenly do their stuff and clasped her hand tighter. 'So, tell me more. I want to hear everything about you.'

She brought my hand to rest against the top of her chest. 'And I want to hear everything about you!'

It was the quick version I got from her that day. The rest would come later, all the little details I needed, but I was already taking down these snippets of information, filing them away to memorise when I was on my own, where I could examine and copy and repeat them to myself so I could fire them back at people when needed.

An actress, learning her lines, starring in the best role of her life, channelling my ever-growing chameleon. A time to shine!

I fabricated an equally happy childhood. All lies. I had loving parents, who I modelled on David and Caroline, my foster parents. I was an only child, too. *How amazing – so much in common!* I'd had lots of pets, running gaily around the farm, where the animals were also thought of as part of the family and treated accordingly. I'd had the space and freedom to play in acres of sun-kissed open spaces. Plenty of fun friends to while away all my free time with. No pressures. Nothing bad ever happened in the fake life of Sam Folds.

'It sounds amazing, Sam.' Her eyes twinkled. 'Very exotic. It makes my life sound boring and dull.'

'But it doesn't at all. Your life sounds perfect.'

Perfect Alissa.

The perfect bitch who'd stolen my life.

THE OTHER ONE
Chapter 23

Alissa wanted answers. I didn't. I already knew the answers, but I had to go along with her. At least for a while. So I dug out my birth certificate and showed it to her. It was a 'certified copy', and as we researched, reading through various websites containing adoption information, huddled together on my threadbare sofa, we realised there was a different birth certificate that neither of us had: one that showed a 'live birth'.

She bit her lip as she read over my shoulder, something she seemed to do a lot. 'So that's why it's got your adoptive parents listed as your mother and father. There probably would've been an adoption order, and then your birth certificate was amended from the live birth, showing our real parents, to the certified copy, showing your new adoptive parents.' She dug out her birth certificate from her bag. She'd had to bring it to Australia with her for the wedding documentation.

This time I read over her shoulder. Hers showed the certified copy, too.

She took a dainty sip of wine and stared at me. 'I'm not imagining things, am I? Not jumping to conclusions? We *have* to be twins.'

I grabbed a mirror from the bathroom and sat back down next to her with it in front of our faces. There was no way on this earth we couldn't be twins.

'God, I'm so confused.' Her eyebrows shot up. 'I mean, my mum and dad . . . well, who I *thought* were my mum and dad . . . were so lovely. I don't know whether to be angry or upset that they didn't tell me at any stage. I'm in shock.'

'Me too. But, like I said before, I don't want to bring this up with my parents right now when they're so ill. And maybe they had a good reason for not telling us. Maybe our mum was a crack whore or something. She obviously didn't care much about us if she gave us up. I don't want to find her, anyway.' I nodded towards the page we'd just read on my laptop that offered advice on how to find birth parents through the system. 'It doesn't change anything for me.' *Yeah, right, ha ha! This will change everything!* 'The only important thing to come out of this is that I've found you. My long-lost sister!'

'I know what you mean. Maybe I'm not ready for that, either, finding out who my real mum is, but . . . I do want to find out about us, for certain.'

A niggle of fear jarred behind my sternum. 'What do you mean?'

'Can't we do a DNA test or something? Just to find out for sure?'

'Great idea!' I tapped away on my laptop and found a lab not far away that could do the test and give us the result within two days, if we made an appointment for the next morning.

That first night we polished off two bottles of wine, talking, talking, talking, until Max appeared and the excited, chattery questions and answers died down a little. It was 2 a.m. by the time Max suggested they leave and that we should meet up the next day to go and do the test.

I couldn't sleep, though. I was wired. Already planning. They were only here for two weeks and there was a lot to do. The first thing was to google Burbeck Developments, which was interesting. I looked up the company accounts for the last few years and laughed out loud. Oh, yes, this was *definitely* going to be worth it. Then I found some articles about a development they'd completed a while back that had been built on contaminated land and Burbeck Developments was passing the buck, not willing to pay for the place to be cleaned up and the houses rebuilt. The more I read, the more I thought Max deserved what he was going to get. Well, who'd have thought he was like that from his charming exterior? Still, I supposed he had to be a bit ruthless for his company to be worth so much. He didn't have a clue what ruthless was yet, though. There were angry quotes from the homeowners who'd effectively lost their life savings tied up in those properties. Some of them were really ill. And still there were *no comments* from Burbeck Developments.

The more I found out, the more I thought that this could be my angle. And it was, until Alissa gave me something much better to work with.

THE OTHER ONE
Chapter 24

We sat in the waiting room of LifeZone Laboratories. Alissa chewed on her lower lip, her right leg crossed over her left, tapping through the air to an imaginary beat. I held her hand tightly and gave her a practised anxious smile. Max was at another business meeting, so it was just the two of us. Just two sisters, ecstatic to have found each other after all these years. What a fairy tale!

A few minutes later, we were called to get our results from the test we'd taken two days before.

We sat down in a bright and airy office in front of a female doctor wearing a requisite white coat over her clothes and a warm smile.

'Here are your results.' She handed us both an envelope. 'You are, as you'd obviously guessed, identical twins.'

'Wow!' Alissa grinned at me and gripped my hand.

'Identical twins are also known as monozygotic twins. At the start of your mother's pregnancy, there was one egg, which was fertilised by one sperm. Usually, a fertilised egg would divide and grow to form one baby, but sometimes after fertilisation it starts to divide and can split. When that happens, each half can grow, giving identical twins.'

'So we are identical in every way?' Alissa asked eagerly.

'You'd think so, wouldn't you? After all, you're derived from just one fertilised egg, containing one set of genetic instructions that combine the chromosomes of both parents. But identical twins are rarely perfectly the same. You may have different birthmarks or scars, for example. One may have a particular illness, while the other may not. You also have different fingerprints.'

'Do we have the same DNA, then?' I asked.

'Technically, yes, you do. According to the basic laws of biology, identical twins share the same DNA, although recent studies have shown that there can be genetic variations between them, and more research is being done on that subject. Environmental influences and lifestyle are thought to contribute to any such differences – you could say this is nurture overcoming nature.'

'Wow, this is so . . . fascinating.' I put on an appropriately fascinated face. It was indeed pretty damn amazing, but probably not for the reasons they both thought. 'So what if one twin committed a crime? Could the police tell them apart if they found DNA at the scene?' I kept my tone deliberately jokey.

'I have been asked that before.' She chuckled. 'It's a very interesting question, and a complex one. Theoretically, it is possible that if there are a number of DNA variants or mutations that differ between them, then these could be used to identify which twin committed a crime. But a test to look for any changes is problematic. One reason is because such changes don't occur in all of your cells. It may be that only a few cells have a particular mutation. For any such test to work, they would have to sequence a lot of DNA to find the base pair difference between the twins. They would also need to know which tissue the DNA came from to compare it with the right tissue in the other twin. There are scientists who've been researching new tests, such as the melting of

DNA, and also exploiting a feature of DNA called "single nucleotide polymorphism", but these are still in their early stages or are expensive. At the moment, with the technology available, it would still be very hard for the police to be able to identify which twin committed a crime if they were relying on DNA, because a standard DNA test would show them to be identical.'

Incredible. Incredible and *lucky! Yee haw!*

Five minutes later, we were out in the car park in the warm sunshine. 'That was so interesting,' I said to Alissa. 'Imagine sharing the same DNA with someone.'

'I still can't quite believe everything.' She blinked rapidly.

'I suppose it could be handy if you ever wanted to commit a crime.' I summoned up a fun laugh.

'Don't forget the fingerprints, though.' She laughed back.

'Only if they found fingerprints, and I guess they'd need to actually have your prints on record, or something, wouldn't they? You know, to compare them to? How would they know your prints weren't mine and mine weren't yours if you'd never had them taken before?'

'Good point.'

'So.' I bumped her shoulder with mine good-naturedly. 'Have you got a criminal record you haven't told me about? I wouldn't want to get into trouble or anything.'

'Me? No, the only bad thing I've ever done is return my library books late!' She threw her head back and laughed, exposing her creamy neck.

It took all the strength I had not to strangle her there and then.

THE OTHER ONE
Chapter 25

Luckily, thanks to Max's business meetings, Alissa and I had a lot of time to spend alone, catching up on all those missed years. I suggested a day at the beach because you can't hide much in a bikini, and I wanted to find out exactly *how* identical we were. After visiting the lab, I'd read that some monozygotic twins had identical birthmarks, while some had identical marks but on opposite sides of their bodies. Barring what was hidden underneath the bikini, I'd get a good look at her to be sure.

I'd also had the brilliant idea of recording a lot of our conversations on my phone. That way, I'd get to write things down later if I missed anything, and it also meant I could practise copying her accent and mannerisms when I was on my own. Ingenious!

We walked to a secluded spot on the beach, dappled with shade from some trees. I spread out a blanket and some towels and put down the cool bag containing drinks and a picnic lunch I'd prepared.

She dropped her Michael Kors handbag on to the sand and arranged her towel neatly, before stripping off her jean shorts and tank top.

I glanced over at her, dressed in a red halter-neck bikini, taking in the protruding clavicle, the lines of her ribs, her flat stomach, the shape of her arms, her thighs. Everything was so similar to my own features. The only difference I noticed immediately was the colour of her skin. She was paler than me, but a few weeks in the sun would sort that out.

She glanced over, watching me as I wriggled out of my sundress, revealing a black bikini. 'It's weird, isn't it?' Her gaze roamed my body like mine had done to hers.

'Completely. Have you got any birthmarks? I don't.' I told her what I'd read on the Internet.

'No.' She pulled down the top edge of her bikini bottoms, showing me her hip. 'I've got two beauty marks here, though.'

I pulled down mine slightly, too, and examined the same part of my body. Nope, no marks there. Still, how many people would get to see that part? Only Max, most likely. And there were ways around that. Sex with the lights off, et cetera. Maybe the sudden urge for a tattoo? But I was already prepared and had also found out that beauty marks can spontaneously regress and disappear suddenly due to the immune system – the perfect excuse.

'I don't think I've got any beauty marks,' I said, turning around so my back faced her. 'Have I?'

'No, can't see any.'

I reached for some sun lotion in my bag. 'Want me to do your back?' I had an ulterior motive, as it gave me a way to do a bird's-eye inspection. You couldn't just copy the big things. It was the little things that counted just as much.

'That would be great, thanks.' She flopped down on to her towel on her stomach and tied her long hair into a messy knot on top of her head that I'd perfect later back at home.

I smoothed in some low-factor lotion for her, committing every inch of her to memory. When I finished, she did my back and we lay down, staring at the sky. She tucked one arm behind her head to prop herself up. So did I. Perfect mirror images.

'I know our DNA is identical, but I keep wondering about other stuff,' I said. 'Like, what about our favourite things? Food, colours, music, books, things like that. Is it nature or nurture that makes us individuals?'

'OK, you go first. What foods do you like and dislike?'

'Well, I'm vegan,' I said. I'd never been able to stomach meat and dairy since the nightmare at the farm.

'How long have you been vegan?'

Since I got free and I had a choice. 'A while now.'

'Is that for health or ethical reasons?'

'Ethical, but as long as you have a balanced diet, the health benefits are amazing. What about you? What kind of foods do you like?'

'I do love veggies, but I also eat meat. I love fish, especially things like fresh tuna and grouper and prawns.' She dug her toes in the sand as she thought. 'Chocolate! I'm a chocoholic. Thai food.'

'What would be your favourite Thai dish then?'

'Pad thai. I just love peanuts. Especially chocolate peanuts!'

'What else?

'Um . . . I hate marrow. Love rocket. Hate curry. Love Chinese.'

'I love Chinese, too!' *Oh, look at us bonding!*

'Mmm, crispy fried beef, egg fried rice, salt and pepper squid. Yum. I like all the stodgy British food, too. Good old fish and chips, shepherd's pie, stew and dumplings.'

'So, what would you have for breakfast, lunch, and dinner on a typical day?' I propped myself up on one elbow.

'I'd probably have toast and jam or maybe Marmite. Then for lunch I'd have soup and a cheese sandwich. Or maybe a ham and cheese toastie. For dinner it would probably be something chickeny. Or fish. Or pasta.'

'Do you like cooking?'

'Yeah, but sometimes I cheat!' She giggled. 'I get these ready meals from a shop called Marks and Spencer. They're fab. And Max can't tell the difference.'

'Does he cook, too?'

'Yeah, he does a mean spag bol. And a great fry-up for breakfast.'

'Are you allergic to any food?' I asked.

'Kiwi fruit. It brings me out in terrible hives.'

After we'd exhausted food, we took a dip in the sea, bobbing up and down. I wanted to keep her in there as long as possible so the sun could do its magic on her skin.

'How about music?' I asked.

'Hmm . . . I like a lot of eighties music, and romantic songs.'

'I like rocky stuff – Nirvana, The Cult, Guns N' Roses. How about books?' I asked her. 'You must've read a lot to be writing a book. How clever is that, I wouldn't know where to begin!'

'Yeah, but you can draw and paint. If I did that they'd just be smudgy little stick men or something.' She threw her head back and laughed. I'd noticed her laugh was throaty. It would take a while to get the right pitch. Difficult, but not impossible. Nothing was impossible if you tried hard enough.

'What's your novel about?'

'It's a romance.'

'Ooh, perfect man meets perfect woman? Tell me more.'

'Well, it's about a woman who's an environmental activist and she falls in love with the CEO of an oil company. Obviously, because of their different core values, it's a rocky road, but they end up together – it's a romance, after all.'

'Fascinating! Where did you get the idea from?'

'It just came to me one day when I was watching a programme about an oil spillage affecting marine life on National Geographic. I thought it could create some good conflict for the opposing characters.'

'How far have you got with it?' I rested my knees on the sand and let the gentle waves bob me to and fro.

She told me how she'd finished the first draft, which took forever, apparently, and that she was going through and editing it now. She'd sent the first few chapters off to some agents and had one who wanted to consider the whole manuscript when it was finished. I wondered how much money authors made. Or how much I'd make if *I* ever published it. Still, money was no object now. Not if Max was worth millions.

'Writing is all I ever wanted to do.' She interrupted my thoughts. 'Being an only child means entertaining yourself a lot – well, you probably experienced that yourself, didn't you?'

'Definitely.' I nodded wisely.

'So, I always read a lot when I was a kid, and I always knew that's what I wanted to do as a career.'

'So Max supports you when you're writing – what a perfect set-up.'

An ecstatic smile lit up her face. 'He's brilliant. I mean, I know he's a lot older than me, but I like that. He's mature, kind, considerate. And good fun. I'm really lucky.'

And rich. Don't forget that part, sweetheart.

'He works a lot, of course. I don't have anything to do with his business, though, so, you know, sometimes he's working long hours and I don't get to see him. But it means I can concentrate on my work, too, and the time we do get together is extra special then.'

'How did you two meet? I want to hear all about it!' I said as we got out of the sea and started on the picnic.

THE OTHER ONE
Chapter 26

'Hi, my name's Alissa Burbeck.' I held out a hand to my reflection in the mirror by way of introduction.

Damn, my voice was too sharp.

'Hi, my name's Alissa Burbeck.'

Better. A little softer.

I tried again.

'Alissa Burbeck. Alissa Burbeck. Alisssssssa Burrrrrrrrrrrbeck.'

Correct it. Correct it. Try again and correct yourself!

I rounded out the vowels, worked on the pitch, accent, cadence.

'I'm an author.' I smiled sweetly. Head tilting.

'I'm an *author*. I'm writing my first book. It's a romance.'

Too flat.

'A romance!'

Gushy. Better. Alissa was very gushy and chirpy sometimes.

'I'd love a pad thai for dinner tonight, Max!' Excited. Girlish.

'Fancy a fuck, Max?' Rampant. Slutty.

'I want you right now, *Mr* Burbeck.' Seductive. Pleasing. Playful.

Was she slutty? Experienced in sex? Did she give blow jobs? Like head? Like it fast and hard? Was she a pleaser? Into something kinky? She seemed more vanilla to me.

I'd learn it all as I went along. If I was ever questioned, I'd say, 'Just trying out some new things, Max. *Max. Max. Maaaaax.*' I rolled his name over my tongue several different ways. 'I want to keep our sex life interesting, darling.' She called him darling a lot. Blah. It was so vomit-inducing. Still, he was OK to look at. I could easily manage to fuck him. And anyway, hopefully it wouldn't be for that long. How much time had to pass before your new husband could die? Six months? A year? Maybe I'd make it look like an accident. Maybe not.

I examined the selfie I'd taken of Alissa and me on the beach with my phone and studied her eyebrows. Hers were plucked slightly thinner than mine. I got out my tweezers and stared into the mirror before plucking away a little at a time.

More of an arch there. Yes. That's it. I sat back and surveyed my face. No more sun for me until Alissa's tan caught up. I definitely had a more golden colour than her right now.

What about her writing? She was left-handed and I was right-handed. Still, people didn't write much these days, did they? They typed into apps on their phones and sent emails. The only thing that might trip me up was her signature, which I'd thought of. I'd downloaded the DNA request form from the lab's website so we could fill it in before we went there, and I'd accidentally on purpose noticed that I'd made an error after I'd got her to sign it. *Oops, sorry about that, I'll throw it away and we can do another one quickly!*

I took it out of my drawer and practised her swirling *A* at the beginning of her name, the loops of the *s*'s as they ran together without her taking the pen from the page, the slightly more heavy indentation of the *k* in her new surname. I practised with my right hand first until it was near perfect. Then I tried with my left.

Hmmm. Messy. I'd never used my left hand to write with. Never experimented. Never had a broken arm that would've forced me to have to try.

Alissa Burbeck.

Alissa Burbeck.

Alissa Burbeck.

Shit. It looked terrible. I filled a page with her signature, scrunched it up and threw it on my bedroom floor.

But I was an artist. I could mimic and copy the brush strokes of other people's pictures. I could do anything.

Could I make myself eat meat though? I thought about Dad forcing me to and pushed the exploding red swirling anger back inside. How was it possible they'd chosen me instead of her? I'd been so close to being her in the first place. It was a cruel twist of fate that she'd got the loving, kind parents and I'd got the insane ones. How could they have let a monster adopt a baby? Things would've been so different if it had been the other way around. I'd been cheated out of everything that should've been mine, and it was only right that I took back the life I should've had. It was only fair.

I straightened up as I looked in the mirror, biting my lip like she did. I could force myself to do anything, to be 'Alissa Burbeck'.

THE OTHER ONE
Chapter 27

'I can't believe we've only got a week left together,' Alissa said to me as all three of us sat in a restaurant.

'It's going too quickly!' I replied, with just the right amount of sadness.

'Have you thought about what you're going to do after we go back?' Max fussed with the napkin on his lap before leaning back and taking a sip of the champagne he'd ordered.

2003 Dom Perignon rosé at five hundred Australian dollars a bottle, don't you know! Lucky Alissa. Or, rather, lucky me!

'Who are you talking to?' Alissa laughed. 'Me or Sam?'

'Well, both of you.' He spread his manicured, now tanned hands on the crisp white tablecloth.

'I'm going to miss you *so* much. You have to come and stay with us really soon,' Alissa said to me.

I bit my lip and inhaled a deep breath. 'I'd love that, but how would I explain going to England to my parents without telling them what was going on?'

'But I really want us to spend more time with each other.' Alissa pouted, like a sad little girl. 'Max and I have been talking and we'd pay for your flights, and you could stay with us. The house is huge, so there's lots of space.' She glanced at Max, as if silently asking him to come up with a suggestion for how to fix things. She'd already told me he was her little fixer. He organised everything for them so she didn't have to worry about a thing. He sounded like a bit of a control freak to me, but whatever.

'How would you explain a twin popping up if you don't want your mum to know?' Max asked Alissa.

'Exactly,' I jumped in, willing my heartbeat to slow down. 'And I can't leave my parents just yet, with both of them so ill.'

Panic! No one can know! For my plan to work, NO ONE can know!

'You haven't told anyone about us, have you?' I asked them both.

'My lips are sealed. It's not my decision to make,' Max said. 'Whatever you ladies decide is fine with me.'

'No, of course I haven't told anyone,' Alissa said. 'I really want to wait until after my mum's passed away. She can't speak now and she's very confused, but even so, I *know* she must've had good reasons for not telling me I was adopted. I don't want our last memories together to be . . . spoiled, if she finds out somehow that I know about it all. I really don't want her upset. I want her to go peacefully.'

'I agree,' I said, not too hastily, demurely looking down at the tablecloth.

'But Alissa can always come out here again to see you so you can spend more time together,' Max suggested. 'No one has to know. We can just say she loved it so much she wanted to come back for a holiday. Or I'm sure we can both come out again soon if things go according to plan with the potential development sites here.'

She threaded her fingers through Max's and leaned her head against his shoulder. 'This is why I love you, darling. You always come up with great ideas. Yes, I'll come out again soon and see you.'

'Brilliant,' I enthused. 'I can't wait!'

'There, all sorted,' Max said as the waiter came to take our order.

I sat back and took a sip of champagne. Every night I'd had dinner with Alissa and Max (with champagne, oh, la di da!), and every night they'd picked up the tab, even though I'd offered several times. *We want to do it! If you can't treat your sister, who can you treat?* I could get used to this. Oh, yeah, I *would* get used to it! Ha, ha, ha!

It was hard enough concentrating on Alissa, but I had to study Max, too, and exactly how they both interacted with each other.

Still, it was all paying off. Every day I was getting a bit closer to what was truly mine.

Alissa took my hand in hers. 'So it's our secret for now.'

I smiled and squeezed her hand. 'Our secret.'

THE OTHER ONE
Chapter 28

Max was at another business meeting with a local developer he wanted to entice into some kind of partnership. No wonder Alissa didn't ask him much about his business. He'd talked to me about it, and it sounded boring, boring, boring. I'd asked him lots of questions, of course, a faux enraptured smile on my face. Not once did he mention The Goldings development, which made me wonder if he was trying to hide it from Alissa. Anyway, if he was going to cheat those poor homeowners, then really, he deserved everything he got.

Alissa and I wandered through a local flea market, browsing stalls. I picked up some items – scarves, earrings, hats, dresses – holding them up to her and saying how they suited her. That brought on a discussion about fashion, and her likes and dislikes. I mentally noted everything down, as usual. Most of her clothes were designer. Mine were more hippie, arty-farty things.

We were grabbing a smoothie at a health-food stall when her phone pinged with a text. She took the phone from her bag, frowned at it, and sighed.

I watched her carefully. 'Is everything OK?'

She rolled her eyes as she picked up her drink from the counter, and we meandered over to a table. 'It's my ex, Russell. We're still friends, but . . . I think maybe we shouldn't be right now, and I don't know how to tell him.'

'He keeps texting you?'

She sighed. 'Yeah. I've been really polite about it. I don't want to hurt his feelings, you know, but he keeps telling me I've made a mistake with Max and that he wants me back.'

I raised an eyebrow. 'Oh? Is he still in love with you?'

'Yeah. We went out for about four years, and then I met Max, like I told you before, and . . . well, the short story is I finished things with Russell.'

I leaned my elbow on the table, rested my chin in my hand. 'What's the long story?'

'Russell wouldn't take no for an answer. I mean, nothing happened with Max at first. He'd send me flowers and stuff and . . . well, I'd grown apart from Russell, fallen out of love with him, and—' She shrugged. 'Max stole my heart. I didn't want to hurt Russell, but I guess you can't help who you fall in love with, can you?'

'So, what happened when Russell knew you were seeing Max?'

'I was a bit worried about how he'd react because Russell could get a bit overprotective sometimes.'

'Really? So, is he a bit of a tough guy?'

'No! Not really. He was always really nice to me. He'd never do anything to hurt me, but he could get a bit jealous, I suppose.' She tucked her hair behind her right ear. 'But I was worried that he might attack Max when he knew we were together, so I thought it was only right to tell him *before* something happened between Max and me, because I knew it was heading that way.'

'Why would he attack Max?'

She glanced down at the floor. 'Well, one night I was in a pub with Russell and this guy was at the bar, really drunk, and he kept making horrible comments about me. How he'd like to fuck me. It was awful. The guy was disgusting. Russell told him to shut up and apologise, and when the guy didn't, Russell smacked him in the face.'

I leaned forward, elbows on knees. 'Wow! So how did Russell take it when you told him you'd started seeing Max?'

'I felt terrible. He was devastated. I can't blame him, really. He thought we would settle down with each other, have kids, the whole thing.' She rubbed her thumb over the phone's screen in her hand. 'Russell wouldn't let it go. Sent me loads of pleading texts. Phoned me late at night when he was drunk. He said he just wanted to be friends. Said he missed chatting to me. So I let it carry on for a while, but I just kept it friendly, *Hi, how's your day? What have you been up to? How's work?* That kind of thing. But then he started turning up places where Max and I were. If we went to the pub in the village we live in, somehow Russell found out and he'd walk in. Or if I went shopping with my mates, he'd bump into me.'

'He was stalking you?' *Oh, this keeps getting better and better!*

She gasped a little. 'No. No, I don't think so.' Then her eyebrows furrowed with concern. 'Well, maybe. I told Max about it and he said we should report him to the police and get an injunction out on him, but I said no. I mean, it wasn't like Russell was actually doing anything horrible. And I still felt guilty about everything that happened, so I played down a lot of it to Max.' She leaned forward conspiratorially.

'Are you scared of Russell?'

'No!' She waved a hand around. 'He'd never hurt me or do anything. He's just . . .'

'Still in love with you?'

'Mmm. Anyway, then he decided to go travelling for a while. He backpacked round Australia for a year, which I was kind of glad about, really. When he came back to the UK, he rented a house in the same village as us, but nothing else happened again until recently. I was dreading him finding out I was getting married, and I wanted to send him a text so he'd hear it from me first. It was only fair.' She tucked her hair behind her ear in two quick movements.

'Was he OK about it?'

'Not really. Now he keeps texting again, asking if I'm OK, and if I'm sure I'm doing the right thing, and that he would always have me back if I changed my mind. I'm a bit worried he might find out about our wedding reception when we get back and turn up to cause a scene.'

'That would be awkward.' *Or quite fortuitous!* 'What makes you think he will?'

She shrugged. 'Just a feeling. The texts are getting more frequent and insistent.'

I quizzed her more about Russell, then steered the conversation back round to the wedding reception. 'So, how many people have you got going?'

She clasped her hands together, her face lighting up. 'We've invited a hundred, but some can't make it, obviously. Max usually arranges everything – he's got to-do lists for his to-do lists.' She laughed. Yes, definitely throaty. 'So I said I wanted to arrange the reception and show him just how organised I can be when I put my mind to it. I drew up this list of party guests on my laptop, lists of food the caterer is providing, lists of music Max wants playing, that kind of thing.' She said it proudly, as if she'd accomplished something amazing, like bringing about world peace or diffusing a nuclear warhead single-handedly.

'It's so exciting! I wish I could be there.'

'I do, too.' She pouted. 'And I'd love to have you in the reception photos with us. Something I could keep forever and look back on as the time I finally found you after all these years.'

Oh, hell, no!

'But you'll have all your good friends there, won't you? What were their names again?' I asked, even though I'd memorised them already in great detail. Practice makes perfect.

'There's Vicky Saunders, my best friend. We've known each other since primary school. She's really sweet. She's a hairdresser. I was bullied a bit at school and she was always really protective of me. She's always been more like a sister than a friend.' She smiled happily at me. 'But now I have a *real* sister! And I can't wait for you to meet her. You're going to love each other. Then there's Sasha Smithers, who's the sister of Leo, Max's best friend. They're the ones I hang out with the most.'

'Yeah, I remember you told me a lot about Vicky.' She sounded really clingy to me, always wanting to spend time with Alissa and do things together. It was an alien concept. And they spoke almost every day on the phone. What on earth could they find to talk about all the time? 'What's Sasha like, then?'

'Um . . .' She did that lip-biting thing again. 'I hate gossiping about people, but Sasha can be a bit . . . well, strange. She likes to be outrageous, and it's as if she does it for attention. She says things sometimes that are a bit rude and hurtful. Like she picks up on your insecurities and homes in on them, bringing them up at every chance she gets, having little digs. Vicky doesn't really like her, and calls her up on it when she says stuff, but then Sasha pretends it's all a bit of fun. I think Sasha just does it because she's insecure herself, so I feel a bit sorry for her, really.'

'Or she's jealous?'

'Maybe. I think she's had a thing for Max for a long time.'

'She fancies him?'

'I don't know.' She shrugged. 'I think it's possible.'

'She doesn't sound much like a friend, then.'

She scrunched her nose up. 'Well, she was friends with Max before we met, so I really make an effort with her for Max's sake.'

I patiently took mental notes in my head as she prattled on about Sasha, wondering if I'd have to watch Sasha carefully. She sounded like a right fucking bitch. This is why it didn't pay to have friends. You either had annoying ones like Vicky who wanted to see you all the time and smothered you, or jealous cows like Sasha. It was much better without all those attachments. No one to annoy you then. A little while later, I said, 'I'm still thirsty, do you want another drink?'

'You got the last one; I'll get these. Same again?' She delved into her bag and retrieved her purse.

'Lovely, thanks.' I watched as she threaded her way through the crowd of people and queued up at the smoothie stall. Then I checked that my phone was still recording.

THE OTHER ONE
Chapter 29

I thought about making it look like a suicide, but, practically, that could be quite tricky. It didn't matter if they knew it was murder. I'd be long gone, anyway, by the time her body was discovered. And technically, I *was* her.

Of course, my fingerprints were all over the apartment. I'd never had mine taken by the police, so they had nothing to compare them to, and hers would also be there, from all the time she'd spent in the apartment over the last two weeks. Nevertheless, I still thoroughly wiped and cleaned the surfaces to get rid of mine. I couldn't leave any trace of me there.

It was their second-to-last day in Australia, and Max had a business meeting in the afternoon, so I invited Alissa over to the apartment. She arrived in a D&G denim mini-skirt (worth $800!) and an Armani top ($420), her bag tucked in the crook of her arm, as usual. The bag alone was worth $450 – I'd googled everything. WTF! That was obscene! I bet *she'd* never had to walk around with her toes poking out of her shoes as a kid.

We hugged at the door and she kicked off her flip-flops (worth $60 – double WTF!).

'I'm so sorry I'm a bit late,' she said. 'I fell asleep in the bath. I'm *always* doing that.'

'Really? Me too.' It was a luxurious habit I'd got into when I finally escaped the psycho parents. Just languishing in silence on my own was something I'd never known before. I wondered briefly if it was nature or nurture that made us individuals. Was Alissa more like me than I realised? I flicked the thought away as she curled up on the sofa and prattled on about her bath routine while I took mental notes and sorted out drinks.

It would be a celebration of sorts. I'd picked out a fruity, crisp white wine that I knew she liked. You couldn't say I never thought of others! I'd already cleaned her wineglass, and wiped off any of my prints before putting it on the worktop with my gloved hands, leaving it ready to fill. She was the only one going to touch that glass.

'I wish I could stay here forever,' she called out from the lounge.

Oh, but you are, my sweet sister. You absolutely are. 'Don't worry, we'll see each other soon,' I said as I put the finely crushed up sleeping tablets in her glass with my gloved hand, followed by a generous helping of wine. I stirred the liquid, waiting for all the tiny flecks to dissolve, then took off the rubber gloves before throwing them by the sink and carrying my own wineglass and a bowl of tortilla chips into the lounge. 'Could you grab your glass from the kitchen and the bottle? I've got my hands full.'

'Of course.' She leaped up to retrieve hers.

When we were settled, we chatted again in the easy way we'd grown used to in such a short space of time. You might think I'd have had second thoughts, pangs of guilt, or, at the very least, anxiety about what was going to happen, but no. Alissa was a means to an end. Alissa had what I should've had all along. Alissa was the reason I'd suffered. I didn't feel guilty. I didn't feel anything.

'I feel . . . a bit . . . woozy.' Her words began to slur as the tablets infiltrated her system. She reached out to put her glass on the coffee table and missed it completely, sending the glass bouncing on to the rug, spraying wine everywhere.

'Don't worry, you're probably tired with all the excitement over the last few weeks. Have a nap if you like.' I swallowed my wine and watched as her eyes eventually closed and she slumped to the side, unconscious, her head on the arm of the sofa, her breathing relaxed and even.

I grabbed the rubber gloves and slapped them on. Then I took a cushion from the sofa and pressed it against her face until her chest stopped moving. A quick check of her pulse confirmed she was dead.

I put my own wineglass and the bowl in the dishwasher and turned it on, before undressing and dropping my clothes into a plastic bag, along with the rubber gloves. Next, I undressed her, leaving her in just her bra and knickers, and put her clothes on me. I lifted the edge of her knickers up and had a look. I couldn't leave anything to chance. No way was I going to mess this up. Every little detail had to be thought about.

Well, well, well, she waxes down there. Everything was off. Not even a strip. I'd have to shave it all quickly at the hotel room before Max returned.

I took one last look around the apartment before picking up her handbag, stuffing the plastic bag with my old clothes inside it to be dumped in the nearest bin.

I shut the door behind me and stepped out into the sunshine, tucking my hair behind my ears as I walked back to her hotel, humming to myself.

Goodbye, Sam Folds.

Hello, Mrs Burbeck!

PART THREE
DUPLICITY

THE DETECTIVE
Chapter 30

I stood on the periphery of the mourners at Max's grave, concentrating on Alissa, taking a mental note of everything. She was at the centre, dressed in the usual black outfit – a loose-fitting dress with long sleeves, black pumps, a black hat with a net veil that obscured her face. Leo stood on one side of her, seeming to hold her up. Vicky was on the other, clutching Alissa's arm tight. Sasha was next to Vicky, dressed garishly in a multicoloured skirt and top with purples, pinks, and greens splashed over them. Whereas Alissa's tears were discreet, shown only by the repeated wiping of her face with delicately lace-gloved hands and the shuddering of her shoulders, Sasha's were full on, with a bit of wailing thrown in. She hadn't seemed *that* distraught when I'd told her about Max's death at Leo's house, but she could've still been in shock at that stage. Maybe it had taken a while to sink in. Was she purposely trying to upstage Alissa, or was she as distraught as she seemed? She'd been friends with Max for as long as Leo had, but was it more than that? Had she been in love with him, like Vicky suspected? Had she killed Max for the simple reason of unrequited love? Compared with Alissa, I doubted

Max would've looked twice at Sasha. The only similarity between them was their height. Did Sasha think that if she couldn't have Max, no one else could? But if so, why had Alissa been allowed to get away that night? If Sasha was crazy with jealousy, why not kill Alissa, too? Or why not *just* kill Alissa?

No, it didn't make sense that Alissa had escaped. The intruder could've shouldered the door quite easily, even if it was a female. It was fairly flimsy, and it had taken the police constable half a minute, a minute at the most, to break through it when he'd arrived on the scene. Or why not wait for her outside, beneath the orangery, which was her only escape route? Why even kill Max when there was a ninety-nine per cent chance Alissa would be in the house if they weren't intending to go after her?

Because it was staged. The killer wasn't after Alissa all along. They were only ever after Max.

I tuned out the vicar's words and thought about the murder scene. I'd gone through the statements and photos, videoed interviews, and forensic reports repeatedly since Stiles had been arrested and remanded in custody by the court pending his trial, and though there was no evidence to contradict Alissa's story about what happened that night, I didn't believe her. Something about her felt off.

Several theories had floated around in my head. The first was that Alissa and Russell had been working together and she was protecting him. Maybe they were still in love with each other, and if Alissa got Max out of the way, she could be with Russell again, with the extra bonus of being about ten million pounds richer. I'd dismissed that, though, because if they were working together, why would she implicate him during the second interview as being at the scene? Surely she'd have described someone else. Unless she was double-crossing him, getting him to do the dirty work for her, and had never had any intention of being with him. But if that was the case, why hadn't Russell implicated *her*? Did he love her so much that he was prepared to risk a life in prison for her? It was unlikely, but not impossible.

I'd stayed on the accomplice theme, wondering if Leo was involved. He'd struck me as maybe in love with Alissa himself, rising to her defence a little too emphatically. Had Alissa been having an affair with him? Had she got him to kill Max? But, no, Leo's alibi of being at a late dinner that night with some colleagues checked out, and he had five other witnesses to vouch for him.

That led me to the unknown fingerprints found in the office. That same set of prints had also now been matched to others found in the rest of the house, including the master bedroom. Who did they belong to? An unknown accomplice? Someone who wasn't in the system and who didn't match any of their closest friends who'd attended the reception? Wilmott had dismissed them as inconsequential, citing Alissa's vague recollection of a removal man who'd helped transfer some of her furniture from her mum's house into The Orchard when she'd moved in with Max a year ago. But, conveniently, she'd said Max had arranged it all and that she couldn't remember which company he'd used, and there was no record of it in Max's financial papers. According to SOCO, though, the prints had been recent. Were they an unimportant little detail, like Wilmott thought, or were they the key to this whole thing? I was inclined to think the latter, but I wondered why, if there was an accomplice, they hadn't worn gloves.

Whether or not there was an accomplice involved, I was now convinced Alissa had killed Max, with or without help, and set up Russell. But if I couldn't find a discrepancy, anything that disproved Alissa's version of events, she was going to get away with it, and I didn't want another sodding Lord Mackenzie case happening again.

The vicar's voice dragged my thoughts back to the ceremony. Vicky handed Alissa a red rose and she took a shaky step forward, closer to the edge of the grave. Her lips moved as she spoke quietly to her dead husband of two short months. Vicky rubbed Alissa's shoulders, tears streaking down her own cheeks. One minute later, Alissa threw the rose on to Max's coffin and then broke down, turning into Leo's shoulder and clutching on to him. Leo spoke words I couldn't hear into her hair as Vicky continued rubbing her back.

Sasha took her own rose and threw it on to the coffin. She glanced up and her gaze met mine. She smiled, not a sad, half-smile that seemed polite. It was more excited, greedy.

She was a bloody oddment. There was something not quite right about her, too.

As others in the crowd began to toss their own roses in final tribute, I turned to Wilmott at my side. 'Are you going to the wake?'

'Of course.' He was staring at Alissa with a barely concealed expression of lust.

'I'm heading back, then. I'll see you later.'

He waved a hand at me dismissively, as if he couldn't care less what I was doing, and walked around to where Alissa stood. He said something. She pulled away from Leo and touched Wilmott's arm in a grateful gesture.

I left Wilmott to fuss around Alissa at the wake, which was being held at Leo's house, and walked back to the unmarked Ford Mondeo on the road outside the graveyard. I was just about to open the door when I heard my name being called.

I turned and Sasha was heading my way, wobbling on the grass in her red stilettos.

'Hi.' She caught up with me. 'I was just wondering if there was any more news on the case.'

I studied her for a moment. That twinkling in her eye. The air of desperation, her outrageous and inappropriate clothes. 'Well, you know Russell Stiles has been charged and remanded without bail.'

She licked her crimson lips. 'Yes, I know that. But I thought there might be something more.' She glanced over to where Alissa stood and her eyes narrowed slightly.

'What are you getting at, Sasha?' I had the feeling that she was good at playing games.

She drew her gaze back to me and smiled again, exposing canines with a smudge of lipstick on them. 'I saw you watching her during the service. You think she was in on it, don't you?'

'Do you think she was involved?'

'Well, don't they say most times it's the spouse? And they *had* only been married a couple of months.'

'I thought you were supposed to be her friend.'

She snorted. 'Well, I am! But I was Max's friend before I knew Alissa. And I don't want to be friends with a killer, do I? I want to make sure I'm safe. And Leo, too. I think he's secretly in love with her, you know. I'm just looking after my big brother.'

'And what about you? Were you secretly in love with anyone?'

She laughed again, but it was more nervous than confident. 'What do you mean?'

'Where were you between 11 p.m. and 1 a.m. on the night Max was killed?'

She pointed a finger at her chest. 'Me?!'

I nodded.

She pulled her shoulders back in a haughty display. 'I was at my art gallery, actually, hosting an exhibition. It finished at one-thirty in the morning, and I've got about twenty-five people who can vouch for me. You can check. Anyway, I was only trying to be helpful. There's no need to be so rude to me.' She turned around and stalked back towards the grave.

I shook my head as I got in the car. She had some kind of agenda with Alissa, but I didn't think she was involved in Max's murder. She was weird, sure, but unfortunately being a weirdo wasn't an arrestable offence. If it was, the prison system would never be able to cope.

I often thought that being a good detective was like being a good actor. To find the offender, you had to get inside their skin and try to think like them, act like them. Which is why I wanted to run through the scene again and see it through the killer's eyes.

I parked in the driveway of The Orchard and took the spare set of keys I'd pilfered from Wilmott's desk out of my pocket. Alissa had told Wilmott she wouldn't be going back to the house in the foreseeable future, that she was going to put it up for sale, and Wilmott had forgotten to hand the keys back to her now that SOCO had finished.

I took the crime-scene photos from the glove box and opened the front door, breathing in a musty, unlived-in smell. I walked down the large, elegant hallway with black-and-white chequerboard tiles, pausing by the door to the lounge, where some of the guests had been during the wedding reception. It was a huge room that overlooked the front of the property, with high ceilings, intricate coving, and a ceiling rose. There were three large grey satin sofas arranged around an open fireplace with an oil painting of a fox hunt in a gilt frame above it. A mahogany sideboard sat underneath the window and a few occasional tables were next to the sofas. It looked like a room that was hardly used and just for show. Nothing looked disturbed apart from the surfaces, covered with fingerprint powder.

I walked through into the spacious kitchen and stood at the window, looking into the vast garden. From here, I had a good view of the carp pond at the bottom with a vibrant pink rose bush at its edge, and the post-and-rail fence that signalled the property's border with the dense wood beyond. I pictured the scene of Alissa standing by the pond at her reception, getting some air, a glass of champagne in her hand as she looked back at the house. Russell appearing behind her, climbing over the fence, approaching her, pleading with her, telling her she was making a mistake. Max coming out and spotting them. The argument that ensued. Russell telling Max he'd get what he deserved and should watch his back. Was Alissa telling the truth about that? Although Vicky and Leo had witnessed some of the altercation, they hadn't heard what had been said first-hand. And Russell couldn't remember because he'd been too drunk. Even if he had said those words, I didn't think it was a threat, not really. Yes, Russell wasn't squeaky clean himself, but I didn't think he was a murderer.

Is that when Alissa came up with a plan to frame him? Or had she calculated it long before that?

I walked up the stairs and turned left, going down the hall and into the office. The chair Max had been sitting at had been moved by SOCO, so I took out the photos, putting them on the desk as I rifled through them to find the ones of Max's body. I repositioned the chair where it had been that night and sat down, staring out of the window in front of the desk, imagining what really happened that night, running through Alissa's story again in my head.

Of course, she'd had to say she'd come into the office and kissed his cheek. If she'd leaned over him, it would explain away the transfer of any hair or DNA on to his body. The music was a plausible reason why Max hadn't heard the attacker, but stabbing someone in the back of the neck also suggested that the victim may have been comfortable enough with the killer to turn his back on them.

What I couldn't work out was how Russell's hair had wound up on Max's body if he really was innocent, like I suspected. He'd never been inside the house. He hadn't seen Alissa or Max since the wedding reception. So where did it come from? I put that thought away for the moment and walked into the master bedroom. The unknown fingerprints found there, as well as in the office and the rest of the house, niggled at me, too. To have access to all areas meant that the prints had to belong to someone who was very close to Max or Alissa, but all of the people they invited to the reception had had their prints compared to the unknown ones and been eliminated. It was another inconsistency that I brushed away for now. I walked into the en-suite and looked around, then leaned over to open the window Alissa had allegedly used as her escape route that night. I hoisted myself up on to the ledge and climbed through, hearing a ripping noise.

When I swung my legs down on to the orangery roof, I inspected my trousers. The catch on the window had torn a three-inch hole in the pocket. I glanced back at the catch. It was what Alissa had apparently snagged her towel on, leaving her naked.

I walked to the edge of the flat roof extension and glanced down, taking in the four-metre drop to the ground. I sat on the edge, then turned around and gripped the edge of the roof with my hands, my chest pressing into the building as my body dangled in mid-air.

Then I let go, landing with a thud on my feet, sending a jolt of pain up into my knees. They gave way and I rolled over, landing on my side, staring up at the roof. It wasn't that difficult, especially if you were younger and lighter than me, as Alissa was.

I stood up, lifting up my heels one at a time as I flexed my legs, checking for any damage. Everything present and correct. Nothing broken.

I rounded the orangery and walked past the side of the kitchen, down towards the pond. I climbed the post-and-rail fence into the woods and looked left. If I ran that way, I'd reach Mrs Downes' house next door where Alissa ended up that night. If I ran right, I'd reach Russell's house a mile away at the edge of the village.

I pulled my phone out of my pocket and turned on the timer app. Then I started running right. The trees were sparser here, so as I pounded over the twigs and decaying leaves, I could avoid getting scratched in the face. Alissa had received no abrasions to her face that night, either. My heart pounded in my chest, my lungs complaining, unused to the burst of exercise, and my back twinged annoyingly.

A short while later, I'd reached the rear of Russell's house. I climbed over the fence, jogged to the shed, and opened it. I crouched down in the area where the knife had been hidden and heard my knees crack. Then I mimed placing a knife there, came out, shut the door, and jogged back to the fence. In the woods again, I ran back the way I'd come. All the way to Mrs Downes' house, stopping at her fence. I pulled my phone from my pocket.

Eighteen minutes and thirty-nine seconds. It wasn't that long, and Alissa was fit and light and could've done it quicker than me.

The forensic pathologist had put the time of death at between 11 p.m. and 1 a.m. Alissa had arrived at Mrs Downes' house shortly before she made the emergency call at 12.58.

Her story was plausible. It added up, but it didn't add up completely. Not to me, anyway.

I took a slow walk back to The Orchard to get my breath back before collecting the crime-scene photos I'd left inside and heading into the woods again. I lined myself up with the carp pond and looked back at the house. Then I flicked through the crime-scene photos, searching for the ones of the Jack Daniel's bottle that Russell had been drinking that day. The bottle had been found at the base of an old oak tree with a naturally hollowed out trunk, just the kind of place to sit and wait and watch. The photos showed the bottle just to the right of the trunk. Next to that was the body of Buttons, Alissa's cat that had ended up with a broken neck.

The cat was bugging me, too. Wilmott thought it proved Russell's insane rage over Max's marriage to Alissa, evidence of his escalating hatred of Max – a pre-existing violence. Psychopathic tendencies. But Leo said he'd chased after Russell into the woods to make sure he'd left and never saw the cat. What did that mean? That someone else had killed Buttons? That Russell had come back another time and done it? That it had died of an accident, falling out of the tree, perhaps? Or was Leo lying for some reason?

I took one last look at the house before locking up and driving back to the station.

No one was in the office when I arrived, so I swiftly deposited the keys back in Wilmott's drawer. I was just limping out – think I'd pulled a muscle in my calf from all that sudden exercise – when Becky appeared.

'God, you look like you're starring in a *Night of the Living Dead* movie.' Becky stared me up and down.

I glanced at my ripped trousers and flicked off the small bits of fern and bracken attached to them. I smoothed down my now windswept hair, conscious that my cheeks were probably still bright pink, too, from all the exertion.

'Ha ha, very funny.'

'Did you go to the funeral like that?'

'No. I've just come from The Orchard.'

She eyed me with a grin. 'Oh, yeah? Why?'

'Seeing if what she said was possible.'

'Was it?'

'Yes, but it's also possible she planted the knife in Russell's shed before she got to Mrs Downes' house, too.'

'Wilmott will go apeshit if he knows what you're doing.'

I shrugged. 'Well, he's had plenty of practice being an ape.'

'Want coffee?'

'Thanks.' I sat down at my desk and concentrated on the paperwork in front of me. I was so engrossed that I didn't see the shadow looming over my desk until it was too late.

'Why have you got that file out?' DI Wilmott snapped. 'The Burbeck case is done and dusted. Didn't I tell you to check CCTV footage for the Brookfield Jewellers robbery?'

I leaned back in my chair, looking up at him. 'I'm still not convinced about it all. There are some loose ends that are unexplained.'

Wilmott blew out an exasperated breath and crossed his arms over his chest. 'Well, the CPS is convinced, so is the court, so am I, and so is Detective Superintendent Greene. Are you deliberately trying to sabotage my first case as SIO? Is that what this is about? Because you're jealous I've got acting DI and you haven't?' His nostrils flared with anger.

Was it? Was that really why I was having trouble accepting Alissa's story? No. There was more to it than that. Much more. Twenty-eight years of copper's instinct more. But Wilmott wanted this case cleared up quickly to make him look like he knew what he was doing. A nice, easy result would do wonders for his new promotion. He didn't want to waste time looking beyond the obvious. He was like a myopic rhino, charging ahead short-sightedly to get to the juicy grass he'd sniffed out and sod anything he bumped into on the way that might take him off course.

'It just seems too convenient to me. Stiles knew he was a person of interest and there were no balaclava, gloves, black puffy jacket, or shoe covers he was allegedly wearing that night found at his house. Yet he still kept the knife that was used to murder Max. Why?'

'Because he's an idiot?' Wilmott raised a sarcastic eyebrow. 'Criminals do stupid things. It's how they get caught.'

'He's not stupid. Why didn't he get rid of it after I questioned him the first time, like he supposedly did with the stuff he wore? Why risk it being found at his house?'

Wilmott rolled his eyes in a *do-we-have-to-go-through-this-again* look. 'Maybe he wanted a souvenir.'

I wasn't going to mention Stiles' protestations of innocence. Most criminals said the same thing. The only difference here was that I actually believed him. And I'd watched his videoed interviews over and over again. I was convinced his body language and reaction to Max's murder were due to genuine shock.

Wilmott shook his head with exasperation. 'He had the motive, the means, and the opportunity! Anyway, I don't know why we're having this conversation. The case is closed. C.L.O.S.E.D.,' he kindly spelled out for me like I was a five-year-old. 'We have undisputable DNA evidence placing Stiles at the scene, the murder weapon hidden at his house—'

'Evidence can be planted. And the murder weapon had no fingerprints or DNA on it from Stiles.'

'Because he handled it wearing gloves! And who do you think planted Russell's hair on Max's body? You're just plucking things out of thin air to undermine my authority here! It's *my* neck on the line, and I'm not letting you stuff anything up for me. You've got nothing left in your life, so you're trying to mess up mine with some kind of rogue agenda!' Wilmott's voice crept higher. 'You haven't been right in the head for a long time.' He glared at me.

I wasn't altogether sure I could disagree with that. 'I may not be right in the head, but I'm right about this!' I said through clenched teeth.

'It's only you who seems to have a problem with this case! We have all the evidence we need. What more do you want?'

'How about the truth? How about the real criminal being convicted for once?'

'Oh, for fuck's sake. Is this about the Mackenzie case again? You should've learned from that already. They almost suspended your arse after all.' He snorted. 'Quite honestly, I'm surprised you're still here.'

'They nearly suspended me because I was digging too deep. It was a bloody whitewash and you know it! We're supposed to be upholding the law, not covering for criminals! How about an innocent person going to prison, then? Doesn't that concern you in the slightest?'

He knocked his knuckles on the desk. 'Hello? Is there anyone there? Russell Stiles is *not* innocent!'

I clenched my fists and fought the urge to knock him off his feet. I thought about telling him again about my suspicions regarding Alissa, but I didn't have any actual proof of anything yet. I considered going to Detective Superintendent Greene myself and laying it out, but his arse had been kissed so much by Wilmott, I'd probably be shot down if I did it now. Plus, he was the one who'd almost suspended me over the Mackenzie case, so he wasn't particularly impartial, and he probably *would* suspend me this time if he thought I wasn't toeing the party line. It was better to act dumb for now. Kind of like Wilmott, actually.

'Well?' Wilmott pressed me. 'Do you have anything to say on the matter?'

I stroked my chin between my thumb and forefinger and pretended to be thinking of something to say in my defence.

'Get on with checking the CCTV cameras that I assigned you for the robbery case.'

Ever since I'd begun to question the Burbeck case, Wilmott had delegated the shit stuff to me. His way of keeping me in my place. He obviously didn't know me that well.

Wilmott snatched the Burbeck file off my desk and glared at me again. 'I do *not* want to hear about this any more!' He stormed into his office, slapped the file on his desk, and started clicking around on his laptop, probably playing Solitaire.

Becky glanced over and raised her eyebrows at me.

I shrugged and left the office.

It wasn't over. Not for me, anyway.

THE OTHER ONE
Chapter 31

I could relax now. Max was dead and Russell was in prison – aww, what a shame. Russell was always going to be a means to an end. An unfortunately fortunate scapegoat. But things had changed rapidly. Almost too rapidly. I'd wanted to wait longer. And I'd actually enjoyed being Alissa – who wouldn't? She had everything she could want. I'd almost enjoyed fucking Max, too, although his kisses were sloppy, like a slick, wet fish on my skin. He'd welcomed the little differences in the bedroom between Alissa and me, thinking I was trying to spice things up. Oh, yes, he'd fallen for everything completely. So had everyone! Flattery always worked wonders for deflecting any conversations I felt were heading in the wrong direction, turning the subject around to them instead. Get people talking about themselves and they love it (and people might call *me* narcissistic – ha!). It's a great way to cover up any little discrepancies. I had a few other tricks up my sleeve, too. Pretending I was distracted from the conversation because some fabulous new plot idea for my book had suddenly burst into my head worked well.

That, and pretending I was busy and had to wrap up the conversation. Weirdly, though, it was kind of nice to be a couple, although sometimes it was really claustrophobic. Sometimes it took a lot of patience not to kill him right there and then. But planning the perfect murder took time and patience and cunning, which I had plenty of. I'd been toying with different accident scenarios. Something that wouldn't ever point to me. An 'accident' would've prevented all this annoying intrusion into my life by the police. But my hand had been forced in the end, though, and I just hoped I was ready for everything. Still, when an opportunity presents itself, you have to work with what you've got. I couldn't believe Russell had killed Buttons. What a bastard. How could he break the poor thing's neck like that? She was such a sweet cat, so friendly and inquisitive. He was crazier than Alissa had thought.

Russell being caught meant I was safe. I could also finally get out of that rank hotel suite with DI Wilmott leering at me, suffocating me, and move into a rented house. *Oh, I couldn't possibly go back and stay at the house, not now. Not after Max was so tragically ripped away from me. I'll have to go somewhere else. I couldn't stand it there.* I mean, that was the appropriate response, wasn't it?

God, Wilmott was so easy to read, the sleaze. And I'd played the sweet, heartbroken widow to perfection. Wilmott thought with his dick and that suited me fine. He wanted to protect me, comfort me. Actually, he wanted to fuck me. But men who think with their dicks are easy to manipulate.

So, I was in the clear. Go, me! Now all I had to do was wait for Max's will to be settled, leaving everything to me, of course, and then get the hell out of Dodge.

I hummed to myself as I unpacked the grocery shopping bags that I'd ordered online and had delivered. Now that Wilmott wasn't breathing down my neck, I was free to be *me* again when I was alone. The house was bright and airy and a good price. I couldn't afford to be seen as overly extravagant right now. That would come later. I'd wanted to leave the county completely, maybe move to an anonymous city, like London, but I worried that it would look too odd, being so far away from 'Mum'. Alissa wouldn't have abandoned her, would she? Alissa would still be living close by, ready to come at the drop of a hat in case lovely Mum unexpectedly got worse or died.

I was avoiding my 'friends', playing the grieving widow card again. *No, I really want to be alone. I'm not good company. No, I'm OK, you don't need to pop round and see me. I'm still coming to terms with things.* That bloody Vicky and Sasha and Leo wouldn't leave me alone, though. They kept ringing up, asking if I needed anything, if I was alright, telling me I shouldn't be alone at a time like this, trying to get me out of the house to take my mind off things. Blah, blah, blah. *Just shut up and leave me the fuck alone!*

I turned on Alissa's iPhone, selected my new playlist that I'd added after deleting all of her romantic, slushy crap, and hit 'Play'. 'Creep' by Radiohead blared out in the kitchen as I put away the food. I laughed. What an appropriate song.

What should I do next today? A clothes shopping trip? No, too frivolous. A distraught widow wouldn't shop. A visit to Mum? Nah, I'd been there yesterday and there was only so much I could stomach. The smell of the nursing home was bad enough, but seeing her gurgling and dribbling made me nauseous. It was gross. Why couldn't she just die already? How long was she going to hang on for? A walk in the fresh air, then? Head down, eyes bright with tears, walking to outrun all the sadness in my life. *Check!*

Then I could spend the afternoon reading. Or watching DVDs. Or, ooh, I know, painting my nails.

I heard the doorbell ring and ignored it, not wanting to have to deal with any of my friends trying to check up on me again.

I opened a jar of peanut butter and dug in a spoon, swallowing a hefty splodge of the stuff. The doorbell rang again. More persistently this time.

I huffed loudly, turned off the music, and walked into the lounge, peering round the edge of the curtain at the bay window.

DI Wilmott stood on my front step, smoothing down his hair.

Oh, for Christ's sake, what does he want now?

I sighed, slapped on my sad face, and walked towards the door.

THE DETECTIVE
Chapter 32

I sat in my car, parked a little way down from Alissa's rented house, watching, waiting for her to slip up somehow. She didn't go out much. From what I'd seen on my observations, she was living a pretty solitary existence. She wasn't singing from the rooftops, celebrating the death of her husband. She wasn't going on wild shopping sprees or out getting pissed and celebrating with her mates.

Maybe I was wrong. Was I losing it since Denise's death, not thinking straight? Maybe I shouldn't be doing this job any more. But I couldn't ignore my gut instinct. OK, I admit there was also a bit of one-upmanship involved, too. If I could prove Wilmott wrong about this case, then *I'd* be walking in the acting DI shoes, and the smug bastard would be taken down a peg or two.

And talk of the bloody devil. Here he was again, hair coiffed up, expensive tailored suit on, carrying a box of . . . what were those? Cakes? This was the eighth time I'd spotted him here when he had no reason to be visiting her if the case was *done and dusted*. And he was supposed to be in a budget meeting right now. At least, that's what he'd told us this morning.

He was obsessed with the woman.

Yeah, I was too, but for an entirely different reason.

I sipped a cardboard cup of now cold coffee and watched the house, slumped down in my seat. My back was killing me in this position. I really was too old for all this crap. But it was all I had left now, the only thin thread holding my life together, stopping me from completely succumbing to the depression that was like a rabid wolf, snapping at my heels. I'd been barely able to keep outrunning it. Had felt it gnawing its way into my brain ever since Denise had gone. If I stopped and let go, if I gave up the job and gave in to it, I knew it would crawl its way into my head and never go away again. Then I'd have to take a long hard look at myself or completely fall apart. Being a detective was the only thing still keeping me sane, which was why I'd backed down on the Mackenzie case when DS Greene had threatened me with suspension. I'd sold out my integrity once because of it – I wasn't going to do so again.

Two hours and twenty-three minutes passed before the front door was opened by Alissa, looking tired and distraught but still absolutely amazing, as if grief had somehow made her even more beautiful. Wilmott hesitated on the step before saying something and heading back to his car.

I twisted in my seat and rubbed at the base of my spine, ignoring the twinges, debating calling it a day and heading off to take some witness statements for the robbery. I'd come back again when I finished work, just like I'd been doing lately.

I reached to start the engine when a van pulled up outside Alissa's house with 'Delia's Delivery Flowers' written on it. A young guy hopped out of the van, which made me jealous of his lithe movements. I rubbed my back again – that running hadn't helped it – and observed him open up the rear doors of the van, lean inside and extract a huge bouquet. He jumped up Alissa's steps two at a time and rang the doorbell.

Her head appeared in the front window then vanished again, before reappearing when she opened the door. She frowned between the guy and the flowers before her face relaxed a little. He handed her the bouquet and a clipboard to sign for them.

I wasn't sure what I was seeing at first. It didn't click straight away. Not until the delivery guy had driven off. And then it hit me.

I drove back to the station, wondering what it could mean if I was right.

~

Becky's gaze was firmly fixed on her laptop when I got back to the office, running through bank statements for a fraud case. Ronnie was out taking some statements from potential witnesses to the robbery – exactly what I should've been doing, too – and Wilmott was nowhere to be seen, as usual, probably picking up a packet of Just for Men.

'How's it going, Sarge?' Becky asked.

'Yeah, not bad,' I said distractedly, sitting at my desk and opening my laptop, typing in the password.

I called up the digital file of Alissa's videoed interview, pressed 'Mute', and forwarded it to the last minute.

I watched. Rewound. Watched again. And again, just to be sure.

When I'd asked her to sign her statement, her right hand had lifted slightly and moved towards the pen, as if she was going to use that hand. It was a quick little flutter. So quick it could almost look as if she was just nervous or fidgeting, but I didn't think so, because of what happened next. It was like she'd suddenly remembered something, and her right hand moved towards the box of tissues instead, taking one out and wiping her nose with it before picking up the pen with her *left* hand and signing.

But the flowers she'd just received . . . they were signed for with her *right* hand. Signed automatically, casually, with no hesitation, and as if no one was watching and she didn't have to remind herself which hand to use.

I leaned back in my chair, steepled my fingers underneath my chin, and watched the now still screen.

What did it mean? Anything? Nothing? Alissa could be ambidextrous. But I'd never met anyone in my life who was. The rate of ambidexterity in the population was incredibly low.

I left a couple of robbery statements I had actually managed to take on Wilmott's desk and said goodbye to Becky. If Alissa's friends couldn't tell me something interesting, then who could?

~

I was betting on Sasha. She seemed to be the scheming, watchful, calculating type. She reminded me of a magpie, the way they hoard shiny things, except Sasha wouldn't be hoarding objects, she'd be hoarding snippets of information, storing them up to use for her own means at a later date. I'm not sure whether her friendship with Alissa was genuine or not, whether she was jealous of her or keeping an eye on Leo to make sure he didn't fall for her, but if Alissa had let something slip, Sasha would be the one to catch it. And was that what her conversation at the funeral had been all about? Was she hinting that she knew something?

Sasha owned Smithers Art Gallery in the nearby town of Hitchin. It was a bright, spacious shop sandwiched between an artisan bakers and a bohemian coffee shop. Sasha was talking to a customer in his early fifties against the far wall when I walked in. She glanced over her shoulder at me, then flashed me a knowing smile, as if she'd been waiting for me all along. She nodded briefly and turned back to the customer.

I headed towards the opposite wall by the window to wait for her to finish, studying a large painting that looked as if someone on acid had been having a bad trip – random splashes of colour everywhere. The price tag was seven grand. I was obviously in the wrong job. I'd got the same effect after I'd accidentally dropped a tin of paint on the bedroom carpet when I was decorating once.

I perused a few more paintings until she wrapped up her conversation and the man left. She walked towards me, teetering on very high canary-yellow stilettos, a thin curve to her lips, and a thought flashed into my head that if you got on the wrong side of her, she'd make you pay.

'Detective Carter. I didn't take you for an art lover. There's more to you than meets the eye, isn't there?' She smirked, as if she was laughing at me. 'I hope you're not going to be rude to me again.'

'I apologise if you thought I was rude the other day, but this is a murder inquiry. We can't pick and choose our questions.' *However much some people would like me to,* I thought.

'What do you think of this piece?' She pointed to an image that had been made from hundreds of bottle tops, depicting a horse's head.

'It's not exactly my taste.'

'What is?' Her gaze swept me up and down. It wasn't subtle, either.

I didn't react, just smiled.

'I heard you were asking Leo some more questions.' She gave me a sly smile. 'I might be able to help you out.' She folded her arms underneath her cleavage, as if trying to draw attention to it. 'Buttons. It was an accident. I saw her fall out of the tree. Leo told me you asked him whether he saw her after he looked for Russell in the woods.'

'Hang on a minute. You're talking about Alissa's cat?' I tried to understand exactly what she was saying, but she seemed to love talking in circles.

'Yes.'

I attempted to keep the annoyance out of my voice and failed. I was losing patience with her attitude. 'What exactly did you see and when?'

'Well, there's no need to be so snippy and rude. I tried to tell you the other day, at Max's funeral, but you were rude to me then, too.' She pouted orange lips at me. 'Anyway, I didn't think it was *that* important. Leo already told you what he saw, and I didn't hear their conversation.'

'*I'll* decide what's important or not.'

She raised her eyebrows. 'I like a forceful man. Are you single, Detective?'

I counted to ten in my head. 'Withholding information in a murder investigation is a very serious matter, Miss Smithers. Just—'

'Sasha. Miss Smithers sounds like a wrinkly old spinster.'

'*Sasha.* Just tell me what you saw.'

She pouted. 'OK, OK, keep your hair on!' She laughed raucously as she dropped her arms and rested one hand on her hip, jutting it out in my direction. 'I'd popped out of the marquee for a cigarette and was standing around the side of the orangery behind a bush, where no one could see me. Alissa was out there, looking back at the house with a drink in her hand. But you know all that.' She waved her hand casually.

'I want to hear it again. Were you watching her on purpose?'

At least she had the good grace to blush, then, as she told an obvious lie and said, '*No!* Of course not.'

'Go on, then. You saw Russell approach from the woods?'

'Yes. He was in a right old state, staggering, so you could tell he was drunk. He fell over the fence as he climbed over it and his baseball cap fell off.'

My heart raced slightly. Funny how Alissa didn't mention Russell falling over. Or that his cap fell off. A cap that she could quite easily have gone back for later and removed his hair from. A cap that hadn't been recovered in the area search by SOCO, either. Vicky hadn't seen the first part, where Russell fell over the fence, as she'd stepped into the garden afterwards, and Leo had caught the tail end of the incident, so he hadn't known, either. And as far as Alissa was concerned, well, if she hadn't seen Sasha, she'd think there was no one else who knew about that bit.

'Did he pick it up again?'

'No. Russell was so pissed he probably didn't even notice. He rolled to his feet, which seemed to take a lot of effort, and staggered over to Alissa. That's when they started talking, but I told you, I didn't hear what they said. Then Max came out and it seemed to get heated. Alissa stepped in between them and then Russell left the way he'd come, going back into the woods. Then Leo came storming down from the house, over to Max and Alissa. They spoke for a few minutes, and Leo went into the woods to check he'd gone.'

'What about Buttons? You said you saw what happened.'

'Well, Leo came back, shaking his head. Then he and Alissa and Max went back into the marquee. I was just about to go back in, too, when I saw a flash of white hurtle down from the top of one of the trees. So, of course I went to investigate. By the time I got there, Buttons was obviously dead. Her head was facing back to front.' She scrunched up her face with distaste. 'Her neck was broken.'

'And you didn't tell Alissa about her cat? Didn't go and fetch her?'

'What was the point? She was already dead. Anyway, I didn't want to upset her at her wedding reception.'

I stared at her, very much doubting that. 'Did you see anything else?'

'No.'

'Did anything strike you as different about Alissa recently? Did she do anything that seemed out of character?'

Her eyes narrowed, her lips curved higher, exposing those pointed canines. 'What an odd question.'

'Not really.'

She tilted her head and tapped the toe of her stiletto on the floor. 'You mean, did she seem like she was plotting to kill Max?'

'I mean, can you think of anything, no matter how small, that seemed different about her?'

'Have you asked Vicky? She saw Alissa more than anyone and they talked on the phone practically every day. But if you ask me, Vicky's always been a bit needy. And if you say something Vicky doesn't like, she bites your head off like a crazy woman!' She curled her lip up, and I wondered if Sasha had any close female friends herself. I had the feeling she preferred to hang out with men. Or maybe she was jealous of Alissa's close relationship with Vicky, and Sasha and Vicky obviously clashed. 'You don't think Russell did it, do you? You think it was Alissa?' She leaned forward. I could smell cigarettes and coffee on her breath.

'I can't divulge anything about the investigation, Miss Smithers.'

'*Sasha*.' She gave me an irritated huff. 'Actually, there was one thing, but it wasn't anything out of character. It was my fault, really.'

'What was your fault?'

'Max told me Alissa was a bit stressed out with the arrangements for the wedding reception and making sure everything went smoothly. It was usually Max who organised everything in that relationship, but she wanted to take on the party because Max had a lot of things going on at work. I don't know what she was fussing about, really. I mean, they had someone to set up the marquee, someone to do the catering and the drinks. It wasn't like she had to lift a finger, as usual.' She rolled her eyes. 'So, anyway, I wanted to treat her to a spa day, as a way to distress her before the party.'

'Distress her?'

'*De*stress her.'

She'd definitely said distress. I wondered if it was a mere slip of the tongue. I'm sure Freud would've had a field day with her. He'd have probably ended up slitting his wrists. And I wasn't convinced she wouldn't make up something she thought I wanted to hear to make her the centre of attention.

'I booked it for the day before the reception, and I'd included a couple of massages and a manicure and pedicure for us both. We were lounging by the indoor pool after lunch and we decided to get a superfood smoothie, so we chose our drinks from the menu, and I went to the juice bar to get them. I had one with mango and kiwi and other bits and pieces, and Alissa had a different mango concoction. Except I accidentally mixed them up when I took them back to our loungers.' She appeared sheepish.

I frowned. 'And why was that a problem?'

'Because Alissa is allergic to kiwi. She has been since she was little. It brings her out in horrible hives, all over her body, particularly her neck. I didn't find out she'd drunk mine and I'd drunk hers until Alissa had gone for another massage and the waitress came over to take our empty glasses. The one with kiwi had a slice of mango on the edge of the glass and the other one had a slice of pineapple, you see. That's how she could tell the difference when she was chatting about whether we'd enjoyed them. Of course, I panicked then, thinking that Alissa would have these horrible hives all over her for the wedding reception the next day, which would look atrocious in the photos.' She bit her lip, as if she was contrite, but I thought it was an act. She didn't look guilty about it at all. 'Usually, the hives came up really quickly whenever she'd eaten kiwi by accident, but when she came back from the massage an hour later, she didn't have any.'

'And did you tell her you'd *accidentally* mixed up the drinks?' I had no doubt she'd done it on purpose as a way to sabotage Alissa's party. What could be worse than turning up to your own wedding reception covered in hives? With friends like Sasha, who needed enemies? Still, enemies were far more likely to tell you something interesting.

'No. I thought she might think I'd done it on purpose.'

'Now why would she think that?' I raised an eyebrow.

'I've got no idea.' She flapped the idea away as preposterous with a flick of her hand. 'But, anyway, as the afternoon wore on, she didn't get the hives, so I thought I'd got away with it and wouldn't have to tell her.'

'And the next time you saw her was the following day, at the wedding reception?'

'Yes.'

'How did she seem then? Had she had a reaction to the kiwi by that stage?'

'No, that's the really strange thing.' She frowned. It was a mixture of disappointment and bafflement. 'She didn't have any hives at all.'

~

I was on my way to see Vicky Saunders when my mobile rang. It was Malcolm Briggs, the gardener, who was now recuperating at home after his operation, so I took a detour to his small terraced house.

He sat in an armchair, his skin a sickly colour that matched his washed-out cream cardigan. He was so shocked when I told him exactly what had happened at The Orchard that he just stared at me blankly for so long that I wasn't sure he'd heard me.

'Are you OK, Mr Briggs?' I asked.

He sat up straighter and winced in pain. I saw genuine tears in his eyes. 'I've known Max since he was a little boy. I started looking after his parents' garden when they bought the house, ooh, probably thirty years ago now. I just can't believe he's been killed.' He wiped his eyes. 'Sorry, I'm not usually like this.'

Denise had been a nurse, and if she was here right now, she'd be comforting him, telling him he was bound to feel a bit down and oversensitive after his operation, the anaesthetic, and the heart attack. I couldn't say that, though – it would sound weird coming from a man. I just did the manly thing and nodded, pretended I hadn't noticed him crying.

'When was the last time you were at The Orchard?'

'Um . . . on the Wednesday, so four days before Max was killed.' He wiped his eyes again. 'I usually only do one day a week there, but when they were having the reception I was there for a week solid, getting the garden pristine for the party.'

'Did you notice anyone suspicious hanging around recently?'

'No, no, I didn't see anyone. It was usually only Alissa there, but sometimes Max worked from home, although he didn't get involved in the garden. He just let me get on with it. Alissa would take an interest in it when she wasn't busy with her writing. She loved sitting outside when the weather was nice, and she always told me what a lovely job I did.'

'Did you witness any arguments between Mr and Mrs Burbeck?'

'I never heard them argue in all the time Alissa lived there. They were very happy as far as I could see. Very happy. They seemed even happier when they got back from Australia, as if marriage had made them a lot closer. I remember the same thing happening with me and my wife. It was as if the commitment made both of us relax a little.'

'Did you notice anything odd happening? Was Alissa acting differently? No matter how small it might seem, it might be important.'

'You can't think she had anything to do with his murder, surely? She's a lovely girl.'

'I have to ask.'

He nodded slightly. 'Of course, I'm sure you do.' He frowned as he thought about the question. 'There was something a bit strange that happened. Before they went to Australia, Max bought Alissa a special rose bush as a wedding gift. He had it named after her – you can do that, you see, with specialist companies. It was a beautiful deep pink floribunda. She thought it was lovely, and asked me to plant it near the pond while they were away. But when she got back, it was like she couldn't remember it. She brought me out a cup of coffee when I was in the garden – said she was taking a break from writing. She often did that, got a bit of fresh air and stretched her legs after being cramped up at the laptop for hours. So we walked around the garden together, and she was admiring what I'd done getting it ready for the reception while they'd been away. We stood by the rose, and I asked her what she thought of it in the new spot. She said it looked really pretty and asked me the name of the plant. It was like she'd completely forgotten about it. Maybe she was just distracted, what with the wedding reception coming up and making all the arrangements for it.'

'Maybe,' I said. Or maybe not. 'Did she seem to forget anything else important?'

'No, I didn't notice anything else.'

~

Vicky worked as a senior stylist at a place called A Snip in Time. I thought Vicky's job might be a sign to start trying to get my act together. Denise used to cut my hair, and I'd neglected it since she'd gone. It wasn't as if I had anyone to try to look good for now, but I supposed I should make the effort of appearing on the surface like I was still holding it together. Even if I was only fooling myself for a short while.

There was only one customer on the shop floor when I walked in: a middle-aged woman sitting under some kind of blow-dryer machine. Vicky was talking to the receptionist, huddled over her shoulder, pointing to an entry in an appointment book.

They both looked up as I approached.

Vicky gave me a slight smile. The receptionist gave me a more *the-customer-is-always-top-priority* one.

'Hi,' I said to Vicky. 'Do you have time for a cut?'

'Actually, yes. I've had a cancellation. Come over.' She walked towards an empty chair by the window.

I sat down. She got a black gown from a cupboard and fastened it around my neck, standing back and looking at me in the mirror. 'Do you just want a trim?'

I ran a hand through my hair. It was way too long, curling at my collar and around my ears. 'Yes. I've neglected it a bit lately.'

She smiled. 'No problem. Maybe I should do it shorter at the sides? Leave it a bit longer on top?' She ran her hands through it, tugging slightly to test the length.

'Whatever you think.'

'Do you want me to wash it or spray it wet?'

'Spray is fine.'

She nodded, dampened my hair first, then pulled a pair of scissors from a belt at her waist. 'Would you like a cup of tea or coffee?'

'No, thanks. How've you been?'

'I still can't believe what's happened. It's just terrible. You think you know someone, and then . . .' She glanced down at my hair in her fingers and blinked a couple of times, as if she was close to tears. 'I never thought Russell could ever do something like that.'

'I appreciate this is still very upsetting, but I wanted to follow up on a few things.'

She sniffed loudly and snipped away vigorously with speed using her scissors. I hoped she wasn't too upset to cut properly so that I'd end up with a lopsided mess. Or worse, half an ear missing. Still, it had to end up better than the style I was currently wearing.

'I thought everything was all finished with now that Russell's been arrested.'

'Not quite. There are a few loose ends to tie up.'

'Oh, OK. Of course, I want to do anything I can to help. Alissa's still so upset.'

'Have you seen her?'

'No. We've spoken on the phone, but she says she's still not ready to see anyone yet. I can understand that. I can't even begin to imagine how I'd feel if my other half was murdered. I sent her some flowers, just to let her know I was thinking of her. But I don't think it's good for her to be moping around in that rental house she's in all alone. She needs people around to comfort her at a time like this, don't you think?' She carried on without waiting for an answer. 'I keep trying to get her out, just to go for a walk or something, but she's not interested. Poor thing. I don't know what to do to help her. I feel kind of useless, really.'

I started off asking some more questions about Max and Russell as she cut so it wouldn't raise any instant red flags. Then I turned my attention to Alissa. 'You've been friends with Alissa for a long time.'

'God, yes. Since primary school.'

'Did you notice any problems with her forgetting things lately?'

'Um . . . no. What kind of things?'

'Nothing specific,' I said, trying to be vague. 'You weren't aware that she'd had any medical problems that might affect her memory? A bang on the head recently?'

'Not that I know of. I always joke with her that she has an elephant's memory. She never forgets stuff.'

'Did you know about her allergy to kiwi fruit?'

'Yes. It started when she was about five. It brought her out in really bad hives. She had some tests done and it was confirmed she was allergic to it.'

'Did you ever see her get hives from it?'

'Yes, before she found out what it was and started avoiding it. They were terrible and lasted for a couple of days.'

I'd read up on the Internet about it. It seemed that while some children outgrew allergies, the majority retained them into adulthood.

'Did you notice anything different about her when she returned from Australia?'

She scrunched up her nose. 'Different? What do you mean?'

'Anything that seemed out of character. Was she behaving differently to normal?'

She frowned slightly. 'No. I only saw her a couple of times alone before the wedding reception – once when I popped into their house for coffee and she told me all about their trip, and once when I came to do her hair at The Orchard before the party.'

'Would you usually have seen her more often than that?'

'Yes, but she was organising the reception, so she said she was really busy with that, plus she was sorting out a lot of things to do with the wedding, changing her name on various things, passports, driving licences, and all that. And, of course, catching up with her writing and going to see her mum. She'd felt really guilty for leaving her for a whole month, so she was making up for it on her return. I did talk to her on the phone most days, though.'

'So you didn't notice she'd changed in any way after her trip?'

'No. She was excited, obviously. What girl wouldn't be after marrying someone like Max? And Australia sounded amazing. I've always wanted to go, so I was asking her loads of questions about it. It sounded like she had a fabulous time.'

'Nothing odd happened?'

'No.' She ran some clippers along the nape of my neck. 'Do you need to know more about what Russell did?'

'No, I think we've got all we need about Russell.'

'Oh, OK.'

'Just one more thing, actually,' I asked casually. 'Is Alissa right- or left-handed?'

'Left-handed.'

And yet, caught unaware by the flower delivery, she'd signed with her right hand.

'You're sure?'

'Absolutely. She's the opposite of me.'

'Was she ambidextrous?'

'No.'

'Did she ever have a hand or arm injury in the past?'

'No. I broke my arm once, and I had to write with my left hand for a while at school. Alissa was really sweet about it, helping me write out my homework because my left-handed writing was almost illegible. I remember her trying to make me feel better about it one day during lessons by her attempting to write with her right hand to match me, but she gave up after a couple of goes. She said it was too difficult. No, Alissa's never broken anything. Why? Is it important? She's not ill, is she?'

I gave her a reassuring smile. 'Nothing to worry about. Like I said, just routine.'

THE OTHER ONE
Chapter 33

The good thing about grief is that most people don't know what to say to you. It's like you've got some contagious disease, and they want to give you a wide berth. They don't want to hang around people who are bawling their eyes out. Don't want to witness snot dribbling out their noses, or smell their unwashed bodies because they're too distraught to shower. Don't want to listen to the endless, 'Why did this happen? I can't believe it. What am I going to do?' All the wailing and carrying on and doom and gloom. Depressing shit. They don't want it to rub off on them. And they don't want to be reminded of their own mortality. That bad, bad things can happen so close to home. Or that they're actually useless, an inconsequential little dot in the universe.

Grief suited me perfectly. I couldn't be bothered to talk to concerned Vicky or bitchy Sasha. And I had the best excuse!

It would've looked a little too weird not to see 'Mum', though. So I went religiously every couple of days. The staff in the nursing home followed the wide berth etiquette perfectly, muttering hellos and condolences, not quite looking me in the eyes, and then leaving me alone in Mum's room, trying to talk to a dribbling vegetable.

Boring.

Luckily, she'd gone to sleep again, so I stared out of her window for a while, pondering what to do with all the money. Where should I go? America? Travel round the Far East? Bali? Thailand? Indonesia? Or the Caribbean? The Cayman Islands? Hawaii? The British Virgin Islands?

The world was a big place. Easy to get lost out there. I knew all about that.

Should I buy a house somewhere or rent? Maybe renting was better. I didn't want to get tied down. I should move around, experience lots of places. A place on a beach would be nice, though. Somewhere I could just step off my property and on to golden sand. I'd want a private beach. Not one with tourists and lowlifes. Somewhere I wouldn't be bothered by irritating people with questions.

I'd been given Alissa's laptop back by the police, so I'd use it later to research some destinations. I'd already read through Alissa's synopsis of her romance I'd found on there when I'd got back from Australia, but it was such utter crap that I couldn't bring myself to read the whole manuscript, and she wasn't going to show it to anyone until it was finished, so I didn't have to pretend I knew what it was about. I'd read better writing on the back of a cereal packet. How had she managed to get an agent interested?

I was itching to paint again, too. I smiled as I thought about picking up some art supplies on the way home. I had too many emotions scrabbling to get out, burrowed under my skin, trying to find their rightful way to the surface. Hmm, good idea.

I popped a dried date in my mouth and chewed thoughtfully. I'd brought them for Mummy dearest, storing them in a little Tupperware bowl for the staff to feed her with later. You couldn't say I wasn't a thoughtful, dutiful daughter.

There was a knock at the door and that policeman was there, peering through the glass panel. What was his name? Sergeant something?

Great. Now I've got both of them trying to get in my knickers.

What was the appropriate face? Confusion? Sadness? Resigned calmness? Before I had the chance to choose one, he walked in.

'Hi, how are you holding up?' he asked.

I sat forward, still trying to chew the remains of the date. I swallowed and gave him a half-smile. The resigned calmness one. I didn't want to overdo things. 'I guess I'm getting through each day,' I said softly. 'Putting one foot in front of the other.'

'I know how you feel. My wife died a year ago. It's not easy.'

'No.'

'But you've got your friends, people who care about you. At some point, you'll feel like talking again. Maybe you could even speak to a grief counsellor. That might help.'

I tucked my hair behind my ears. 'Maybe. I'll think about that, thanks. Um . . . what are you doing here?'

'I was just passing and thought I'd stop in on your mum. Like I said, I know it's hard when your spouse dies. I thought perhaps you weren't getting in to see her as much as you'd like, so I popped in for a visit with her. My dad was in a nursing home for a while and visits were the highlight of his day.' He smiled, his gaze staying on me for a little longer than necessary. But it wasn't desire I saw in his eyes, like with Wilmott. It was something else. Something dangerous.

I turned my head back to Mum. 'You're right. It is tough getting out of bed some days. The only thing keeping me going is knowing she still needs me, even though a lot of the time now she doesn't even realise I'm here.'

He sat down on the plastic chair on the opposite side of Mum's bed. The plastic made a farting sound, which made me want to laugh. I stifled it and watched him watching her.

'I used to read to my dad a lot,' he said. 'He liked that. Does your mum like being read to?'

'Yeah, she does.' I leaned over and held Mum's hand in mine, stroking it gently. 'It's very kind of you to come in and check on her, but there's no need, really.'

'I bet with you being a writer you must've read a lot of books. Didn't Stephen King say, "If you don't have time to read, you don't have the time, or the tools, to write"?'

'Well, yes, very true. He definitely knows his stuff.'

'I read your novel that was on your laptop we recovered from the house.' He smiled, but there was something chilly in his voice. 'I'm not really a romance man, give me a good thriller and I'm hooked, but it was very good.'

I swallowed and willed an embarrassed blush to appear. 'Thanks. I wish you hadn't, though. It's not a final draft yet. I'm still working on it, and there are parts of it that still need a lot of attention.'

'No, I suppose no artists like people seeing their work until it's at the finished stage. Sorry, but we had to go through everything thoroughly.'

I smiled, wondering where he was going with this. 'I understand.'

'It's pretty amazing to be able to write a book. It's one thing to come up with an idea, but to put it all down on paper like that in a cohesive story is a great accomplishment. You should be really proud of yourself.'

'Thanks.'

'I loved the heroine, Justine. Although she was compassionate and loyal, she had a quirky, feisty edge to her. And, of course, the hero, Cameron, was, I suppose, typical for a romance novel – strong, good-looking, rich – but I liked the conflict between them because he was a CEO of an oil and gas company and she was an environmentalist trying to stop them fracking. Where did you get the idea from?'

I recalled what Alissa had told me when I'd asked her the same question. 'It just came to me one day when I was watching National Geographic.'

'And Justine's bitchy friend with the hidden agenda added a new dimension and a few twists I didn't see coming, trying to sabotage their relationship. Was she based on anyone you know?'

Damn. I didn't know the answer. I improvised on the spot, making up something vague. 'Not really. I mean, there are plenty of bitchy people in the world to draw from.'

'How about that other guy, the secondary character, the one who worked with Justine . . . what was his name again?' He scrunched up his face, as if he was thinking.

Shit. I didn't have a clue what his name was. I hadn't read the whole thing. *Shit, shit, shit!*

DS Carter clicked his fingers together, trying to remember. He glanced at me expectantly, waiting for me to jump in and tell him.

I thought fast and said, 'I'm sorry, I'm really too upset to talk about my book right now.' I bit my lip and looked down, tearing up on demand. I wiped my eyes and thankfully he shut up about it.

'Of course. I'm sorry. I didn't mean to upset you. I understand completely.'

Mum snored then and jerked awake, blinking rapidly with watery eyes.

I sniffed and leaned in towards her. 'Hi, sleepyhead. How are you feeling?'

She slurred something that could've been 'water' or 'daughter'. The muscles on the right side of her face were droopy and didn't work properly. God, I hoped I never ended up like that. It was horrific to look at.

I poured her some water into a beaker with a straw and put the straw to her lips. She sucked slowly, water dribbling down and dripping off her chin. What a state. When she finished, I folded up some tissues and dabbed away the water. Then she turned to the policeman and muttered something that sounded like, 'Agh ooe we ooo.'

He smiled at Mum. 'I'm DS Carter, Mrs Stanhope. Just thought I'd pop in and see how you are.' There was an undercurrent of something in his voice. Something suspicious and questioning.

Mum lifted her left hand, the good side, and it hovered shakily in the air, as if she wanted to touch him.

He took it in his and patted it. 'You're lucky to have such an attentive daughter.' He smiled at her, then me.

The smile was broken by Mum's voice, talking garbled nonsense that no one could make out, dragging his gaze back to her.

He patted her hand again and stood up. 'Well, I'll be off now. You both take care of yourselves.'

I stood, too, just to be polite. 'Thanks for coming and checking up on us. It's very kind of you. I'm sure it goes above and beyond the call of duty, so it means a lot. It makes me feel safe.' I glanced down demurely as I said the last part, letting my lashes flutter on my cheeks, as if I was about to have another cry-fest.

'It's nothing,' he said. And then he was gone.

I walked to the window that overlooked the car park and watched Carter get into his car, knowing I'd have to do something about him.

THE DETECTIVE
Chapter 34

I'd double-checked with SOCO and no baseball cap had been found in the area where Russell fell over the fence. To find out more, I needed to speak to the man himself.

Stiles was being held on remand until his trial. I called the prison ahead of time to arrange a visit and went through the various security checks and obtained a 'Visitor' badge before I was asked to wait in a small, windowless room painted an institutional grey.

I leaned against the wall and waited. Ten minutes later, the door unlocked with a clattering sound of metal on metal. It swung open, revealing Stiles in front of a prison officer.

'Oh, great!' Russell stopped in his tracks, his face turning an angry shade of red, and looked back over his shoulder to the guard. 'Do I have to talk to him?'

The guard shrugged like he couldn't care less.

'Then I want to go back to my cell. They'll only try to pin something else on me.'

'I think you'll want to hear what I've got to say, Russell.' I stepped forward and took a seat on one of the chairs bolted to the floor, keeping my eyes on his.

'Shall I bring you tea and cucumber sandwiches while you're having a nice chat?' The guard laughed.

I glared at the guard. Russell glared at me, a muscle in his clenched jaw ticking away.

'It's in your best interests to talk to me,' I said.

Russell's lips narrowed, weighing me up. Maybe something in the tone of my voice made up his mind, and he walked towards me, slouching down in the chair on the other side of a metal desk.

'Lovely.' The guard pulled a sarcastic smile. 'I'll be outside. Bang when you need me.' He shut the door and relocked it.

Russell leaned back in the chair, one leg outstretched, one knee jigging away, an angry scowl scrunching up his face. 'What do you want, then? I shouldn't even be talking to you without my lawyer.'

I leaned my elbows on the desk and got straight to the point. 'Look, I don't think you killed Max Burbeck.'

He shot upright in his chair. 'Then what am I fucking doing in here?'

'I said *I* didn't think you killed him. My colleagues don't agree with me. They think you're guilty.'

'So . . .' His mouth flapped open and closed as he tried to think of the next thing to say.

I beat him to it. 'I think you were a convenient scapegoat.'

'For who?'

'Alissa Burbeck.'

He shook his head and blew out a breath. 'You think Alissa killed Max? No way, man. She'd never do anything like that. She hasn't got a bad bone in her body.'

Which is basically what everyone had told me about her all along. And why I was having trouble accounting for all the inconsistencies mounting up.

'I don't want an innocent person going to prison over this.'

'I'm already *in* prison!'

'You know what I mean. I need your help.'

'You need *my* help? That's a good one!'

'OK, let me put it this way. I need your help to help you.'

'Like I keep saying, I don't know anything. I didn't kill Max, and I don't know anything about who did.'

'When I interviewed you, you said you hadn't seen Alissa since the wedding reception.'

'Yeah, that's right.'

'So she never came to your house?'

'No.'

'Did you always leave your shed unlocked?'

'Yeah. I kept most of my work tools in my van. There was nothing expensive in the shed so I didn't see any point in locking it.'

Which would explain the ease of someone getting inside it and planting the knife. I pulled out the crime-scene photos from my briefcase on the desk and flicked through to one of the knife. 'Have you ever seen this before? Do you know where it came from?'

He leaned forward and studied it. 'No! I told that other inspector bloke the same, but he didn't believe me. I've never seen it before in my life.' He looked up at me, genuine shock and righteous outrage in his eyes. I'd interviewed hundreds of people over the years, and even though some people could lie their arses off really convincingly, the tell was in their eyes. There was always something there that they couldn't hide, no matter how good they thought they were. Russell's eyes told me the truth – that he hadn't killed Max. Alissa's, on the other hand, spoke of something distant and unemotional, even when filled with tears.

'Was your house broken into recently and you didn't report it?'

He frowned. 'No. And I've got good locks on the doors. I would've noticed if someone had tried to get in.'

'Did you ever notice anything out of place in the house? Anything that struck you as a bit strange?'

He glanced down at the metal desk, thinking. 'No.'

'Has anyone else got a spare key?'

'No.'

'I was trying to work out how Alissa managed to get one of your hairs planted on Max's body, and now I have a theory about it.'

'Alissa didn't do it. She wouldn't do something like that. She couldn't have.'

'Look, I can't help you unless you help me. Get your ideas about Alissa out of your head right now. Even the most unlikely person is capable of murder given the right circumstances. Do you use a hairbrush or comb?'

He pointed to his short hair. It had grown a bit since I'd last seen him, but it was still only about three inches long. 'Do I look like I need one? No, I don't own a brush or comb.'

'And before you turned up at the wedding reception, when was the last time you'd seen Alissa?'

He shuffled in his chair but didn't say anything.

'When was it?'

'A few months before. Before they went to Australia. I saw her in town and followed her.' He avoided my gaze, looking down at his knees.

'When you were stalking her.'

'I wasn't—' His head snapped up level with mine. 'Are you trying to set me up? Do the good cop, bad cop thing? Get information from me by pretending to help me?'

I placed my arms out wide in a gesture of sincerity. 'No. I just want the truth.'

He studied my face for a moment before his own relaxed slightly. 'I didn't talk to her or anything. I was just watching.'

'Tell me again what happened when you gatecrashed the reception at The Orchard.'

'I don't remember much about it. I was really pissed. I know I was sitting there by a tree, watching the house from the woods, drinking JD and smoking. And then I saw Alissa on her own and wanted to talk to her. Then, the next minute, I *was* talking to her. Then Max came over and . . .' He shrugged. 'He must've asked me to leave, I guess. I don't know. I was pretty wasted. I woke up the next morning in a bush in the woods near my house. I'd had some kind of blackout, I think, on the way back, and I couldn't even remember being at The Orchard at first.'

'What were you wearing?'

He stared off to his left. 'Um . . . a T-shirt and jeans. I had to chuck them away because when I woke up I'd been lying in a pile of bird shit. Why's that important?'

'Were you wearing a cap?'

He chewed on his lower lip, a blank look on his face, which was gradually replaced by something animated. 'That day . . . yeah. Yeah, I was. I had a baseball cap on when I went there. It was beige with a black Nike tick on it, but I don't remember having it on when I woke up. I haven't seen it since, actually, so I must've lost it somewhere between The Orchard and waking up in the woods.'

I thought back to the search of Russell's house. No baseball cap had been found there, either. 'You're certain about that?'

He nodded emphatically. 'Yes. I'd totally forgotten about it until you said, but that could explain where my hair came from, couldn't it?'

It certainly could. If Alissa had seen him lose it and came back later to retrieve it. I knew from my own experience of wearing them that they could easily snag a hair in them. A hair for someone to plant as irrefutable evidence that Russell was at the scene of the crime.

'Didn't your lawyer ask you where the hair could've come from?' I asked, angry with myself because I should've asked the right questions before. Angry with Sasha for withholding information.

'No. He doesn't seem like he knows what he's doing. I've only got legal aid. I can't afford anyone better. What do you think, though?' He placed his hands on the desk, palms down, and leaned forward eagerly.

'I think she set a trap and you walked right into it.'

~

This time when I knocked on DI Nash's door, she opened it. She wore crumpled tracksuit bottoms and an old rugby shirt of Spencer's that had probably been white at one time, but now looked as if it had been washed in with the darks and had a dirty blue tinge to it. The long auburn hair she usually wore straightened and glossy was tied up in a messy, knotted ponytail. She had dark smudges under eyes that were empty and lost.

I wanted to hug her, but she wasn't a touchy-feely kind of woman.

'Meals on wheels.' I held up a plastic bag.

She tried to smile, but her lips just formed into a tight line. 'Stop bringing me food. I can look after myself. You're acting like a bloody mother hen.'

She didn't mean it. She was trying to be brave. Takes one to know one.

I shrugged. 'Are you going to let me in or what? Because I'm starving.'

She groaned and threw her hands up in the air with a sigh. Then she walked back into the house, towards the kitchen. 'It's not chow mein again, is it?' She took a couple of plates from the cupboard and set them on the kitchen table, which was littered with piles of unopened post.

I glanced around the room, taking in the sink full of dirty dishes, the half-empty bottle of whisky on the worktop.

'Cleaner's day off, is it?' I grinned, trying to lighten the mood.

'Shut up.' She rolled her eyes at me. At least it was a reaction.

I pulled out cartons of curry and rice. Put one set on her plate and one on mine. I wasn't going to ask her how she was. That much was pretty obvious, and besides, I knew Ellie well. She'd only tell me things in her own good time.

She handed me some cutlery and sat down, staring at the food. I heaped half the rice and prawn dopiaza on to my plate and tucked in.

A couple of minutes later, she was still staring at it. 'I don't want to talk.'

'Well, stop talking, then, and eat.' I forked in another mouthful and said, 'I actually want to talk to you. I need some help.'

'You need my help?' She snorted. 'I'm not in the mood to help anyone right now.'

'It's about the Burbeck case. The one I told you about.'

She finally removed the lid from the rice and dolloped a couple of spoonfuls on to her plate. 'I'm not interested. I don't want to hear anything about work. It was the *job* that got Spencer killed.' She looked up, her eyes flashing with tears and anger.

I reached out and put a hand on her arm.

She shook me off and looked away, swallowing hard. 'Actually, I don't think I'm going to come back. I don't think I can do it any more.'

I paused, fork in mid-air. 'You have to do what you think is right. But I don't think you should make a decision right now. Give it some time. You're still grieving.'

'Shut up!'

'Two shut ups in five minutes – you're slacking, Ellie. Normally I get a lot more than that.'

'This is what I love about you. You're so sympathetic.'

I pulled an incredulous face. Ellie was hard as nails. Usually. She didn't do tea and sympathy. She did straightforward and objective. Softly-softly wasn't exactly my forte, either. I was happier interrogating criminals than dealing with emotions. But sometimes emotions deal with you, rather than the other way around.

I put my fork down. 'I'm sorry. He was my friend, too.'

'I know.' She blinked rapidly, holding back the tears, afraid to cry, to show weakness in front of me.

'Just let it out. I was a bloody mess after Denise, and you saw all that. You were the *only* one who saw it. I may not be Dr Phil, but I *do* care about you. I hate seeing you like this. I want to help,' I said, even though nothing I could ever do would help. I couldn't bring her husband back. I couldn't magically turn off her emotions. Couldn't suck the grief out of her.

She inhaled deeply. 'I know. Just ignore me.'

'Look, maybe thinking about something else will help for a while.'

'So you've got an ulterior motive for coming round all the time and hassling me, then?'

I looked her in the eye. 'No. I come round because I'm worried about you.'

She nodded briefly. 'Yeah, I know. Sorry.'

'Don't apologise to me.'

She swirled the rice around her plate with her spoon. 'What's the investigation about? Robbery, wasn't it?'

'Murder.' I gave her the details again, since she obviously hadn't been listening to me the first time I'd told her about it. I ended with, 'I think Alissa killed Max and framed Russell. Yes, I know Russell was stalking her, and we found one of his hairs on Max's body and the knife in Russell's shed, but I think the evidence was planted.'

'Tell me about the scene.'

I ran through Alissa's account of that night. 'Her DNA was obviously all over the house, and one of her hairs was found on Max's body, which can be explained away by her kissing him beforehand. I did a re-enactment of the scene, even climbing through the window and down to the garden.'

'What did that tell you?'

I sighed. 'That it's entirely possible it happened as she said. But I don't believe her. She's got a motive to the tune of ten million quid. She could also easily have taken a detour that night, run through the woods to Stiles' house at the edge of the village, which is in a straight line from hers, planted the evidence in his unlocked shed, and *then* gone on to her neighbour's house. It would be well within the parameters of Max's time of death.'

'Any other forensic evidence found at Stiles' place, apart from the knife?'

'No. Which is strange. If he took the time to get rid of the gloves, shoe covers, clothing, and balaclava, why not get rid of the knife, too? Especially when he knew we were taking an interest in him.'

'What about Stiles' hair found on Max's body? Where did it come from if it was planted?'

I grinned, telling her about what Stiles and Sasha had told me. 'And there's one set of recent fingerprints in the office and the rest of the house that are unaccounted for. They don't match any of their closest friends who were at the wedding reception.'

'An accomplice?'

'I thought so at first. I've been watching her to see if she'd lead me to anyone else, but she hasn't. Her phone and computer records were checked and she hadn't contacted anyone we haven't accounted for. She could've used a throwaway pay-as-you-go phone, I suppose, or an Internet café, but I don't think so.'

She chewed on the skin around her thumb, thinking. 'So how do you think she did it?'

'I think she stabbed him in the back of the neck while he was working, maybe crept up on him if he was listening to music, or maybe she put the music on afterwards to mask that he was comfortable enough in her presence to turn his back on her. Her prints were found on his laptop, but she told me she'd used it before. Then I think she planted the hair she'd got from Russell's cap on Max's body. When she removed the knife, because it went straight into the spinal cord and his blood pressure dropped rapidly, there was very little blood loss from the wound. It's possible she didn't get any fluids from him on to her. And even if she did, I think that's when she had her bath to wash away any evidence.'

'Did SOCO examine the plugholes?'

'Yes, they didn't find anything.'

'OK, so she had a bath *after* she'd killed him, then climbed out of the window and ran to Stiles' house to plant the knife before running to her neighbour's and making up the masked intruder.'

'That's my theory.'

'Naked? Because she apparently lost the towel as she was climbing through the window.'

'One of the reasons Wilmott thinks she's got to be innocent is because she ran away naked.'

She frowned. 'How does he work that one out?'

'He thinks if she'd planned it, she would've been wearing a bath robe instead.'

'If I'd killed him in those circumstances, it's exactly the kind of thing I'd have done to make it seem like I was innocent.'

'But apart from that, Wilmott sees her as a victim and completely disregarded her as a suspect from the beginning. I'm pretty sure he wants to bloody shag her.'

'He wants to shag anything with a pulse.' She scoffed. 'What was DS Greene thinking, appointing him ADI? Wilmott doesn't know his arse from . . . well, from his mouth, actually. They both spout a load of shit! You should've had that job.'

'Thanks.' I picked up my fork and drew a circle in the rice left on my plate.

'So who do the other prints belong to?'

'Well, this is going to sound really strange, but I don't think Alissa is who we think she is.'

'What do you mean?'

'I don't think she's actually Alissa Burbeck.'

She snorted. 'What are you talking about? She's an imposter? Don't you think someone would've mentioned that by now? Her friends? Even if one of her friends was in on it, which is a ridiculous idea, people from her mum's nursing home know who she is.' She shook her head. 'And you think *I'm* losing it?'

I leaned my elbows on the table. 'When you put it like that, it sounds crazy, but hear me out. When I did a videoed interview with her, she hesitated about which hand to use to sign the statement. I wasn't sure that's what it was at first – thought it was her being nervous or traumatised – but now I am. She made a move as if to sign it with her right hand, but then seemed to check herself and signed it with her left. Then later, I was doing some observations on her house, and she signed for some flowers with her right hand.'

'So what? Maybe she sprained her wrist climbing out of the window, or maybe she's ambidextrous.'

'No, she was thoroughly checked out at the hospital. She had a couple of scratches on her stomach from climbing out of the window, a bruised heel from jumping to the ground, along with abrasions and cuts on her feet from running through the woods, but that was it. And her best friend Vicky says Alissa is definitely left-handed, not right, and has never had an arm or hand injury.'

She stared at me, a big *So?* written across her face.

'You're right-handed. Have you *ever* written with your left hand in your life? Ever signed your name with your left hand?'

'No.'

'And how many things have you signed over the years?'

'I don't know, thousands.'

'And it's instinctual, isn't it? You don't hesitate, like she did in the interview, before correcting yourself. When she signed for that flower delivery, she didn't think she was being watched, she wasn't under pressure, it was instinctual to do it with her right hand.'

'That doesn't prove anything.'

'No, but you have to admit, it's a strange inconsistency.'

'Why don't you just get her signature analysed? Compare the one you witnessed when you took her police statement with another document?'

'I thought of that, but we don't have any other documents with her signature on to compare it to. I can't go to her bank and get a copy without proper authorisation, which Wilmott isn't going to sign off on, is he? The case is supposed to be closed. But there are more inconsistencies with her.' I told Ellie about the rose bush named after Alissa that she'd also forgotten.

'OK, that is strange, but maybe the gardener is confused about it. Or maybe Alissa was distracted, thinking about something else at the time, or just forgot.'

'No, I don't think so. According to Vicky, who seems to know everything about her friend, Alissa didn't have any kind of health problems that would make her forget things. Alissa has also been allergic to kiwi fruit since she was five, but suddenly she isn't any more.' I told her what Sasha had told me.

Ellie sat back, raising her eyebrows. 'That's really interesting.' The sarcasm oozed from her voice, but at least it was better than sadness. 'Some people say they're allergic to something when they're not, they're actually intolerant to things. And people can grow out of intolerances or allergies anyway.'

'It was definitely an allergy, not an intolerance. And from what I've read, it's unlikely the allergy disappeared.'

'Is that all you've got to support your bizarre theory?' She stood up, grabbed the whisky bottle and a couple of tumblers, and poured us both a shot. She sat down, tucking her feet up on the chair, cradling her arms around her knees. 'It's a big stretch.'

'There's something else, too. I went to visit her mum at the nursing home, just to confirm whether Mrs Stanhope was in any fit state to give me any information about her daughter, but it turns out she can't speak properly. She's had a couple of strokes. But when I got there, Alissa was there, too, and I asked her some questions about her novel. The document was on her laptop when it was seized.' I sat back with a smile on my face. 'So I started asking her questions about it, trying to catch her out. And she couldn't remember the name of one of the secondary characters in it.'

'When was the document last looked at?'

'It was last saved the day before they went to Australia. It could've been looked at since then. But it's not like she wrote it a couple of years ago and forgot some of the details. This woman, who's supposed to be Alissa Burbeck, doesn't even know her character's name and he has a big part in her novel!'

She took a long sip of whisky. 'OK, let me humour you, because I know what you're like. And, yes, I do find it very weird that she doesn't seem to know who her characters are. But first of all, you've got nothing you can *prove*.'

'I know that. That's why I'm talking to you about it.'

'Like you said, you're never going to get a warrant to seize anything else without Wilmott's approval, and he won't go along with that because he always thinks he's right. Why not go to DS Greene with this, though?'

'Because he's threatened me with suspension once over the Mackenzie case to stop me digging further, and I'm still fucking angry about that. How do I know I can trust him with this? And anyway, Wilmott will tell him a load of bollocks about how I'm just trying to undermine him and make him look bad. Not that he needs any help with that. And you're right, I've got nothing concrete yet. They'll just say I'm losing the plot because I'm—' I stopped abruptly.

'You're what?'

I picked up the whisky and topped up my glass. Downed half of it, savouring the burn in my throat.

She reached out and touched my hand. 'Because you're depressed?'

I looked up sharply at her. Looked away. I thought I'd been doing a good job of hiding it. Thought pretending to be OK was easier than actually being OK. But obviously I wasn't that good an actor. Not in Alissa's league, anyway.

'I know you are. Don't you think I haven't noticed it over the last year? Maybe it's my fault, not pushing you to see someone, talk to someone properly, the force psychologist. But I know you. I knew you'd never do that, so I was hoping you'd work through it in your own time. And now I know exactly how you feel.' Her voice sounded small, faraway.

I had thought about talking to someone professional about how overwhelmed I'd been. How nothing seemed to be getting better. But I'd bottled it. I didn't want someone telling me how I *should* feel.

'I don't know what to do with myself, either,' she carried on. 'I can't accept Spencer's really gone. I can't believe he's never going to walk through that door again. And I don't know how to live without him.' She blinked rapidly, trying to hide the tears that were forming.

I squeezed her hand and then let it go. 'Look at us. We're a right bloody pair.'

She sniffed, wiped her nose with the back of her hand and sat up taller, as if trying to compose herself again. 'But we're still better than Wilmott, even if we're depressed to shit!' She swigged back some more whisky. 'If Alissa's not who she says she is, then who exactly do you *think* she is? How could she get away with it without someone noticing?'

'Because she's someone who looks identical.'

'A sister?'

'An identical twin.'

'But no one else has mentioned a twin, have they? Her friends? Her mum's carers? Max's colleagues and friends?'

'No. Alissa's supposed to be an only child. But what if she was adopted? What if there's another twin out there pretending to be her?'

I pulled out a copy of the birth certificate belonging to Alissa Burbeck, née Stanhope, from my pocket and handed it over. 'There are two kinds of birth certificate. One is a certified copy, and one is a certificate of live birth. Alissa's is just the certified one and was probably issued after an adoption order took place to show the new adoptive parents' details only. It would succeed the original live birth certificate because that one would've had the birth parents' names on it instead. I've got an appointment with an adoption social worker tomorrow to see if I can find anything out.'

She took another swig of whisky and cradled the glass to her chest. '*If* you're right – and I'm not totally convinced yet – but if you are, and this woman isn't Alissa Burbeck, then what has she done with the *real* Alissa Burbeck?'

THE OTHER ONE
Chapter 35

Ever since I'd seen that detective sergeant at the nursing home, I'd had a bad feeling about him. What was he really doing there? Checking up on me? Trying to see if Mum could tell him anything? Had I slipped up somehow? I'd been disciplined. Focused. So it couldn't have been me. Not possible. But . . .

But he suspected something; I was sure of it. And it had to be something to do with Alissa's novel. Why hadn't I read all of it when I'd had the chance? What an idiot! But even if I'd got a few details wrong, I'd explain it away by saying I was upset, distraught, confused, couldn't think straight at the moment.

Still, I'd been keeping my eye out for him whenever I left the house in case he was following me. Not that I'd been out much. I'd been painting again, which felt *amazing*! It was therapeutic to let it all out as I counted the days. I hadn't seen DS Carter anywhere else, hadn't spotted him lurking outside the house, but it didn't matter. I had a plan worked out. All it needed was a little seed planted with Wilmott, because I couldn't risk Carter spoiling things. Russell's trial was still months away, and his guilt spoke for itself. The hair, the knife, the evidence of his obsession with Alissa – oops, I mean me, LOL! It couldn't be disputed. Even if DS Carter had doubts about me, he couldn't prove a thing. Still, I had to be vigilant. I didn't want him to find out who I really was before I got my money and could disappear somewhere else. Wilmott was wrapped around my finger, the stupid, blind, ignorant idiot. All I needed was a little teary episode and it would be bye-bye DS Carter. I didn't come this far for it all to fall apart.

I called Wilmott, and he was only too happy to drop everything straight away to pay me a visit. I put the finishing touches to my mask, pinching at the skin around my eyes to make it red and swollen, letting the tears fall. Crying was easy. All I had to do was think about one of the murdered cows from the farm and out came the floods.

I looked at myself in the mirror, prepared just the right scared expression, and opened the door when Wilmott arrived.

He held a bouquet of tulips in his hand and was about to offer them to me, but stopped when he saw my face.

'Has something happened?' he asked. 'It sounded quite urgent on the phone.'

'I think someone's been following me.' I blinked rapidly, letting the tears flow with ease. 'I'm . . . I'm really frightened.'

Wilmott glanced up and down the street before saying, 'Come on, let's get you inside and we can talk.' He placed a hand on the small of my back, guiding me into the lounge, sitting down next to me. Our thighs were touching as he put his arm around me, and I rested my head on his shoulder.

'I'm . . . I . . . I keep seeing this strange car following me, and I'm worried that . . .' I trailed off for a hiccuping sob. 'What if Russell's got one of his friends to start following me? To scare me into not talking at the trial? I mean, he must be crazy to have murdered Max. What else could he do to me?'

Wilmott pulled me tighter towards him. His aftershave was overpowering and fresh, as if he'd splashed half a bottle on himself in the car on the way over. I fought the urge to push him away and breathed through my mouth. He probably thought I wouldn't notice his thigh pressing harder against mine.

'Russell Stiles is a very calculating and nasty individual. I wouldn't put anything past him. Did you get a registration number for this car?'

'Yes.' I nodded vigorously. I'd taken a note of it when Carter had been at Mum's nursing home.

'Where have you seen it?'

'Um . . . when I've been out walking. I sometimes go to the park to clear my head. It's hard being cooped up here all the time on my own.'

'Well, that's why I keep checking up on you. I know it's a terrible time for you, and I'm here to support you every step of the way.'

'I know, and I want to thank you for being so concerned. You've been so kind and helpful.'

He stroked my back. He actually stroked it, the pervert.

'I'm really worried that someone is after me.' I sniffed loudly and pulled away, clutching his arm tightly, eyes wide with fear. 'What if Russell's trying to get one of his friends to *kill* me to keep me quiet?' I gasped, shivering.

He took my hand in his. 'You can count on me. Try not to worry. Let me have the registration number of this car and I'll check it out.'

I nodded and walked towards my handbag in the corner of the room, retrieving a scrap of paper. 'It was a Ford Mondeo.' I handed it to him.

'OK, I'll do a check on it. Can I get you something to drink? You're very pale. Do you have any brandy or something like that?'

I gave a shivery little nod and pointed towards the kitchen. 'In the cupboard next to the oven. Thanks. I think I need one. I've been really scared.'

He came back with a tumbler containing a couple of inches of brandy and pressed it into my hands, his own hands enclosing around mine. 'I'm glad you called me. It was the right thing to do. You should've done it sooner. I don't want you to ever be frightened again.'

I brought the glass to my lips with shaky hands. I thought about saying something else, but didn't want to go overboard with it.

Wilmott dialled a number on his mobile as he paced up and down. He spoke into it, asking for details of the car, then listened for a while and stopped pacing, a frown etching into his forehead. 'What?'

More listening.

'You're sure?' A pause, and then, 'Right, thanks.' He put his phone back in his suit jacket pocket and sat next to me. He took my hand in his again, his sweaty palm against my cold one. Yuck. I cringed inwardly. 'It's nothing to do with Russell Stiles.'

'How can you be sure?' I widened my eyes.

'I thought the plate sounded a little familiar. It's actually a police vehicle.'

I pressed a hand to my chest, breathing deeply, drawing a subtle amount of attention to my cleavage, which I noted Wilmott's eyes strayed to. Men so easily give themselves away. I'd read something once that said men don't have the same peripheral vision as women. We can do a full up and down sweep of someone without moving our eyes, but men can't. They have to physically move their eyes up and down, which, of course, gives them away every time. He'd be talking at my tits again in a minute, like usual.

'Oh, thank God for that!' I said, blowing out a breath of relief. 'But . . . why has this policeman been following me?'

Wilmott steered his gaze away from my tits (*yep, caught ya!*) with a puzzled look in his eye. 'Are you sure he *was* following you?'

'Absolutely. I've spotted him several times. Sometimes I've seen the car parked outside, too. Just sitting down the road, as if there's somebody watching me.' I hadn't, but, hey, might as well throw that in there as well. 'And Detective Sergeant Carter came to Mum's nursing home when I was there, too.'

'He what?' Wilmott barked. 'What for?'

'Um . . . well, he said he was just passing and wanted to pop in on Mum because he thought I may not be getting in to see her as much as I'd wanted to after what had happened. But I think . . . I think it was an excuse, and he'd been following me. He started asking me questions, badgering me. I was really upset. He treated me like I was a criminal.' I bent over at the waist and sobbed, my shoulders shaking up and down. 'He made me feel awful.'

Wilmott pursed his lips tightly and rubbed my back gently. 'Right, well, trust me, it won't be happening again. I'm so sorry you've been upset by all this. I'll be having serious words with DS Carter, don't you worry.'

I clutched his hand, twisting on the sofa so my knees touched his, looking into his eyes. 'Thank you so much. I don't know what I'd have done without you after . . . after Max.'

He licked his lips, puffed his chest out, and smiled with pride. He opened his mouth to say something more, probably wanting to suggest he moved in with me to protect me.

Yes, *so* fucking easy to read.

THE DETECTIVE
Chapter 36

'I want you back in the nick right now!' Wilmott shouted down the phone at me, dispensing with any preliminaries.

I pulled my mobile away from my ear to save my eardrums. 'What's up? I'm still making enquiries into the robbery.'

'Just get back here, now. I want to talk to you!'

'Oooookaaaay,' I drawled. 'I'll be—' But I didn't get to finish, as Wilmott hung up on me.

I dropped the phone in the centre cubby and started driving. Someone had his designer underwear in a twist.

As I parked in the police station car park, I saw Ronnie hurrying out the door. 'What's up with Wilmott?' I asked. 'He sounded like he was going to have a heart attack when he summoned me back.'

'I don't know, Sarge. But he looks like it, too. I'm just off to take some more statements.' He smiled proudly.

I left Ronnie to it and ambled up the stairs. There could only be one reason I'd been summoned. He knew I was still looking into Max's murder.

I walked into the CID office and clocked Wilmott in his office in the corner of the room, reading a file.

Becky glanced up from her desk as she gathered some papers together and stuffed them in her bag. She pulled a *you're-in-trouble* face.

I raised my eyebrows casually at her in response, giving my *do-I-care?* face.

I knocked on Wilmott's door and walked in.

'What the fuck do you think you're doing?' he barked out as he stood up.

'Um . . . standing in your office?'

He glared at me. Wrong answer?

I pointed at the chair. 'Can I sit down first?'

Wilmott blew out a frustrated breath. Was that a yes or no?

'What the fuck am I doing about what, guv?'

'I've had reports that you've been harassing Alissa Burbeck.'

I did my best incredulous look. 'Harassing? Harassing *how*, exactly?'

'She called me up earlier in a very distraught state, wanting to see me.'

I fought the urge to say, *I bet.*

'When I got there, do you know what she said?'

I thought this was probably a rhetorical question, so I didn't waste my breath with a reply.

'She told me she'd spotted a vehicle following her. Then lo and behold, when I do a PNC check, it's one of ours. And then I find out you've been using it! You've also followed her to her mother's care home, asking her inappropriate questions, badgering her. You've been sitting outside her house and watching her. She was in a devastated panic, worrying that it was one of Russell's friends trying to frighten her, or worse! Now, what I want to know is why.'

I could just imagine the scene. Alissa crying on to his shoulder in a fake fit of panic. Oh, she was good. Very good. A first-class actress.

'Why are you still involved in this case when I've expressly told you on several occasions that she's never been considered a suspect? And what were you doing at the care home when the case is over?' His face turned an angry shade that matched his salmon-coloured shirt.

'I was just following up on a few loose ends.'

'There are no loose ends! How many times do I have to tell you? Stiles killed Max Burbeck and that's the end of it. You seem to have become obsessed with her!'

I opened my mouth to say, *Actually, I could say the same about you.* But then I'd have to admit I had been following her to notice him turning up there all the time.

'You're not a team player, and you seem to be incapable of following any kind of order,' he carried on.

Oh, great. Any minute now, he's going to come out with the 'There is no I in team' rubbish.

'I've also just received some complaints from Leo and Sasha Smithers regarding your conduct when questioning them about this case, and about your attitude. Your work is also late and shoddy. You should've finished those robbery statements ages ago and we're no further forward on the investigation! You obviously resent my promotion to acting DI, and even though DI Nash has carried you and puts up with your sloppy and outdated way of working, I will not. The bottom line is, you don't seem to be up to the job any more, and it's a bloody liability having someone like that on my team. You've had a lot of slack in the last year because of Denise, but you've lost the plot and—'

I'd tried to tune out his rant until he mentioned Denise's name. That's when something exploded inside and all the anger, the pain, the emptiness of losing her came back again. Her name on his tongue sounded vile, something ugly, and I wasn't having that.

Before I knew what I was doing, I'd launched towards him, pinning him against the wall, my fists clenching the collar of his shirt. Wilmott was taller than me, but what I lacked in height, I made up for in width. 'You've got no idea what you're talking about! And how dare you blame anything on Denise! She was worth a hundred of you, you arrogant, jumped-up prick! I watched my wife *die*! She wasted away right in front of me, in agony. It would've been our wedding anniversary tomorrow, you bastard! And you have no idea how that feels, because the only person you care about is yourself!'

Wilmott's eyes widened with surprise as he squirmed against the wall, trying to get away. 'That's assault, that is! You're assaulting a police officer!'

'Call yourself a police officer? Don't make me bloody laugh!' I gripped his shirt tighter with my left hand, my right swinging back for the punch that would feel so good when it connected with his face.

'Go on, give me one more excuse to get you slung out for good!' Wilmott sneered in my face.

'*Carter!* Let him go! *Right now!*' Detective Superintendent Greene shouted out behind me.

I whipped my head around. Greene stood in the doorway. His face wasn't quite as red as Wilmott's, but it was heading in that direction.

'*Now!*' Greene commanded.

I let Wilmott go, pushing him against the wall as I did so in a final act of defiance. One of Wilmott's shirt buttons slipped through my hands and bounced to the floor.

'Wait for me in my office,' Greene snapped at me.

My jaw tightened as I walked through the now empty CID office. Clenching my fists, I headed up the corridor to Greene's office and paced the floor, fuming, taking deep breaths as I tried to calm down.

A few minutes later, DS Greene walked in. He closed the door, rounded his desk, and sat down. 'Have a seat.' He nodded towards the chair opposite him.

'I'd rather stand, sir.' I had too much adrenaline flowing through me to sit still like a good boy.

'Sit!'

I stared at the chair. Clenched my fists again. Then did as I was told.

'I can't believe what I just witnessed. What the *hell* was that all about?' He gave a furious shake of his head.

'He provoked me.'

'How?'

'He was disrespecting Denise.'

He sighed. 'Obviously, you have my deepest sympathies about Denise. Her death has affected you very badly in the last year, and I fear that the stress and grief is also affecting your rational—'

'Of course it's affected me!'

'And you're not thinking clearly.'

'With all due respect, sir, I'm thinking perfectly clearly.'

'I disagree. This is impinging on your judgement now.'

'My judgement is fine. It's everyone else's that's the problem.'

'Do you know how paranoid that sounds?' He gave me an exasperated look. He pursed his lips and leaned back in his chair. 'DI Wilmott has told me that you're doing everything you can to undermine his promotion. And that you've become obsessed with the Burbeck case. By Alissa Burbeck in particular.'

'I'm sure he has. Actually, he's the one who can't seem to keep away from her. In work time, too. Maybe you should ask him about that.'

He ignored my tone and said, 'He was also concerned that it was affecting your other work, and that your actions seem to be becoming increasingly inappropriate and erratic. And I have to say I agree after what's just happened. Look, you *can't* go around assaulting other officers, flying off the handle and acting like a loose cannon, questioning things that are above your rank, trying to sabotage DI Wilmott's authority, and looking for things that don't exist! I know working so closely with people at times means things can be frustrating, but that kind of behaviour is completely inexcusable.' He pinched the bridge of his nose, giving me his *this-will-hurt-me-more-than-you* look. 'I think you need some help, Warren. Professional help to deal with the grief and depression that is clearly—'

'The only help I need is being allowed to actually do my job and ask the right questions.' I blew out a sharp, frustrated breath. 'First the Mackenzie case, and now this. What's the point of policing if you're not allowed to actually police?'

'We've been over the Lord Mackenzie case before,' he snapped, picking up a biro from his desk and fiddling with it. 'You know the way things work. It was a direct order from the top to stop the investigation. My hands were tied. And besides, there was no evidence that he was involved in the theft.'

'And fraud. And if I'd had time, I could've found the evidence that connected him to it.'

Greene threw the biro on to his desk. He probably wanted to throw it at me. 'This isn't a discussion; it's an order. Your standard of conduct, job performance, and mental well-being have been called into serious question. I have no choice but to suspend you from duty for your own welfare at this time, pending an investigation into your conduct. You will receive a letter in due course calling you for a meeting to discuss this further. You will continue to receive full pay. But in the meantime, I would strongly recommend you contact occupational health and make an appointment to see the force psychologist, because I'm sure that's what will be recommended anyway. Now go home, calm down, and try to get yourself together until then.'

'What?' I stared at him. 'You can't do that.'

'I'm doing it for your own good.' He pointed a finger at me. 'I can't have detectives with their own agendas on my team. It puts too much pressure on the other officers at a time when we're desperately short-staffed. And it could be dangerous, too – a serious health and safety risk for everyone. So take my advice and—'

I didn't want to hear the rest of the bollocking. I'd heard enough. I stood up and walked to the door, cutting him off mid-rant.

'I'll need your warrant card before you leave!' His voice drilled into me from behind.

I strode back to the desk, pulled it out of my pocket, and slammed it on top of a pile of files. Then I stormed into the men's room and splashed cold water on my face, catching my reflection in the mirror – the bloodshot eyes, the untucked shirt, the skew-whiff tie. Was I losing it? Looking for things that didn't even exist? I didn't know any more. So what if I was about to flush my career down the toilet? I wasn't even sure I cared.

I ran a hand through my hair. Adjusted my tie and tucked in my shirt. I left the nick, to give the semblance that I'd taken on board what Detective Superintendent Greene had said, and then completely disregarded him. Protocol was the last thing on my mind. I knew Alissa was the real killer. Now all I had to do was prove it.

THE DETECTIVE
Chapter 37

The adoption social worker looked young enough to be my daughter. If I'd ever had one. Denise and I had tried for years, but it wasn't meant to be. There was a lot that was never meant to be. I thought things were supposed to get easier with time, but they seemed to be getting worse. Maybe it was Spencer's death that had brought all the emotions back. I tried to blank out the thoughts of Denise and concentrate on Tina Bell's red hair as she perused the file in front of her.

She glanced up nervously and smiled. 'I'm afraid I can't let you take copies. I'll, um . . . need a warrant from you for that. Or a judge's order.'

'That's OK. I just need the information at this stage. We're making preliminary enquiries on a possible murder suspect.'

'Of course.' She nodded emphatically, trying to appear knowledgeable and professional when it was obvious she'd only been doing the job a short while. Still, that helped me. If she'd been a more experienced social worker, she may not have given me anything without a warrant or a look at my warrant card, which was probably currently locked in Greene's office drawer.

'There was an adoption order for Alissa on the twenty-fourth of April, 1992. She was adopted by . . .' She read a few more lines. 'Rita and Bernard Stanhope. I have details of the birth mother, although it's noted that she expressed a wish for her information not to be revealed should anyone try to locate her in the future. That's not unusual.'

'That's OK. It's not her I'm interested in at the moment. Is there any mention of another sibling?'

'Um . . .' She bent over, perusing more of the document in front of her, then tapped the page. 'Yes.'

I leaned forward expectantly.

'The birth mother had twins. Alissa, who was adopted by the Stanhopes.' She looked up and smiled awkwardly. 'Sorry, I just said that, didn't I?'

I smiled politely, willing her to get on with it.

'And then there was Samantha, who was adopted by John and Elizabeth Folds on the thirteenth of March, 1992.'

My heart rate kicked up a notch. 'Do you have the Folds' details?'

'Um . . .' She read through more papers, running her finger down the pages. She flipped through another couple of documents and glanced up again, squinting apologetically. 'Sorry.'

'It's OK, take your time. It's good to be thorough.'

'Ah! Yes, I've got something here. The address at the time of the adoption order was Dentonbrook Farm.'

I wrote that down in my notebook. 'Can you tell me anything else about the Folds?'

She perused a few more pages. 'John was thirty and Elizabeth was twenty-five when the adoption took place. John was a farmer. Elizabeth was listed as a housewife. It would appear that they couldn't have children of their own and desperately wanted to adopt a baby. They obviously passed all of our screening methods at the time. There's not much more I can tell you, really. A social worker visited them several times at the farm before the adoption, and also a couple of times after the order was granted. Everything appeared to be in order and our involvement ceased twenty-three and a half years ago.'

'Why weren't Alissa and Samantha adopted by the same family?'

'We have to work with what we've got at the time. Not many prospective adoptive parents are looking for twins, especially with their first child. It can be a very demanding and stressful situation caring for two babies right off the bat. So it's not uncommon for twins that young to be separated.'

I stood to leave. 'Great, thanks, you've been a big help.'

She blushed.

~

It was a long shot. The address for John and Elizabeth Folds was twenty-three years old. How many people stayed in the same house all their lives these days? I'd checked the electoral roll, directory enquiries, and other databases, but there were no listings for them.

Dentonbrook Farm was out in the sticks. Their nearest neighbour that I passed on the way up a single-lane track was half a mile down the road. A sign on the metal gates creaking in the breeze announced that this was the right place.

I drove over the cattle grid and up a concrete drive. When I got out, I was hit with the smell of manure, the sounds of frantic mooing filling the air.

I took a path forking away from a cluster of barns towards a whitewashed farmhouse at the side of the property. I knocked on the door and waited. Either no one was in or they weren't answering.

Retracing my steps, I headed back towards the barns. On the way, I saw a few stalls with cows in, but the rest were empty. It looked a bleak and desolate place.

'Hello?' I called out. 'Anyone around?'

A man in his mid-fifties appeared from one of the barns, dressed in wellies and a navy boiler suit. 'Alright, mate? Can I help you?'

'I'm looking for John and Elizabeth Folds.'

'Nah, you've got the wrong place. I own this farm.'

'They used to live here about twenty-three years ago.'

He scratched his head. 'Well, I've been here fifteen years. Bought it off a bloke called Davidson, not Folds.'

'I'm DS Carter, and I'm trying to trace the Folds. Do you have a forwarding address for this Mr Davidson anywhere?'

'Afraid not.'

Bugger. 'Did you buy the farm through an estate agent?'

'Yeah, Barnworth & Co. were selling it for the Davidsons. They specialise in farms and smallholdings.'

'OK, thanks.'

I trudged back down the path and got in my car, where the air was cleaner. I googled Barnworth & Co. on my phone, got the number, and gave them a call. Unfortunately, they hadn't acted as agents for the Folds, but pointed me in the direction of the lawyer the Davidsons had used during their sale of the farm to see if they had any information regarding prior owners.

So an hour later I was sat in the office of Ian Dunn, waiting for him to finish trawling through his computer records.

'I'm afraid there was no forwarding address given by Mr and Mrs Folds at the time the Davidsons bought it from them,' he said. 'They were emigrating to Australia, so they didn't have one to give the lawyer who acted for them. Sorry I can't be more help.'

I grinned. 'Thanks, you've actually been a big help.' As I walked out, I phoned Becky. 'Is Wilmott still in the office?'

'No, he left about ten minutes ago. Said he had a dentist appointment.'

'Getting his teeth whitened again, is he?'

She laughed. 'You're not his favourite person right now.'

'I'm deeply upset by that.'

'Yeah, right. I can't believe you've been suspended! Someone said you'd hit him?'

The station was already rife with Chinese whispers. 'Unfortunately not. I just pinned him up against the wall. Maybe I should've hit him. It would've felt bloody good. Look, I'm obviously not supposed to be in the nick at the moment, so can you do me a huge favour?'

'What?'

'Can you get me something from the Burbeck file?'

She paused for a moment. 'What do you want?'

'I need copies of their bank statements.'

Another pause. 'Are you sure about this? I don't want you getting in any more trouble.'

'Look, I know Alissa Burbeck killed Max. I just need to prove it. And I'm not backing down again like I did with the Mackenzie case. Will you do it or not?'

'Only if you buy me lunch.'

'That's blackmail.'

'Yeah, but you can't arrest me now, can you?'

'Ouch, that hurt. When and where?'

'Pizza Express in an hour.'

~

Two and a half hours later, I was on DI Nash's doorstep with a bag of cold beers and a hot pizza that I'd got to take away for her.

She looked a hell of a lot better. Her cheeks had colour in them for the first time in a long while, and her hair was glossy and sleek, as if she'd finally washed it.

'So,' she took the tops off two beers and handed me one, 'what's going on with the Burbeck case?'

I took a long swig. 'Apparently, Alissa knows I've been keeping my eye on her. She told her little lapdog Wilmott, who told me to leave it alone. I kind of lost it when he brought up Denise and, well, the short version is DS Greene suspended me.'

Her mouth fell open. 'He *suspended* you?'

I filled her in on exactly what had happened.

She shook her head, eyes narrowed. 'This is really about Lord Mackenzie, isn't it? They want to keep you in line. If I'd been there working on that case, I wouldn't have bowed down to pressure like Wilmott would. He'll do exactly what they tell him to.'

'Then you probably would've been suspended, too.'

'It's all wrong. We risk our lives every day doing this job. Spencer died, and what for? So influential people like Mackenzie can be protected? We can't even bring him to justice because of who he knows?'

'Well, I did bow down then because I thought I had too much to lose. It was the job that kept me getting out of bed every day, putting one foot in front of the other. I thought if I lost that, there would be nothing worth living for. But I won't back down this time. This isn't the police force I joined, and I don't want to be part of that. You've got me thinking about giving it up, too. After this case is over, I'll go quietly. Retire. Maybe go away somewhere. Spain or something, I don't know. I could sell my house, get a nice apartment and have some money in the bank. It's not like anyone's going to miss me, is it?' I rubbed my hands across my face.

'I'd miss you. And I definitely can't see you in the Costa del Retirement, taking up golf and lying on a beach. You'd go mental within a week!'

She was right. But it was tempting to just pack up and go somewhere else. Even as the thought formed, I realised all I'd really be doing was trying to outrun myself. How far would I have to go to do that? And if I did retire, it would mean even more time on my hands to think about what was missing. Catching criminals was far easier than confronting reality.

She gave me a concerned frown. 'Don't let my situation influence you.'

'It's not you. It's everything. I've had enough.'

'You're worrying me now. You're not going to do anything stupid, are you?'

'Define stupid.'

'You know what I mean.'

I shrugged off the question. 'Apparently, I'm not a team player,' I said, just for something to say to change the focus of the conversation.

'Depends whose team you're on.' Ellie grabbed a slice of pizza and shovelled it into her mouth, chewing vigorously.

'Hungry?' I eyed her.

'Actually, it's the first time I've felt hungry since . . .' She trailed off. No words were needed. 'So what else did you find out about "Alissa Burbeck" before you were suspended?' She made quote marks in the air with her fingers when she said Alissa's name.

'I thought you didn't want anything to do with the job, either?'

'What else are we going to talk about? Death? Dying? Being depressed?'

I told her about the adoption of Alissa and Samantha, and how the Folds had apparently emigrated to Australia. 'Which is where Max and Alissa just happened to have come back from.' I raised an eyebrow.

Ellie finished chewing, swigged some beer, and regarded me thoughtfully. 'So, Alissa is really Samantha?'

'Yeah.'

She whistled.

'None of Max's or Alissa's friends have mentioned a twin, so I don't think anyone else knew about her, which also makes me think they've only just recently found out about each other. And it makes sense that Alissa met her twin in Australia, because if they'd met here, someone would've noticed them together, and they must've spent a lot of time in each other's company for Samantha to thoroughly get to know Alissa and step into her shoes so easily that she could pass herself off as the real deal.'

'OK, so if Samantha came back to England with Max, pretending to be Alissa, how come no one has noticed any significant changes in her? I know they're identical, and since you told me about this case I've been researching identicals. It would be easy to pass for the other visually, but what about voices? They're not always the same. Surely Samantha would have a different accent if she was brought up in Australia, too. And there can be other things, like birthmarks – one could have one, one might not.'

'What do actors do when they're preparing for a role?' I took a swig of beer. 'They mimic voices and mannerisms, don't they? Samantha could be very adept at that.'

'How did she fool Max, though? Their relationship would've been far more intimate than those she had with her friends. He must've noticed something different about her, surely.'

'Maybe he didn't know about Samantha? Maybe Alissa met her and kept it a secret for some reason so there was no reason to suspect an imposter. Or maybe Samantha and Alissa spent enough time with each other for Samantha to copy the way she walked and spoke and dressed.' I finished my beer and opened another. 'People see what they want to, don't they? If their eyes were telling them it's Alissa in front of them, they could put any little discrepancies down to her wedding nerves or being distracted because she was organising the reception.'

Ellie slid another slice of pizza on to her plate. 'Perhaps he did start to realise something was wrong and that's why she killed him. She did slip up a few times after all – the novel, the kiwi fruit she didn't know she'd drunk, the rose bush. Even though she's done a very good job of being Alissa, maybe it wasn't good enough to convince Max long term. You can never know all the details of someone else's life, no matter how much you get to know them.'

'I think she was planning to kill him all along.'

'And stitch up Russell.'

'Yeah, it was very convenient for her that he'd been stalking Alissa *and* he had a previous history of violence.'

'It sounds really far-fetched, doesn't it?'

'Yeah. Which is why I've got to be certain before I do anything about it.'

'She's very clever and calculating.'

'Psychopaths are great liars.' I glanced at the last slice of pizza. Ellie had polished off most of it. Hopefully that was a good sign.

'Why kill him after only eight weeks of marriage? Why not wait? It would always look more suspicious, and we'd always look at the spouse closely.'

'Not if you're under her spell, like Wilmott is. He's been blinded by her. She's the kind of woman who could get under your skin. Manipulative but stunning.'

'She's got under your skin.'

'Yeah, but not in the same way.' The only woman who'd ever be under my skin was Denise. 'But maybe you're right and something happened that did tip off Max and he needed to be silenced quickly. So how can I prove all this?' I had my own ideas, but I wanted to take Ellie's mind off thinking about Spencer 24/7. Getting her involved in this was the only way I knew how to do that. 'I need your help.'

'You know, monozygotic twins have the same DNA.'

I quirked an eyebrow. 'That would explain a lot.'

'But.' She held a finger up. 'They don't have the same fingerprints.' She leaned forward, her eyes sparkling, but for once they weren't filled with tears – it was excitement I saw in them. A hint of the old Ellie who sunk her teeth into a case. 'You said there were some unidentified prints found all over the house, including the office and master bedroom. They have to be the real Alissa's prints.'

I nodded with interest, as if it was the first time I'd thought of it.

She tilted her head, tapping her fingertips on the table, a far-off look in her eye. 'So, if Samantha is pretending to be Alissa, then Alissa must be dead.' She sat upright and gave me her full attention. 'Unless Alissa is actually in on it, too, and she's hiding out somewhere until this is all over and Max's estate is passed on to her. Then she can split it all with Samantha.'

'No. It doesn't fit her character, does it? Everyone who knew Alissa said she was a lovely, sweet woman who was very much in love with Max.'

'Anyone can commit a murder. You know that.'

'No, that doesn't feel right. I think Alissa, the *real* Alissa, is dead. And if she met Samantha in Australia, then that's where it happened. Samantha kills Alissa, steps into Alissa's shoes, and comes back to England with Max. Four weeks later, Max is dead.'

She pointed the tip of her beer bottle at me. 'Whereabouts in Australia did they go on their honeymoon?'

'The east coast.'

'Was there anywhere they spent a significant amount of time?'

I retrieved the bank statements Becky had copied for me from my briefcase, looking for signs of credit-card bills.

Ellie cleared the table to make room and I slapped them down, searching through them. I flicked back to the dates in question and studied them in detail.

'It looks like they spent a few weeks in a place called Noosa.'

'Then that's where you need to start looking.'

THE DETECTIVE
Chapter 38

I set my alarm for 6 a.m., which would be 3 p.m. in Queensland. After being passed around a few times, I spoke to a detective and explained the situation so far, leaving out the fact that this was off my own back. He told me to email him the unknown fingerprints from our scene and he'd see if they could find a match. If Samantha had disposed of Alissa in a way that meant she'd never been found, then I'd be out of luck. If she hadn't, they would probably have assumed the body was that of Samantha Folds, but hopefully they'd give me the evidence I needed. I also sent him the digital files of Samantha's fingerprints, the ones taken from her at the hospital the night Max was murdered, which, luckily, I'd downloaded on to my own laptop before being suspended. If they'd found a crime scene for Alissa out there, I was praying Samantha's prints would be all over it.

Now I had to sit back and wait.

I scarfed down a quick breakfast and headed to a local florist to pick up a bunch of pink and cream lilies. I'd hardly ever bought Denise flowers when she was alive. She didn't really go in for random acts of romance. It was what you did on a daily basis that counted. All those actions and words that built up over the years showing you cared, that you loved someone, were far better than a one-off gift of impersonal flowers. But I'd taken to buying them since she'd gone because what else could I give her now?

As I drove to the cemetery, I tried to quell the gaping sense of loss again. Today we would've been married thirty years. Maybe I should've felt lucky that we'd had all that time together, but I was still far too bitter for that. I forced myself to think about the Burbeck case instead because I could feel the tears pulsing painfully behind my eyes, and if I let them fall, I didn't know if I had the strength to ever stop them again.

I knew I was right about Samantha. I was so close now, and it would be worth it to watch Wilmott's fall from grace when I presented my bombshell. When I got a result on this case, *I'd* be the one walking in the ADI's shoes, delegating the crap out to Wilmott. Except . . . I'd only just been talking about retiring. So what did I want now?

I parked up and ripped off the cellophane from the flowers, leaving the plastic in a messy pile in the passenger footwell. Slowly, I walked to Denise's grave. There was an elderly woman standing in front of a fresh headstone, clutching her handbag in front of her chest, weeping. I looked away and wondered if she ever felt like giving up, too.

I kneeled down in front of my wife's grave and removed the previous flowers which were now dried and discoloured, replacing them with the fresh ones. I sat back on my heels and stared at the inscription: 'In Loving Memory of Denise Carter. Tragically Taken Too Soon. Remembered Always.' It sounded too inconsequential. How could you sum up the wonderful, warm, kind-hearted woman she'd been in just a few words? My soulmate. That one person in a million. I hadn't had a clue what to put on there at the time. How was I supposed to decide that? It wasn't meant to happen. There should've been plenty of time. *We* should've had more time.

'I think I'm falling apart,' I whispered to her, rubbing my hands over my face and letting them rest on my cheeks. 'I need you here. I need you to tell me what to do with my future. I don't know how to get through each day without you.'

A voice in my head said, *You've got to let it go.* But I didn't believe it was a message from Denise. It was just my subconscious speaking, and it made no sense to me. Let what go? Denise? The job? The Burbeck case?

Tears filled my eyes. I let them fall down my cheeks, tasting salt on my lips, and felt everything I'd held in for so long cracking open. I didn't know if I believed in an afterlife. All I knew was that I desperately wanted to be with Denise again.

I left the cemetery an hour later and went home, forcing myself to eat something. I watched the clock to take my mind off my dead wife, the hands getting closer together and further apart, hoping that the Australian police would get back to me today, but knowing, because of the time difference, it was highly unlikely.

At 6.30 p.m., I was back at Ellie's house with a Burger King takeaway.

'I'm sick of eating all this rubbish,' was the first thing she said to me. 'Come in. I've got some pasta on the go.'

I smiled inwardly. Another sign of improvement.

'Any news from Australia?' She glanced over her shoulder as she stirred the bubbling tomato sauce.

'Not yet.' I looked at my watch for the hundredth time that day and leaned against the worktop as she drained the tagliatelle.

'If you get something positive, what's your plan? You know you should go to Wilmott first with it. He is SIO on this.'

'And let him take all the glory? Actually, I was hoping you'd come back and then I wouldn't have to.'

She shook her head. 'I don't think I am coming back.' She put her hand on her hip, the steam from the boiling water swirling in the air. She glanced at me cautiously.

'You can't leave me there with bloody Wilmott! You have to come back.'

'For you or for me?'

'For you, of course.' I paused sheepishly. 'Well, OK, for me, too.'

'Anyway, you said you were going to retire.'

I slumped down on the chair and tried to make sense of all the confusion in my head.

'I need a change,' Ellie continued. 'I can't go back to the same nick Spencer worked at. I can't face all the memories. It's too much. There are so many ghosts of him here, all over the house. I can't have those ghosts at work, too. I'd never get through this. I'd never move on.' She dumped pasta into two bowls and spooned on the sauce without looking up. I got the feeling she was also talking about me.

I sat at the table, shook salt over my dinner, and just stared at it, the realisation suddenly kicking in. I couldn't go on like I had been, wallowing in grief, trying to take my mind off it with work, hardly ever sleeping because I was afraid to close my eyes and see my wife's face and know I couldn't touch her again, hold her, keep her safe. I needed something else in my life, but I had no idea what. I'd thought work would heal me, keep me occupied, stop me thinking about her, help me move on. But that hadn't been working out too well.

'I'm not giving up. I'm just . . .' She waved her fork around in the air. 'I just need something different. I need a challenge. Things have changed now, and *I* need to change with them, or I'm going to fall apart. Surely if anyone can understand that, it's you.'

'Right now, I can understand that completely.'

'I need to fix myself. *Do* something other than mope around the house.'

'But what are you going to do? You've been a copper for twenty-five years.'

'What are you going to do if you retire?'

I shrugged.

'Take up sudoku? Cooking? Crochet?'

'I couldn't think of anything worse,' I said.

'Exactly. You're a copper, too. It's in your blood. It's who you are. You've never known anything else.'

'But the way things are at work . . . the likes of Wilmott being promoted, the chief constable putting pressure on Greene to quash investigations into people like Mackenzie, it's just wrong.'

She put her fork down on the edge of the plate, rested her elbows on the table, and laced her fingers together. 'I've been headhunted for another job.'

'That was quick.' I raised my eyebrows.

'Quick? It's been three months since I went on compassionate leave.'

'God, yes, it has. It feels like yesterday still.'

'It feels like a lifetime since he's been gone, but you've made me realise that I need work more than ever now. To stop me going mad.'

'Well, it's not working out so well for me, is it? Maybe you should take a good look at my situation.' As soon as it was out of my mouth, I held my hands up in appeasement. 'Sorry, I shouldn't have said that. I'm just an angry old man. Ignore me. What's the new job?'

'I'd still be a DI. It's just in another unit. The government are setting up a National Wildlife Crime Enforcement Unit. I think it's something completely different that I can get my teeth into.'

'Wildlife crime? How will a bit of poaching and fox hunting be a challenge?'

'No, that's the stuff the rural officers will still deal with. This is the big stuff. Illegal wildlife trafficking, endangered species. It's a huge enterprise now – the third biggest criminal industry in the world, worth billions every year. And a lot of it goes to fund terrorism and other types of organised crime. After they called me about it, I started doing some research – there's some seriously nasty stuff going on out there. It would blow your mind. Before I came into CID, I worked with the guy who's been tasked with setting it up. He thinks I'd do a good job, and I think I would, too. I need something completely different, away from this place, but where I can still be a DI. It sounds like exactly what I need right now.'

I sat back and eyed the spark of excitement on her face. An overwhelming rush of jealousy hit me in the sternum. How come Ellie could move on so quickly and I couldn't? I swallowed it down. I had no right to be jealous of her. I was being irrational and selfish. I should be pleased for her. What the hell kind of person was I turning into? Denise would've severely kicked me up the arse.

'And you know what the best bit is?' she asked, grinning slightly.

'You get free safaris?'

'I get to pick my own team. I want you to come with me.'

THE DETECTIVE
Chapter 39

I tossed and turned again, fluffing up my pillow, huffing to myself. There was too much running around in my head to sleep. Again. I gave up at 3 a.m. and turned on the TV, flicking through channels just for a bit of company.

I could understand why Ellie needed a change. A challenge. And now that she'd put that thought in my brain, I was starting to want one, too. I'd been slowly turning into a sad, lonely old bastard. Not that I'd ever admit it to anyone except her, of course. Yeah, a change of scenery could be a good thing.

I picked up the photo of Denise that I kept by my bed and touched my fingertip to her face, tracing the lines around her eyes. She'd thought they made her look old, but I disagreed. She'd only grown more beautiful to me as she got older. They were just marks of all the times we'd laughed together over the years. Like the rings in a tree trunk, they were evidence of the life we'd had. We'd always talked major decisions through. She was the first person I went to. The last person I spoke to at night. A memory flashed in my head. I was twenty-five, and

I'd been involved in a long and complicated investigation into a child murder, one of my early cases as a detective. The prime suspect had always been the father, but the evidence against him was flimsy and the CPS declined to prosecute. I'd been down after that, an overwhelming feeling of hopelessness and anger taking over me, so it affected our home life in the end. Denise was her usual sympathetic, supportive, and helpful self, but I couldn't stop thinking about the child. How we'd failed her, let her down. How justice hadn't prevailed. Denise had sat me down one day and said, 'You're an amazing detective. Never doubt that. You can't fail because you never give up! You have to accept what you can't change, and change what you can't accept.' She was right, of course. I couldn't accept that the father would get away with it, so when everyone else gave up, I kept digging and digging, and eventually found the evidence we needed to convict him.

Even at that young age, before she'd blossomed and grown, Denise was a special woman. My rock. My inspiration when things were hard. No wonder she'd been an amazing nurse.

But that was over now. There was just a gaping hole in my life, and sometimes it felt like I was slipping through it. I'd wanted to stay in the same house after her death, even though the memories were too much to bear sometimes, but at least it had meant I was closer to her. Ellie was right about the ghosts, though. But if Ellie got this job and brought me into her team, I could move to London, where the National Wildlife Crime Enforcement Unit was being set up. It would be too much of a pain in the arse to commute every day.

It's what I needed, too. Finally. A fresh start. A new chapter. I'd hated the thought of change. It felt like a betrayal to Denise of some kind. But now I thought it was the *only* thing I could do to fix myself. And maybe all good changes were preceded by heart-crushing devastation, by soul-destroying loss. Now I listened to Denise's words anew. I couldn't give up. I had to change what I couldn't accept any more.

If I went with Ellie, I thought her enthusiasm and strength could start to rub off on me. Help me to move on instead of festering away. CID hadn't been the right place for me for a long time, but I hadn't known what to do with myself in the last year. Hadn't thought about the new possibilities that really could be out there. Now I thought, finally, there was an answer.

'What do you think, Denise?' I asked her photo. 'Should I go with Ellie?'

She didn't answer, but my mobile phone rang instead.

I looked at the screen and saw the international dialling code for Australia. 'DS Carter speaking.'

'Hi, this is DS Warwick. I hope I didn't wake you up. I'm not sure what the time is over there.'

'Nah. I wasn't sleeping.' I put Denise's photo back on the table. 'Have you got something for me?'

'I have.' And as he spoke, my heart raced and a satisfied grin snaked up my lips.

After I hung up, I had a shower and got dressed. Then I had hours to kill before heading into the office to brief Detective Superintendent Greene, so I surfed the web, looking for flats to rent in London and researching the National Wildlife Crime Enforcement Unit and the types of cases they were expected to handle. An unfamiliar buzzing coursed through me. Something I hadn't felt in a long time. Excitement.

At 8 a.m., I was in the fingerprint office, calling in a favour with Amy, one of the techs, to quickly do a comparison with the ones DS Warwick had sent me from the crime scene in Noosa. Luckily, Amy's department was based at Police Headquarters and not at the station, so she wasn't aware of the suspension looming over me. I'd managed to wangle my way in without my warrant card, following a civilian who was going into the building. Still, when I dropped my bombshell on Greene, the suspension would be lifted and I could leave in a blaze of victory. I wondered if Ellie would want Becky on her team, too.

She was solid. Did all the grunt work thoroughly and conscientiously. She was married, though. Would she want to up sticks or commute? I doubted it.

I sat in a café, sipping coffee and waiting for Amy to ring. I opened up DS Warwick's email again and stared at the crime-scene photos attached to it of the apartment in Noosa. Samantha and Alissa were absolutely identical, no doubt about it. But Samantha hadn't been as clever as she thought.

I was on my second espresso when my mobile rang. I snatched it up from the table.

'Hi, it's Amy, over in fingerprints. I've got a match for you.'

If she'd been in front of me, I probably would've kissed her. I listened as she talked, then hung up, gathered my things, and headed to the station.

Someone had very helpfully left the rear door wedged open with a tall metal ashtray, so again I avoided the embarrassment of having to go to the front desk and wait for someone to collect me. So much for security. I slipped inside and took the stairs, spotting DS Greene in the corridor, heading towards his office.

I followed him. 'Sir, can I have a word?'

DS Greene cast a surprised look over his shoulder. 'What are you doing here?'

'I've got some information you'll want to hear.'

He studied me for a moment, probably wondering how unstable I was and whether I was about to grab him by the scruff and throw him against the wall. 'OK, you'd better come in, then.' He stepped into his office, shrugged out of his jacket, and hung it on a coat stand in the corner. Then he sat down behind his desk, eyeing me carefully as he prepared to speak. I knew from the frown in place that it wouldn't be anything particularly good, so when he opened his mouth, I jumped in there first.

'I need to talk to you about the Max Burbeck murder.'

He blew out a frustrated breath. 'Not this again! The case is over. You've been suspended! What part of suspension don't you understand? Have you booked an appointment with the force psychologist yet?'

'With all due respect, sir, ADI Wilmott doesn't know what he's talking about with this case. He's become so obsessed with Alissa Burbeck that he never looked at it objectively from the start.'

'Oh, what, and you have? Come on, Warren. The—'

'Some new evidence has come to light. Evidence that proves what I've been trying to tell him all along. Russell Stiles is not guilty. He was framed for Max's murder. Alissa Burbeck killed him. Except she's not actually Alissa at all.'

DS Greene looked at me as if I was talking Arabic. But the more I talked, the more his face turned from disbelief to shocked confusion to intrigue.

He leaned away from his desk and said, 'Right, let me get this straight in my head. You're saying Samantha Folds met her identical twin Alissa Burbeck in Australia, then murdered her, leaving Alissa's body in her flat, before taking on her identity and returning to the UK with Max Burbeck, where she murdered him and framed Russell Stiles.'

'Well, that's the short version.'

'That sounds ridiculous.'

'I know.' I brought up a few files on my laptop and turned it to face him on his desk. 'I've been in touch with our counterparts in Australia. The dead body of who they thought was Samantha Folds was discovered in Samantha's flat, near to where Alissa and Max had been staying. She was found three days after they returned to the UK. She'd been drugged and smothered. They had no leads and were still investigating. Samantha's photo driving license was found in the flat with her. It was rented by Samantha, and she was identified by someone who knew her.'

'But you think this isn't Samantha Folds' body?'

'No. This is really Alissa Burbeck. The prints taken from that body match the *real* Alissa Burbeck's prints found at The Orchard. When our SOCO collected them, we had no one to match them to, you see. Until now.'

DS Greene rubbed at his forehead.

'That's not all, though. When the Australian police dusted for prints, they found a wineglass and bowl in the dishwasher. Fortunately, there had been a power cut and the dishwasher had turned itself off. On the glass and bowl they recovered prints belonging to Samantha Folds. Prints taken by our SOCO when she was at the hospital following Max's murder, posing as Alissa Burbeck.'

'Bloody hell. You're absolutely sure about this?'

'The evidence is undeniable. So we have Samantha Folds placed at the murder scene of Alissa Burbeck in Noosa and we can arrest her on behalf of Noosa police for that murder.'

'Right.' He steepled his fingers. 'But do we have any proof she killed Max Burbeck? The knife was found at Stiles' house. What about Stiles' hair found on Max's body?'

'The knife was planted at his house by Samantha Folds.' I explained about Russell's missing cap.

'You don't think he was involved at all? As an accomplice?'

'No. He was a convenient scapegoat. I don't have all the answers yet, but I will. Samantha met Alissa and Max in Noosa, obviously learned a lot about both of them, then planned the whole thing. We can prove she took on Alissa's identity, and she had the motive to kill Max.'

He glanced back at my laptop again. 'Do you think she'll confess under pressure?'

'I don't know. She's very controlled. We'll have to see what happens. Even if she doesn't, I think the CPS will get a prosecution based on all the other evidence and circumstances.'

He leaned back in his chair. 'Good work, DS Carter. Why didn't ADI Wilmott pick up on all this?'

Of course, I took great pleasure in informing him how Wilmott had acted completely inappropriately with 'Alissa', disregarding all lines of enquiry because of his apparent obsession with her, the dates and times of his visits to her when he was supposed to be working, the little gifts he'd brought her.

'And I didn't come to you earlier because my opinion didn't seem to count for much these days.' I got that little dig in there and felt a moment of fleeting triumph. 'Plus, I had no actual proof.'

His lips tightened into a thin line. 'Well, DI Wilmott seems to have pretty much fucked up this case.' He leaned his elbows on the desk. 'Right, I want you to arrest Samantha Folds. And ask ADI Wilmott to come in here, please.'

I allowed myself an inner smirk and headed for the door.

'Wait. You're going to need this.'

I turned around. Greene opened his top drawer, took out my warrant card, and tossed it in my direction.

THE OTHER ONE
Chapter 40

I could set my watch by Wilmott. He'd turn up every morning on his way to work to 'check' on me. Often during the day, and on the way home, too. He was obviously lying about where he was, because when people called him, he'd say he was in meetings or checking out a lead on something. Everyone lies. Everyone wants something they don't have. Everyone thinks the grass is greener. That's the law of nature. That's just how we are. Some people spend their lives miserable and bitter because of it, rotting from the inside out. And other people deal with it. Take action. If you don't like something, then stop moaning and change it! Like I did.

Of course, I'd encouraged Wilmott. I had to have him on my side. I knew that from the beginning. Recognised the weakness in him. The arrogance and self-gratification. The ego and narcissism. But there are right ways and wrong ways to do things. It couldn't be so obvious that it looked as if I'd sleep with him right after Max was dead. That wouldn't do at all. I had to be cunning and calculating, manipulative. So sometimes when he touched me in his accidentally-on-purpose way, or when he was supposed to be comforting the new widow, I let his hand or thigh or arm linger a little too long. I wore clothes that exposed a shoulder, the creamy swell of my tits, a bit of thigh. I knew his gaze followed me across the room, could see him staring out of the corner of my eye. The promise was there, under the surface, lying in wait for him. *One day you'll have me.* At least he thought it was. I had him under control, and he, in turn, had that arsehole sergeant under control. I hadn't seen Carter lately. Hadn't bumped into him. Wilmott had told me he'd been suspended. Ha ha!

It was 8.45 a.m. when Wilmott knocked on my door bearing gifts again. I didn't comment on his newly whitened teeth, or the fact that his hair was a darker shade of brown than before and the grey at the temples had miraculously disappeared, or his disgustingly overpowering aftershave that made me want to chuck up all over him.

I smiled. It had been an appropriate amount of time since Max's death to allow for occasional smiling.

'You're so thoughtful,' I said, opening the door. 'What would I do without you?'

He grinned, showing too much teeth. It was arrogant and smarmy all rolled into one.

He held a cardboard tray with two cups of takeout coffee and a paper bag in his hand. 'Coffee and muffins.'

'You know how to start my day off right. Come on in.' I led him into the lounge, swishing my hips, letting him take in the lacy thong sitting higher than my short black skirt. Maybe I'd give him a flash of it when I bent over. If he was a good boy.

I sat on the sofa and curled my legs up to the side, facing him. He'd get a good look from there, anyway. 'You don't have to do this, you know. I bet you're really busy, aren't you?' I removed the lid from my coffee and drank it, trying not to gag on the milk. Trying not to think of Jennifer and Lulabelle and the other cows on the farm. I banished the image and put the coffee back on the table. I'd just throw it down the sink when he left.

He shrugged smugly. 'I'm the boss now, so I make my own hours.'

'I bet it's exciting, though, isn't it? Police work? I bet you come into contact with all sorts of people.'

He took a sip of coffee and licked his lips. 'Since I've been promoted I've been in the office more, dealing with reports and budgets and reviews, instead of running around doing the boring grunt work.'

I placed my hand on his arm, letting it linger there a moment. 'You're great at your job, I can tell.'

His mobile phone rang then. He pulled it from his pocket and eyed the number, then rolled his eyes. 'Carter. What does he want? He's suspended. He's probably calling me up to beg for his job back.' He laughed viciously before jabbing the 'Off' button, sending the call to voicemail. 'He hasn't been bothering you lately, has he?'

'Oh, no, thanks. I'm grateful for what you did. It was just so creepy, him following me. I was worried he was going to turn into another stalker like Russell.' I glanced down at my knees, my hair falling across half of my face.

'No one's going to hurt you now. Not while I'm looking out for you.' Wilmott reached out and moved a lock of my hair away from my face with his fingertips. 'You know that, don't you?' He looked deeply into my eyes. It was an *I-want-to-fuck-you* look.

I smiled back innocently, pretending I couldn't read it. *Of course I know, you dirty bastard.* I nodded gratefully, demurely. 'Thank you. I—' Before I could say anything else, his phone rang again.

He glanced at the number flashing up. 'Bloody Carter again! Honestly, I've been stuck with the most useless team ever. Ronnie can't even take a piss without supervision, Becky looks like a dyke, and Carter's a head case!' He put the phone on the coffee table and let it ring out this time.

'Maybe you should take it. It could be important, couldn't it? I mean, you've got an important job.'

Wilmott puffed his chest out slightly. 'They can do without me for five minutes. And I'm not talking to Carter. He can go through the proper channels if he wants his job back. I'm not listening to his whining. I've got better things to do with my time. Now, where were we? What were you going to say?' He twisted on the sofa to face me, his arm sliding along the headrest closer towards my shoulder.

'I was wondering if there'd been any updates on Max's case. Is there anything else I should know before Russell's trial? Because what if . . . what if he gets away with it? What if he gets out and tries to kill me?'

'Please don't worry your pretty head about that. The case against him is solid. He won't be getting out any time soon, I can assure you.'

'You're absolutely sure?' I bit my lip.

'Definitely. You're safe, Alissa. You're safe with me.' Then he stood up and said, 'Sorry, can I just use your loo? Coffee always goes straight through me in the mornings.'

'Of course, you know where it is,' I said, wondering if he thought that statement would get me wet. What a loser. He had a lot to learn about women.

His phone bleeped with a text while he was out of the room. I picked it up, wondering if it was Carter again. I clicked on 'Messages'. Yes, it was him.

I opened the message and a blast of heavy heat pressed against my spine.

New evidence re Alissa Burbeck. DO NOT approach. Call me URGENTLY.

THE DETECTIVE
Chapter 41

I walked into the office, my mobile pressed against my ear, listening to Wilmott's phone ring.

'Sarge! Are you back?' Becky glanced up from some paperwork and her face lit up. At least someone was pleased to see me.

'Yeah, I'm back.' I grinned. 'Where the hell is Wilmott? He's not answering, as usual.'

'He said he was in a meeting at Headquarters.' Ronnie stopped making coffee. 'Nice to have you back.'

'Thanks. Ronnie, can you keep trying to get hold of him?' I handed him my mobile phone.

'What's going on, Sarge?' Becky asked.

'It's a long story, and I don't have time to explain everything now. But Alissa Burbeck isn't who we thought she was. She killed Max and framed Russell. I'm heading out to arrest her.'

She raised her eyebrows. 'It's what you thought all along, isn't it?'

'If only Wilmott had listened to me in the beginning.' I glanced over at Ronnie, busy dialling numbers and trying to get hold of Wilmott. I paced up and down.

'No luck,' Ronnie said eventually.

'I was waiting for Wilmott out of courtesy, but I'm not waiting any more. If you see him, Becky, tell him DS Greene wants a word. Ronnie, you're coming with me.' I took my phone back. It was too complicated and time-consuming to explain everything, so I rattled off a brief text to Wilmott that he'd understand.

Ronnie jumped up, excitement plastered all over his face, hurrying to keep up with me as I strode out of the building and into the car park.

I got in the unmarked pool car, reversed out of its spot, and pulled out of the nick on to the main road, tyres squealing. I drove up the dual carriageway, undertaking a car hogging the fast lane and sounding my horn at them.

Ronnie held on to the door handle as I swung back into the fast lane and approached the roundabout. The queue was about half a mile long. Rush hour traffic. Great. Just bloody great. I slammed my foot on the brake.

'You should've gone the other way,' Ronnie said, trying to be helpful.

'Yes, I know that now, thanks very much.' I glanced at him. 'Get the blues out, then.'

He opened the window, reached out his arm, and fixed the blue light on to the roof.

I turned on the siren, waiting for the cars to part enough for me to get through, shouting at everyone to move, even though they couldn't hear me.

THE OTHER ONE
Chapter 42

A hundred thoughts ran through my mind as I deleted the text. I'd always had an escape plan. You have to, don't you? So I was prepared. I wasn't prepared for Wilmott being here when I needed to run, though.

I couldn't waste time thinking about it. I had to move. Right now. Right fucking now! They would *not* arrest me.

I turned Wilmott's phone off and slid it down the side of the sofa. I heard the toilet flushing from out in the corridor and rushed into the kitchen. A knife. A knife. That's what I needed.

By the time Wilmott came out of the toilet, I was prepared.

'Where are you?' he called from the lounge.

'In the kitchen.' I didn't need to say more. I knew he'd follow me.

He poked his head round the door and smiled.

I faced him, leaning my back against the worktop, the knife handle gripped firmly in my hand behind me. The neckline of my top had slipped down my shoulder, exposing my red, lacy bra.

'Are you OK?' Wilmott stepped into the room, his gaze darting between my bra and my face.

I smiled back at him. This time it was brazen. I moistened my lips with my tongue. My eyes hooded with desire. 'I really want you to hold me. I need you to make me feel safe again.' I tilted my head. Watched him walk towards me. Saw the greed light up his face.

He got closer.

Closer. So we were a few inches apart.

Stopped.

His gaze danced over my face, down my body. 'Are you sure?'

I threw a little mix of vulnerability into my expression. 'Very sure.' My voice was husky as I parted my lips, jutting out my chin, daring him to kiss me. Daring him to take what he'd wanted for so long.

His hands touched my cheeks as he angled his face towards me, his eyes closing a fraction of a second before his lips touched mine.

A fraction of a second before I plunged the knife into his stomach.

THE DETECTIVE
Chapter 43

Half an hour and two narrow misses with other cars later, I yanked on the handbrake outside Samantha's house before the vehicle had even come to a complete standstill.

'That's DI Wilmott's car.' Ronnie jerked his head towards the red Audi A5 convertible further up the road as I scrambled out on to the pavement.

'Shit!' I muttered, taking the front steps two at a time.

I banged on the door. It was too complicated to get into the whole Samantha/Alissa scenario on the front step, so I called Alissa's name. 'Police, open up!'

Nothing.

'She must be here if Wilmott's here,' Ronnie said. 'And her Mini's here, too.'

I hammered at the door again.

Still no response. 'Go round the back,' I told Ronnie. There was an alleyway along the side of the property. 'Get over the fence and check the rear.'

Ronnie dashed off as I peered through the front window into the lounge. The curtains were open, but no one was in there.

I banged again. Heard a thud and Ronnie make a noise as he launched himself over the rear fence.

'Wilmott? Are you in there?' I called out through the letter box. I couldn't see anyone through the small slit. There were no noises coming from within. No signs of life at all.

'Sarge!' Ronnie called out from somewhere around the back. 'Call for an ambulance! Wilmott's on the floor in the kitchen. There's a lot of blood. I'm going to force an entry.'

'Fuck!' I radioed the control room and told them an officer was injured and to get an ambulance en route immediately. Then, radio still in hand, I launched my shoulder into the front door.

It was sturdy. Hardwood. It didn't budge.

I heard the sound of breaking glass at the rear and legged it up the alleyway. By the time I'd climbed over the fence, there was a metal bench lying on its side and the double-glazed rear door to the kitchen was smashed.

Ronnie crouched over Wilmott, who was unconscious, blood oozing from around the knife sticking out of his stomach, creating a patchwork of red on his shirt.

I crunched over splinters of glass in the doorway. 'You stay with him. Ambulance is on the way. I'll check the house.' I didn't expect Samantha to be hanging around anywhere, waiting for a nice cosy chat over tea and biscuits, but I checked the lounge and downstairs toilet before bounding up the stairs and looking around the rest of the house.

She was gone. Of course she was.

I ran back downstairs and radioed the control room again, giving them an update. If Samantha hadn't taken Alissa's car, she couldn't have got that far. Unless she had another vehicle stashed away somewhere, which I wouldn't put past her. 'Get in touch with Passport and

Immigration and circulate her details,' I told the communications operator.

'Which ones? Samantha Folds or Alissa Burbeck?'

'Both! I want the CCTV operators informed. Either she's on foot or she's in another vehicle. She can't have waited for public transport or to call a taxi. And where's the bloody ambulance? DI Wilmott's in a bad way.'

'It's en route. It should be there soon.'

I passed on a few more instructions and then crouched down next to Wilmott. He didn't look good. His face was pale. Blood had spread over the floor in a pool of slick, sticky red. His breathing was shallow.

'Should I press on the wound?' Ronnie shrieked, a panic-stricken expression on his face. 'I know that helps with blood loss, but I'm not sure about when there's still a knife in there.'

If he died, it would be my fault. I should've told him I was on to her before. Should've told him everything. A little inner voice told me I'd tried and he hadn't wanted to know, but still, it didn't make me feel any better at that moment.

'You could push it in further by pressing on it. The ambulance should be here soon. You wait for it, OK? I'm going to drive around and see if I can spot her.'

I left through the front door without waiting for an answer, got in my car, and did a sweep of the area.

'Where are you, you crazy bitch?'

THE OTHER ONE
Chapter 44

I didn't know what had gone wrong. There was no evidence to connect me to Max's murder. There couldn't be. I supposed it didn't matter now. The only thing that mattered was getting away. If they started poking around more into my life, it wouldn't take long for them to find out who I really was. What I'd done.

I laughed to myself as I joined the motorway, heading towards Heathrow Airport, in the old Ford Fiesta I'd purchased for a few hundred pounds. I'd parked it a couple of streets away from my rented house. It was taxed, so no one would even pay it any attention. I'd given a false name and address to the person I'd bought it from and never registered it. By the time they realised where I'd gone, I'd be on a plane to somewhere.

The bad bit: I'd never get my hands on all of Max's money now. I slapped my palm repeatedly against the steering wheel. Stupid. Stupid. Stupid. I'd squirrelled away money from Max when we'd got back from Australia. *Yes, of course I have to pay the caterers and the marquee hire in cash for the reception.* I'd bumped up the price and got five grand, just like that. And when he'd kissed me hard, got the money from the safe in the house, and counted out the notes, I'd tucked away the combination in my head.

Fifty grand he'd had in that safe. Who keeps that kind of cash in the house?

I'd taken bits and pieces out of our savings account and current account, too. Not huge amounts at a time, which would've seemed too suspicious. Three hundred here, two hundred there. So I'd amassed seventy grand in cash. Not as good as ten million, but at least it meant I could get away. I could feed myself until I decided what to do. What my next goal was. I'd opened an account in a new bank in the name of Samantha Folds months ago. Then I'd transferred most of the money to the Cayman Islands. I had five grand in cash on me. Not enough to raise any alarms at the border.

The good bit: the really good bit, actually, that I realised now after my initial panic had cleared, was that they still didn't know exactly *who* I was yet. That text from Carter had said Alissa Burbeck. *Not* Sam Folds. Not the real me. The me I still had a passport for. The me no one would be looking for because I wasn't Alissa Pathetic Burbeck.

It wasn't ideal. I admit that. But it wasn't all lost, either. Life was all about adapting. I'd done it so many times before, I could easily do it again.

The new question was: where should I fly to first?

Answer? Whichever the hell flight left first. *Check!*

THE DETECTIVE
Chapter 45

She'd disappeared. The frustration and adrenaline slammed through me as I drove around the nearby area, searching fruitlessly for any sign of her. Patrol cars were out looking, too. She could be anywhere by now.

The communications operator's voice was the sweetest thing I'd ever heard when she called me on the radio.

'Go ahead,' I said urgently.

'We've got something. A CCTV operator has been reviewing footage and spotted her getting into a black Ford Fiesta in a nearby street forty-five minutes ago. Index number Alpha-two-three-X-ray-Tango-Bravo. It's been circulated. The motorway cameras have picked it up on the M25. Stand by for more information.'

I did a U-turn in a residential street, tyres squealing as I headed towards the A1M, where I could pick up the M25 motorway. She was going to the airport, I was sure. But which one? Heathrow or Gatwick?

I floored it, my heart racing.

The control room called again. 'One of our operators is talking to the Road Policing Unit. They've just spotted the vehicle on CCTV leaving the M25 at the Heathrow slip road.'

'Alert the airport police.'

'Received.'

'Is there an update on DI Wilmott?'

'He's at the hospital. Critical condition. They're not sure if he'll make it.'

I gripped the steering wheel tight and pushed the accelerator down.

THE OTHER ONE
Chapter 46

I hadn't had time to change my clothes before I'd left the house. I'd washed my hands, of course, but there was blood on my top, so I'd just grabbed a long black cardigan and pulled it on, doing up the buttons to hide the stain. I could easily buy something else to wear from one of the duty-free shops, anyway.

I approached the British Airways desk, which, thankfully, had no queue. 'Hi, I'm feeling like a spontaneous trip.' I smiled sweetly. 'Can you tell me which flights you have leaving soon?'

The woman with an over-processed perm and too much make-up on didn't even bat an eyelid at my odd request. She smiled back. 'I've always wanted to do that. Book a couple of weeks off and just go somewhere spontaneous. Go on an adventure and not know where until the last minute.' She leaned forward. 'The thing is, I'm too much of a planner. I like to research places so I know exactly what there is to see before I go. It's great in theory, but I don't think I could really do it.'

Do I look like I care?

My smile was in danger of becoming tight against my cheeks. 'So, what flights do you have?'

She turned her attention to her keyboard and prattled on again.

Shut the fuck up!

I glanced around, checking out a couple of armed police walking around casually, hands resting on their guns. I averted my gaze back to the woman.

'I'll look for flights leaving in around two hours because it will take you at least that long to get through check-in and security.'

Two hours?

I tapped my foot. 'What about first-class tickets? Don't you get priority boarding and check-in?'

'Yes. You *could* also purchase a priority pass to fast-track through the security queues, too, if you like.'

'Yes. I want all of those. So how soon can I get a flight?'

She typed away again. 'The next departure we have is for Paris, leaving in an hour and five minutes.'

'I'll take that, please.'

'Wonderful! I'm so jealous.' She giggled. 'What's your name, please?'

'Samantha Folds.'

I tapped my foot as she took my cash and printed out pieces of paper.

'I hope you have a lovely time. I hear—'

I didn't catch the rest of her annoying conversation. I was already rushing towards the BA check-in desk.

Luckily, there was no one in the queue for first class, and I whizzed through the check-in process before rushing towards the security area. There were people winding around barriers in a horrifically long swarm, waiting to go through the X-ray machines. I looked frantically for the fast-track queue and breathed a sigh of relief. Only two people there.

I joined in behind them and put my bag on the conveyor belt, even managing to summon up a smile as I stepped through the metal detector.

At passport control, they scanned my passport and checked my boarding card to make sure the names matched up. I breathed deeply. It wouldn't do to panic and blow everything now.

The uniformed man looked up from my passport and studied me for a moment, a stern expression on his face. He typed a few things on his computer. Studied me again. Then he handed me back my passport and boarding card. 'Have a nice trip.'

In the departure hall, I looked around for a clothes shop, spotting a Ted Baker.

I walked into the stuffily hot shop and headed straight for the summer dresses, sliding them along the rack as I checked out the sizes. I picked up the first I found in my size and rushed towards the till, thrusting it towards the woman behind the counter.

'Oh, this is really pretty,' she said. 'I've got one of these.'

'That's nice,' I said, watching her remove the security tag, tapping my feet and glancing at my watch.

'Did you see the one in red, too?' She pointed over to the rack. 'That colour would really suit you, and it's on sale at the moment, too. Fifty percent off.'

'I'm in a hurry, actually. My flight's about to leave soon.' I forced myself not to scream in her face to get a move on, and I thrust some money at her.

'Oh, sorry.' She rang up the purchase, folded up the dress, and put it in a paper bag, then handed me the change.

I quickly scanned the departure screens, looking for my gate, then power-walked in that direction. When I got there with thirty-five minutes to spare, I went into the toilets, stripped off my top and skirt, and threw them in the cubicle bin, then put the dress over my head. I heard a slight ripping as I hastily dressed. Hopefully I hadn't done any major damage, but I didn't have time to check it now. I pulled my cardigan back on and walked to the boarding gate.

There was a queue of people for the commoners' boarding, but the line for first class was empty. I skittered to a stop, took a deep breath, and breezed calmly up to the uniformed male member of staff, conjuring up a relaxed smile.

He scanned my boarding card, checked my passport and voila – as they say in gay Paris! – I was heading down the corridor towards the plane.

THE DETECTIVE
Chapter 47

My contact at Heathrow Police was a detective named DS Paul Browne. He was currently on the radio to patrol units on the airport floor, and had emailed photos of Samantha to phones and computers. We'd established that she'd already gone through passport control before we'd had the chance to circulate her details.

We had operators on the lookout for her, checking the real-time CCTV cameras, while others reviewed any footage that had already been recorded. More were speaking to the various airlines, trying to confirm which one she'd bought a ticket from.

Thousands of people moved around the airport every second. It would be hard going to spot her in amongst the throngs of people.

She could not get away, though. I wouldn't let her. But I felt useless just doing nothing and leaving it to DS Browne's team.

I ignored the twinge in my back, the tension tightening up my shoulders, and I clenched my fists, wondering if Wilmott would make it. He was in surgery right now to repair his wounds. That was all they knew so far.

Sweat beaded on my forehead as the feeling of hopelessness kicked in. What if she managed to slip through my fingers?

A little while later, we had a result.

'British Airways flight to Paris, leaving in . . . twenty-five minutes,' DS Browne said to me. 'Come on, let's go.'

DS Browne got on the radio and started talking to the boarding gate staff as we rushed to the airport floor.

A few minutes later, Browne's radio crackled and sprang to life, and a voice on the other end said, 'Samantha Folds has boarded the plane.'

'OK, I don't want anyone to approach her. We're on our way.' He fired off other instructions to someone else on his radio, something about holding the plane. I wasn't listening. The pounding of blood in my ears drowned out everything else, and I just had one thought.

Gotcha!

THE OTHER ONE
Chapter 48

'Champagne, madam?' The flight attendant held out a tray towards me with several glasses of bubbly on it.

What a stupid question! Of course I want some!

'Thanks.' I took a glass and sipped. Shame it was so small. I needed a serious drink. Still, when we took off, I'd ply myself with some more.

She offered the tray to the middle-aged, balding man next to me in the aisle seat, who took one, before turning to me.

'Are you travelling on business or pleasure?'

I groaned inwardly. I didn't really want to get into a conversation with anyone right now. And how cheesy was that line? My mind was racing, making it hard to think.

'Holiday,' I mumbled, picking up the in-flight magazine from the seat holder in front of me. I flicked through it, all too aware that the dress I'd bought was very low at the front, flashing too much cleavage for my liking right now. At the moment, I wanted to be as inconspicuous as possible.

I could tell without looking up that the man was staring at my tits, so I pulled the edges of my cardigan closer together.

'Cheers,' he said, pushing his glass closer to mine, almost in front of my face. How rude. 'This is always a nice way to start a trip, don't you think?'

Blah, blah, blah. Just shut up and let me THINK!

I chinked my plastic glass with his and tried to tune him out, giving the appearance of reading the words on the page, when really they were all swimming together.

A picture of Wilmott's face as the blade slid into his skin flashed in my head. The look of surprise, the gasp, his mouth and eyes opening wide, the split-second shock of it all. Then, before he could react, I'd done it again, and again. He'd slid down my body, arms clutching at my hips, my thighs, my calves, until I'd kicked him away and left him on the floor.

Did I feel bad? No. Not in the slightest. He shouldn't have been such a feeble idiot. They would've found him by now, but did it matter? Did it matter? Did it matter? I tried to think through the question, unsure, a panicky pressure making my nerves tingle. It took every little bit of effort to stop my whole body fidgeting.

Think. Think!

No, it didn't matter. They thought Alissa had killed Max and that's who they'd be looking for. They didn't know about Sam Folds, so I was safe. They wouldn't be looking for that name on any flights from the UK. Yes, safe. Why was I even worrying about it at all? Ah, relief.

I took another sip of champagne and felt better as I thought about my new adventure. Where would I go from Paris? Or should I stay in the city a while and do some sight-seeing? Should I fly to another place? Hire a car and drive down to Italy? Tuscany would be nice. All that delicious wine and food. Yum. Plenty of scenery to paint. Hopefully some wildlife, too.

I turned a page in the magazine, an article on Santorini catching my eye with several glossy photos showing whitewashed houses built into a cliff. They had blue shutters that were in stark contrast with the brightness of the buildings and sunshine.

Hmmm, that looks nice. Somewhere to add to my list of possibles for the future. I could picture myself on a terrace overlooking that view, sipping icy cold retsina, eating olives and mezze, painting away. The light would be amazing there. Maybe I could set up a stall selling my artwork to tourists again. Or island hop. Yes, life wasn't so bad at all, despite the rather major fuck-up of not getting all the money I'd wanted. But I was free. That was the main thing.

I glanced up suddenly, realising we'd been sitting on the tarmac for ages and no other passengers had come on. I glanced at the door at the front of the plane. It was still open. I looked at my watch, noticing a fleck of blood on the face. I wiped it against my cardigan, but it didn't come off, so I scratched at it with my fingernail. How long were we going to sit here for? Didn't they know I had places to go? What was the hold-up?

The attendant caught my eye as she walked past, closing the overhead lockers.

'Will we be taking off soon?' I asked.

'Yes, not long now. Would you like another glass of champagne while you're waiting?'

I gave her a gracious smile. 'That would be lovely, thanks.'

'Me too.' The man next to me held out his glass and seemed to think that this was his cue to start chatting again.

'What's your name?' he asked, leaning closer so I could smell his disgusting garlic breath.

I edged further away towards the window and picked the first bland name that came into my head, not looking up to meet his eyes. *Can't you take a hint?!* 'Sarah.'

'Lovely to meet you. I'm Bruce.' He thrust his hand towards me to shake.

I nodded with disinterest and still didn't look up. A shadow fell over my magazine, and I reached out my hand for a refill from the attendant returning with my champagne. She was very efficient. I liked her.

When the champagne didn't materialise in my glass, I glanced up. DS Carter and another man in a black suit stood in the aisle next to my seat.

No. No, no, fucking no!

Black Suit flashed a card at Bruce. 'Police. Please get out of your seat, sir.' He indicated with a sweep of his arm for him to move further down the plane.

Bruce didn't need asking twice – he scrabbled away towards the rear of the plane, quite quickly for a fat man, until he was beyond my vision. DS Carter watched me with a slight grin on his face.

My stomach lurched, forcing the champagne back up into my throat. Fireworks shot through my skull. It felt like fingernails were scratching at my skin.

Then DS Carter started talking. 'Samantha Folds, I'm arresting you on suspicion of the murders of Alissa Burbeck and Max Burbeck, and the attempted murder of Richard Wilmott. You do not have to say anything, but it may harm your defence if you do not mention, when questioned, something you later rely on in court. Anything you do say may be given in evidence.'

The world started swirling in front of my eyes, and I didn't hear the rest of his words. They were just white noise.

White noise scratching at the screaming darkness inside my head.

PART FOUR
LOVE

THE ONE
Chapter 49

No, no, no, that just wasn't how it was supposed to turn out. AT ALL!
You think you know people, and *I* was the one who knew Alissa best,
but . . . well, that was strange. I should've guessed, I suppose. I should've
picked up on it. But Samantha was so good an actress I hadn't noticed
a thing. To me, the imposter walking around in her shoes was still the
Alissa I loved more than anything in the world. My soulmate. The one I
had to keep to myself. I didn't spot it coming. Who could predict that?
Turns out Samantha and I are a *lot* alike, even though I can't stand that
thought.

When you think about it, we're all actors and actresses, aren't
we? All playing a part. And we all have secrets. But when our secrets
collide . . . Boom! It's devastation.

The wedding reception was when the idea first came into my head.
I couldn't let it be that final. Max didn't deserve Alissa. He couldn't have
her. She was mine. I'd loved her since we were six years old. Before I
even knew what love was. Before I knew how someone could get under

your skin like that and take hold of your heart, like a tree taking root in the ground. Tough, solid, impenetrable, all-consuming love.

Growing up, other people began to notice Alissa, too. You couldn't exactly *not*, looking like she did. Even then, she was so beautiful. But they didn't feel the way I did. They were jealous of her. Spread rumours about her. Bullied her. And of course I stuck up for her. I was there for her in every hour of need. Of course I was. I always would be. I punched one of the ringleaders in the face once. Got my own back in many different ways. There was nothing I wouldn't do for my girl. You could never say I wasn't loyal. That I didn't protect those I cared about. And it all worked in my favour for a long time, pushing us closer together. I was the one she could rely on. The one who was always there for her, no matter what happened.

We were eleven when we had our first kiss. I'd waited all that time on the sidelines, watching how the boys looked at her. Wanted her. But they couldn't have her. I knew her better than she knew herself. She just didn't realise it yet. We were sitting in the park after school in a secluded spot where no one else would notice us. The sunlight was behind her, casting an ethereal glow around her hair. She looked like an angel. She was *my* angel. Alissa was just casually talking about boys, worrying about how to French kiss properly, like teenage girls do, worrying she'd be embarrassed when it happened for the first time and not wanting to look like an idiot. She'd had slobbery pecks on the cheek before from some of the lads, but she'd never been *really* kissed before. So I told her we should practise, to get it right for when the time came.

Alissa giggled. 'You mean, practise on each other?'

I shrugged and smiled, giving the impression that it was the first time I'd ever considered kissing her. I thought maybe if I kissed her I'd get it out of my system, this obsession I had with her. But I didn't want just any girl. I wanted her. Always her. 'Why not?' I laughed too.

She smiled. 'Yeah, OK, why not? So, how should we . . .'

I scooched closer towards her so that our faces were an inch apart. She looked so serious, concentrating, as if she was about to commit every detail to memory, just like me.

'Wait! Which way are you going? Left or right?' she said.

I angled my head to the right. 'Here.'

'OK.' She leaned her head to the left, moving in closer so I could smell the strawberry chapstick on her inviting lips.

And then it happened. The moment I'd been fantasising about for as long as I could remember. My lips touching her soft, full ones. Our tongues entwining together. I'd waited so long for it, and the reality was better than the fantasy. A million times better. I thought, *This is how I want to spend the rest of my life – kissing you!* I kept my eyes open as her lids fluttered closed, wanting to make sure it was really happening, wanting to savour every second. But then she pulled back suddenly, embarrassed.

She giggled again. 'Oh, my God! I can't believe we just did that!' She glanced around nervously, as if hoping no one had seen.

I wanted to lay myself bare and tell her how much I cared for her. How I'd look after her. Be everything she needed. I was about to tell her that it was meant to happen. How good we'd be together. How I'd always be there for her. Have her back. Give her what she wanted. I grinned easily, ecstatically, and stared at her beautiful face, wanting to trace it with my fingertips, kiss her eyelids, her cheek, every part of her. My whole body throbbed with desire. And now we'd kissed, surely it would be the beginning for us.

But no.

She leaped to her feet and grabbed her school bag, pulling me to my feet and linking her arm through mine as she dragged me away from the park.

I opened my mouth to tell her how I felt, the words burning a hole in my tongue.

'Thanks for that,' she said happily. 'Now I won't feel like a real dork when I get to kiss a guy. You're such an amazing friend.'

The words in my mouth morphed into a thick, choking feeling. She couldn't see me yet for what I was. The One for her. But it didn't matter. I had all the time in the world to make her see the truth.

Eventually, she started seeing Russell. I didn't give away my feelings, but I knew he wasn't right for her. Of course not. I knew she'd see it herself in the end and we'd get to share that kiss again and more. Much, much more. When they broke up, I couldn't sleep, couldn't eat. The anticipation that finally *now* was the right time for us. Of course she'd wanted to experiment with him – it was natural, normal. But now it was over, it would be *our* time.

Except it wasn't.

If Max hadn't taken her away from me, it would never have happened. But he did, so it *did* happen. Over the years, I'd been patiently waiting for her to see what was in front of her eyes, but now all she saw was Max, and I couldn't have that. No way. She belonged to me, not him. And if he was out of the way, finally it would happen for us, I knew it. All the pieces would click into place for her.

I tried subtle little ways to get rid of Max, but they didn't work, so I bided my time, waiting for an opportunity, pretending I was happy for them both. I always knew he couldn't have her. No one else could. It wasn't right. It wasn't fair.

The anger built up. Alissa didn't know what she was doing, marrying him. *I'd* have the final say in it all.

I toyed from the start with the idea of framing Russell, because he was still as obsessed with her as I was, and if Max was out of the way, would she take up with Russell again? Would Russell get to be happy with her in a way I couldn't be unless I had her to myself? My plan was to take both of them away from her and she'd have no one to turn to except me.

I knew Max and Alissa's routines inside out. I'd made it my business to know over the years. I knew he never locked the back door or set the alarm until he was going to bed. Knew the curtains were usually kept open. I watched the house from the woods, seeing the office light on, seeing Max's silhouette working away in there, hearing the music carry even through the window. Then I'd seen the bathroom light go on – Alissa's nightly bath routine that she'd told me about, during which she always fell asleep. I knew she'd be safely out of the way when it happened, as I couldn't allow her to get hurt, and my plan meant she wouldn't seem guilty, because the police wouldn't suspect her, I was sure, if she managed to 'escape' from the killer. I'd watched Russell as well and knew he went night fishing every Sunday. Alone. It was perfect. The answer to everything.

The day of the wedding reception was like a gift. I'd watched Alissa step out of the conservatory and head down to the pond on her own. I was about to go and talk to her when I saw Russell approach. She didn't see him fall over the fence and drop his cap, but I did. When they'd all gone back into the marquee after it happened, I saw Sasha heading down towards the bottom of the garden from some sneaky hiding place. I watched her go into the woods, wondering what she was up to, but she came back a few minutes later and disappeared into the house. That's when I went down to the bottom of the garden myself, picked up Russell's cap, and stuffed it in my bag, knowing the hairs in it would come in handy.

DS Carter never even checked out an alibi for me that night because he was convinced it was all Samantha. So what if she'd only really killed that inspector and my amazing, sweet Alissa? What's that old Meatloaf song? 'Two Out of Three Ain't Bad'? Samantha deserved to pay for what she did. For taking everything away from me. She needed to rot in hell for what she'd done. Although she looked exactly like her, she wasn't beautiful on the inside, too, like Alissa.

I'd thought I was about to have it all. Now I had nothing.

It was the end, alright. Just not the ending I'd planned so carefully.

So it was time to leave. There was nothing left for me here any more.

TWO WEEKS LATER
THE DETECTIVE
Chapter 50

I sat in the bedroom, surrounded by piles of Denise's clothes, sifting through them, each one sparking some kind of memory – a weekend away here, a night in a pub there, a birthday celebration, Christmas. I'd been at it for a week, unable to carry on for too long each time before the choking sensation threatened to overwhelm me. But finally, it was time to do this. To let her go. To exorcise the ghosts.

I'd put the house on the market and found a buyer in the first week. Now it was time to pack everything away. I'd handed in my notice at work. DI Nash and I would start at the National Wildlife Crime Enforcement Unit in eight weeks. Part of me was scared, apprehensive, but the other part felt alive for the first time in a long while. Of course, DS Greene had begged me to stay. The acting DI job was mine, he'd said. I'd earned it. My blaze of glory had materialised, but the victory was hollow. Wilmott was dead, and that was my fault, even though no one else shared this view. Of course I felt guilty. Denise's death should've taught me that life was too short to let petty jealousies and squabbles get in the way. I should've tried harder with Wilmott, and then maybe he'd still be alive. Now I had to live with his death on my conscience. Whether it was really a result of his actions or mine didn't matter to me. Denise would've told me to rise above everything and stop looking at things from my own perspective all the time. To put myself in his shoes for a while. Sadly, it was too late for me and Wilmott now. But it wasn't too late to change. To learn from my mistakes and become a better person.

Sam Folds had been charged with all three murders and had been remanded in custody until her trial. When I'd interviewed her, she'd taken great pleasure in telling me how she'd met Alissa, got to know her, murdered her. How she'd stabbed Wilmott in cold blood. When she'd started talking, it was hard to shut her up. She wanted me to know everything. She was gloating, bragging. But the one thing she denied vehemently was Max's murder. She said she'd been planning it, but someone else had got there first. That everything really did happen that night as she'd described. It was bugging me *why* she wouldn't admit to Max's murder when her confession to the other two practically spilled out of her as soon as she'd been arrested. But I thought she was just playing games, wanting to get the upper hand, trying to prove how clever and calculating she really was.

I shook the thoughts away and finished filling yet another black plastic sack with Denise's clothes. I loaded it into the car next to the five that were already in there and drove towards the cancer charity shop in town, certain that was where Denise would've wanted them to go.

I parked outside the shop and heaved two bags inside. The woman behind the counter was pricing up some clothes, which were spread out next to the till.

'I've got a few clothes for you.' I dumped the bags at the side of the counter.

'Oh, great, thank you.'

'I'll just go and get the rest.'

Two trips later, I'd unloaded the last of them. I walked back out into the fresh air and stood on the pavement, taking in a few deep breaths to quell the guilt. I glanced around at the shoppers bustling on the pavements – mums pushing buggies, an elderly couple still holding hands even though they looked to be in their eighties, the back of a man further up the street, wearing a beanie hat with messy blond hair poking out underneath, hands tucked in the pockets of his jacket. People going about their business, oblivious to all the bad things in the world.

I ran a hand through my hair. It had grown since Vicky had cut it. Maybe I should get another trim while I had time so it would be nice and neat for my new job. I could kill two birds with one stone – get a haircut and see how Vicky was doing. She'd been distraught when she'd found out Alissa was dead. She'd been inconsolable when I explained exactly what had happened out there in Noosa. How Alissa had been found and what Samantha had done.

A Snip in Time was only at the other end of the high street, and I wanted to delay going back home, since all traces of Denise's possessions had now been taken away.

I window-shopped on the way down the road, browsing at the window of a bookshop. Maybe I'd buy a thriller on the way back and settle down with it for the night. Further up was a small hardware shop with a sale on lawnmowers displayed outside. I perused the window, looking at some trowels and spades. I wouldn't need any of those if I was moving to a rented flat in London. Maybe I should get rid of all the gardening stuff in my shed now, too. Have a complete clear out. Be ruthless. I did need some filler and white paint, though. When I'd removed some photos of Denise from the wall to pack up, I'd noticed chips in the plaster where I'd bashed the nails in all those years before. I'd have to make good before the new owners completed.

I walked up one aisle, past protective work masks and gloves and overalls, looking for Polyfilla. I was about to turn into the next aisle when I spotted a box of plastic shoe covers. I picked it up, looking at the picture of them on the outside of the cardboard. They were blue. It sparked off the fake description of the killer that Samantha had given on the night of Max's murder, and I thought again of all the lies she'd told.

I shook it off. The case was finished. I put the box down, found the filler and paint, and headed to the till.

Carrying my purchases in a plastic bag, I wandered down to Vicky's shop. The bell chimed as I opened the door. It was busier than it had been the last time I was here. There were a few girls cutting hair and one dabbing dye on to a woman's roots. The same receptionist was there, giving me the same smile.

'Hi.' I glanced around, looking for Vicky. 'Is it possible for Vicky to fit me in for a trim?'

'Oh, sorry, but Vicky's left. You're the policeman, aren't you?'

'Yes.'

She glanced down at the open appointment book on her desk. 'Tina can do it if you want to hang on for about twenty minutes.' She looked back at me.

'When did Vicky leave?'

The beaming smiled wilted to a sad one. 'Well, she didn't come back after what happened with her best mate being killed. She phoned up the boss and said she was leaving. She said that nothing was keeping her here any more so she wanted a new start and she was going to move somewhere else. I've been trying to get hold of her on the phone, actually, but it's just been going to voicemail. She left some things here in the staff room, and I left her a couple of messages about it, but she hasn't been back to pick them up.'

'Right.' I nodded, thinking I'd better check up on her at her flat. 'She was very upset about what happened. I should just make sure she's OK. Do you want to give me her things and I'll take them round to her?'

'Oh, great, thanks. The boss wanted me to throw them away if she didn't come in by this weekend. I told her that in one of the messages, but maybe she's not bothered about them.' She disappeared into a door marked 'Private' and returned a few minutes later with a large white carrier bag stuffed full. 'Here you go.'

I took the bag and headed back to my car. As I opened the boot to put it inside, the handle split, spilling some of the contents out. A single black glove fell out, along with the sleeve of a black puffy jacket. I stared at it for a while, and something Vicky had said flashed into my head.

It's hard not to love Alissa.

What had the receptionist just told me? *She said that nothing was keeping her here any more.*

I pushed everything back in the bag, shut the boot, and started the engine. The feeling started as a tiny niggle, but it mushroomed the closer I got to Vicky's flat, the more my mind raced. Was Max's murder not about money and deception and stealing someone else's identity all along? Was it really about love? Had I focused too hard on Samantha and got it all wrong?

I parked in the communal car park and pressed the buzzer on the intercom system for Vicky's flat, a prickle of unease running through me.

No answer.

I looked around the car park, not knowing which car she drove and wondering if it was still here, or whether she'd disappeared now.

I buzzed again.

Nothing.

I tried a few different buzzers, and when someone answered, I said, 'Police. I need to get in to talk to someone.'

'Well, why don't you buzz them, then?' a cocky male voice said.

'I've tried.' I attempted to dampen my growing frustration. 'Can you just let me in, please?'

'How do I know you're really police and this isn't a scam?'

'If you come down to the entrance, I'll show you my warrant card.'

A pause on the other end. Then they must've thought better of getting involved, and the door unlocked.

I swung it open and took the stairs to Vicky's second-floor flat instead of waiting for the lift.

I strode down the corridor and banged on her door. Waited.

I pressed my ear to the wood. There were no sounds coming from inside. Was I too late? Had she done a flit?

I banged again. 'Vicky? It's DS Carter.'

There was no letter box because there were postboxes downstairs in the hallway for mail. Nothing to look through to check if I could see anything.

I banged again. 'Vicky! Open up, please.'

I knocked on her neighbour's door, and a thirty-something woman opened it.

'Hi, I'm DS Carter. I'm looking for Vicky Saunders. Your neighbour.' I pointed to Vicky's door. 'Have you seen her recently?'

She tilted her head, thinking. 'Um . . . yes, I saw her yesterday. She was taking a load of rubbish bags down to the bins outside.'

'Do you know what car she drives?'

'No, sorry.'

'OK, thanks.' I went to Vicky's door again and shouldered it while the neighbour watched me.

The door didn't budge.

'Hey! Are you allowed to do that?'

I ignored her and put all my body weight behind it. It groaned a little under my weight, but wouldn't open.

I whipped my phone from my pocket and called the control room, asking for a unit to come up with a battering ram.

'What's going on?' The neighbour leaned against her door frame. 'Is she in trouble or something?'

'I think you should go inside,' I said. 'I may need to speak with you later.'

She stood there for a few more minutes before reluctantly heading back into her flat and closing the door.

I waited by the communal entrance for uniform to arrive, fidgeting. When they got there, we legged it back up the stairs, and they made light work of the door.

The smell hit me as soon as it was open. I recognised the stench of death straight away. 'Stay here,' I told the young constable, and left him hovering outside in the hallway.

I walked down the narrow corridor into the first room, which was the lounge.

And there she was. In her bra and knickers on the sofa, just how Alissa had been left when she was killed, in what I thought must've been her final tribute to the woman she loved. Packets of empty tablets littered the floor and coffee table. A pint glass had fallen from her hand and rested against her thigh. Her eyes were glassy, dead.

I grunted out some kind of sound.

'Have you found her?' the PC called from the doorway.

'Yeah.' I sighed. 'Looks like suicide.' I walked back towards him. 'Have you got any gloves?'

He opened a pouch on his equipment belt and pulled out a pair of latex ones.

I slapped them on. 'Thanks. Can you let the control room know?'

I left him there speaking into his radio as I wandered around the flat. I opened the door to her bedroom and stopped dead.

Framed photos of Alissa were all around the place. Hanging on walls, standing on the bedside cabinets. It reminded me of Russell's spare bedroom where he worked out in front of Alissa's picture, except worse.

I sighed again and opened the cupboard, searching through it.

There was nothing incriminating in the house. Nothing that proved she'd killed Max, apart from the black jacket and gloves downstairs in my car that she'd thought would be thrown away by the staff at A Snip in Time. Of course not. She'd want Samantha to take the fall for it – the ultimate payback for killing Alissa. But I thought I knew exactly where to look.

I called SOCO and they arrived fifteen minutes later while I was eyeing several overflowing, industrial-sized wheelie bins in the car park.

'Oh, God.' Emma Bolton scrunched up her face when I told her I needed all of it checked. 'I hate rubbish. I'd rather deal with a dead body than all that crap.'

An hour later, Emma called me over to a bag she'd been removing the contents from. 'Think you'll want to see this.' She held up a balaclava and a pair of black combat trousers with a tiny fragment of now dried bracken caught around the button of the leg pocket, bracken that I knew without a doubt had come from the woods at the rear of The Orchard. The same stuff that had collected on my trousers when I'd run through the woods to Russell's house. She bagged it as evidence and then retrieved an open box of shoe covers with the same packaging as I'd seen in the hardware shop just down the road from Vicky's salon.

'What's that?' I said, as Emma pulled out a black book from the bottom of the bag.

She handed it to me. The pages were soggy and stained, but still readable. As I flicked through, words caught my eye here and there. *She has to be with me . . . Get Max out of the way . . . Now it's only a matter of time . . . Love Alissa more than anything.* I turned the pages to the last entry.

I can't go on now she's not here. I can't recover. She was my world. And I don't want to live in a world without her.

I knew that feeling well.

I'd been wrong all along. Yes, I'd caught Sam the Psycho. But I'd been so hell-bent on proving I was right that I'd been blinkered, just like Wilmott.

I was right about one thing, though. Love was both a blessing and a curse. Love could destroy you. If you let it. But maybe the biggest curse was not losing your love, but never being loved at all by the one who stole your heart.

ACKNOWLEDGMENTS

Firstly, I'd like to say a *huge* thanks to readers, reviewers, and book bloggers for choosing my books! The idea for *Duplicity* first came about when I was thinking about identity theft. But what if it went a step further than just stealing your online presence or your credit cards and ID documents? What if they stole your life, too? There was only one way I could see someone pulling off a deception like that, and that's what unfolded in the pages of this story. I hoped you enjoyed the outcome, and if you did enjoy it, I would be so grateful if you have time to leave a review or recommend it to family and friends. I always love to hear from readers, so please keep your emails and Facebook messages coming (contact details are on my website: www.sibelhodge. com). They make my day!

For anyone familiar with Hertfordshire, the village of Waverly is a figment of my imagination! It might not be the ideal place to live, anyway, with a stalker and a murderer on the loose!

A massive thanks goes out to my husband, Brad, for supporting me, being my chief beta reader, fleshing out ideas with me, and putting up with me ignoring him when he's trying to talk and my brain's overloaded with plot noise.

Big thanks to D.P. Lyle, MD, for all of his information on knife wounds, and for all the amazing advice he gives freely to authors on his blog and in his books.

Thank you to Jenny Parrott for all of her editing suggestions, and to John Marr and Alex Higson for catching all the things I didn't. Big, big thanks to Emilie Marneur for all of her help, advice, and support over the last few years, along with Sammia, Sana, Hatty, and the rest of the Thomas & Mercer team. It's very much appreciated.

And finally, a loud shout out and hugs to all the peeps in The Book Club on Facebook for your enthusiasm, fun, and amazing support of authors!

ABOUT THE AUTHOR

 Sibel Hodge is the author of UK and Australian #1 bestseller *Look Behind You*. Her books are international bestsellers in the UK, USA, Australia, France and Germany. She writes in an eclectic mix of genres, and is a passionate human and animal rights advocate.

Her work has been nominated and shortlisted for numerous prizes, including the Harry Bowling Prize, the Yeovil Literary Prize, the Chapter One Promotions Novel Competition, The Romance Reviews' prize for Best Novel with Romantic Elements and Indie Book Bargains' Best Indie Book of 2012 in two categories. She was the winner of Best Children's Book in the 2013 eFestival of Words; nominated for the 2015 BigAl's Books and Pals Young Adult Readers' Choice Award; winner of the Crime, Thrillers & Mystery Book from a Series Award in the SpaSpa Book Awards 2013; winner of the Readers' Favorite Young Adult (Coming of Age) Honorable award in 2015; and a New Adult finalist in the Oklahoma Romance Writers of America's International Digital Awards 2015. Her novella *Trafficked: The Diary of a Sex Slave* has been listed as one of the top forty books about human rights by Accredited Online Colleges.

For Sibel's latest book releases, giveaways and gossip, sign up to her newsletter at www.sibelhodge.com/contact-followme.php.